I0738203

Take Me Home To Woodstock
A Novel

By
Sally Cissna

Appleton, Wisconsin
2023

Copyright 2023 by Sara L. Cissna

SuLu Press
1230 South Telulah Avenue
Appleton, Wisconsin 54915

Publisher's Cataloging-in-Publication Data

Take Me Home To Woodstock/Sally Cissna
Paperback ISBN 978-0-578-25378-7
1. HIS054000 HISTORY/Social History
2. FIC008000 FICTION/Sagas/Family Sagas
3. SOC026000 SOCIAL SCIENCE/Sociology/Women/Religion.
I. Cissna, Sally. II. Take Me Home To Woodstock.

Disclaimer: The stories herein are not factual accounts but rather flow from letters and the imagination and memory of the author. However, the general history of the families, the newspaper articles, and the era are as accurately represented as possible. These accounts are not meant to characterize or disrespect any person or group, past or present. While some words or ideas may challenge twenty-first century sensitivities, including the author's, these terms are true to the times and necessary to the story.

Cover design: The picture on the cover is a Wienke family photograph taken around 1904 of Lincoln Avenue. The house on the back cover is 365 Lincoln Avenue, the home that John Wienke is planning to build at the end of this book.

Separators: The *** indicate time passing between sections. An extra space but lack of *** means something happening later but on the same day.

News Articles: The news articles included herein are, to the best of the author's ability, exactly as they were printed. Spelling, grammar, and lack of cultural awareness is accurate in the day and paper, as is the editorializing therein regarding issues such as peace, war, and humanity.

Second Edition

Dedicated
To

The families of

John Wienke and Ida Doering

May Ida and John's legacy forever be.
preserved in the generations to come.

And to the people of Woodstock, Illinois,
the pretty little village where
John and Ida made their home in 1902.

Ida Helen Louise Doering   John Francis Wienke
Before they knew each other (Circa 1890)

Thanks

Without the time and support of the following individuals, this book would never have come to fruition.

Thank you to my friend, Liz, for being my cultural reader and unofficial counselor. Your ear for a writer's truth and a reader's reactions to the controversial areas of this enterprise was greatly valued – along with the lively discussions over our two-margarita lunches.

Thank you, Shari, my friend and most enthusiastic reader. Your constant encouragement kept me productive, and our long friendship makes me happy.

Thank you to my niece Becky who proofread as she read the first draft of the book aloud to her mother Marian. Getting a family perspective on the story was so important along with finding those infernal typos.

An enthusiastic thank you to my editor and mentor, Juliet, without who this project would never have gotten off the ground. She was the rational voice calling in the wilderness who sat me down to develop a timeline, among other things.

Thank you to the Carmel Crisp Writers Group, who have over the last year, acted as my sounding board and brainstorming group, as I organized and reorganized my short narratives into a cohesive book. You, my friends, are the best!

Thank you to Sarah who brought her creative ideas and skills to the project.

And finally, without the love and support of my life-partner and spouse, Rebecca, I would not have had the ability nor the time to do the research necessary, or for that matter, to write at all. Thank you for your patience and encouragement, for your knowledge of many things, and for being the primary shareholder in this undertaking.

The Wienke Home
At the edge of Oakland Protestant
Cemetery, Woodstock, Illinois (Circa
1900)

The Wienke Brothers
From Woodstock, Illinois
Circa 1885
Front (R to L): Emil, Charles, William, August (Ed).
Back: Robert, Frank, John, Albert.

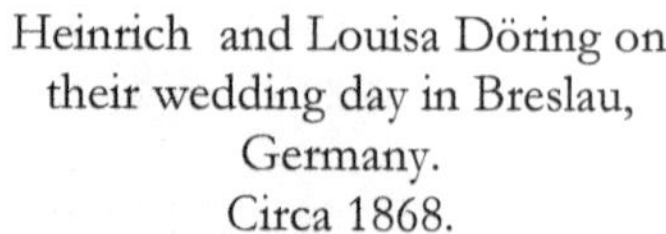

Heinrich and Louisa Döring on
their wedding day in Breslau,
Germany.
Circa 1868.

Henry and Louisa Doering of
Whitewater, Wisconsin.
Circa 1890

The Doering Family of
Racine, Wisconsin
Circa 1893.
Front: Ida Doering.
Second (L to R): Clara
Doering, Emma Von Natzmer
Ardelt, Dorothea Steiner
Doering. Back: Louisa Ardelt
Doering, Carl Ardelt, and
Emma Doering Fisher.

New Year's Eve
(1911)

Cold, crisp air greeted John and Ida Wienke as they climbed down from the train to the platform in Woodstock. John looked about for the horse and sled that was to meet them and carry them home. The train was several minutes early, but it was too cold to wait long. Then he heard the jingle of far-away sleigh bells approaching – and a robust, jolly elf drove his trusty steed off the roadway coming forward for their pickup. The driver had a ruddy face and a winter beard frosted white with his breath. He wore a red stocking cap and a scarf over a heavy sheepskin coat. Their dear friend, Roger Kaufman gave a hearty, "Whoa, Gertie!" He pulled on the reins bringing the sleigh to a skidding stop on the ice-covered surface.

"*Guten Abend!*" he shouted to those assembled on the platform.

"*Guten Abend!*" John, Ida, and eight-year-old Helen answered in unison.

"*Wie geht es?*" Roger's voice echoed in the cold air. Then noticing the two sleeping little ones slung over shoulders, he shushed himself laying a gloved finger to his lips.

"We are doing just fine." John answered for the whole group.

He sprang from the sleigh and took Dodi out of Ida's arms. "Here, my dear. Let me take this burden from you," he said, lowering his voice. "Better that you just have yourself to worry about on this icy night, especially—"

"In my condition." Ida finished his thought, placing her free hand self-consciously on the swelling at her waist. "She's not such a burden, although I'd like it if she would stop growing quite so round." As Ida transferred the child to him, she noted his transport. "I see you brought the sleigh. We feel like royalty."

"Oh, I've been up to Queen Anne's for service this evening. The station was on my way home." Roger cradled the sleeping five-year-old on his shoulder and gave his other hand to Ida to step down off the wooden planks onto the ice-covered gravel. "Here you go then. Be careful. The footing is less than perfect, and we wouldn't want you to fall."

Ida took his hand and stepped gingerly down. She felt her foot slip, but then it caught on the gravel poking through the ice, and Roger guided her over to the sleigh and allowed her to pull herself up into the rear seat of the sleigh without assistance and handed Dodi up to her minimal lap.

Roger turned his attention to John who had one handedly gathered the luggage to the near side of the platform. Roger grabbed up two bags at once and loaded the luggage beside Ida and Dodi. Helen climbed up to the middle position in the front. John made his way to the sleigh and climbed up, sheltering seven-year-old Mamie's face from the cold blast with his gloved hand. All they needed was for her to get sick again.

Roger jumped up and took the reins. "I'll have you home in a jiffy. Cold night, aina?"

"Sure is," said John. "The train was warm by comparison even without heat."

"Great way to travel, but certainly not perfect. Come on Gertie, let's go. Hold tight to your precious cargo!"

As the roan began to pull, the sleigh slid sideways rather than forward, and Gertie had to put her back into it to get the sleigh to follow her out onto the street. The Village of Woodstock lay quiet on this night of transition. Tomorrow would begin a new year with its promise of prosperity, but they heard no revelry as was common for such a night. Not a sleigh or sled in sight. As they left the station and headed for the square, the quick clop of Gertie's feet was the only sound and the moon above the only light.

"Where are all the people?" Helen's small voice floated into the silence.

"Hunkered down in front of the fire, I would guess." Roger said a little too loud.

But then they rounded the corner onto the square. The park was lit with hundreds of electric bulbs so that even the air above the square shimmered with all the colors of the rainbow.

Helen's eyes were saucers. "Oh, how beautiful! Do you think there will be fireworks tonight, Papa?"

"Maybe. But, I hope, we will all be sound asleep by then." John couldn't pull his eyes away from the spectacle on the square.

Bang! Bang! Rat-a-tat-tat! Firecrackers broke the crystalline silence. Gertie was taken by surprise and shied away from the sound, sending the heavily loaded sleigh into a skid. They spun, and Gertie lost the ability to control the momentum. Bags flew from the rear seat as Ida clung to Dodi with one hand and the front seat with the other. John lost purchase on the front seat and slipped one foot out to stand on the right runner, hanging on tightly to Mamie and the front rail. Roger pulled Helen to him as he, too, clung to the front rail. The world slowed and the sleigh was made an arc around a distraught Gertie.

They came to a stop facing the wrong direction on the one-way street around the central park. Gertie had somehow kept her feet, and they, the sleeping children and all, had stayed on the sleigh. A silent moment ticked by as everyone remembered to breathe.

Mamie opened her sleepy eyes and looked around. "Woodstock." She sighed and laid her cheek against her father's rough wool coat.

John smiled. "Yes, we are home in Woodstock," he whispered to the top of her head. Mamie smiled a little and slipped back into sleep.

Roger clambered down, making comforting sounds to Gertie whose breath came in frosty steam puffing from her nostrils. He retrieved the bags and was back in a flash of good humor.

Roger looked at Helen. "We meant to do that. Gertie and I have been practicing our skating all week just for you."

Helen giggled.

"It's a bit icy." John was the champion of understatement.

Roger chuckled. "Yes, Ice storm yesterday, don't cha know. You may not have electricity at your place. The whole town was out. The power is certainly back on here on the square." He carefully turned Gertie in a half circle. "We best walk Gertie. No more skating. We have to get these folks home in one piece."

The horse walked up Cass Street, past the old grocery shop and turned right on Throop, past Ida's brother Herman's house. They continued left on Judd, past the place where Helen had lost her mittens on the way to "Papa's 'tore." Gertie pulled onward, turning right on Tyron and then left on Lincoln Avenue. The way was circuitous, but it was always nice going through the square when coming home. Half-way up Lincoln, Roger gently reined Gertie to a stop in front of 365, the house that John built.

"Here we are!" Roger announced. "Home Sweet Home!" Helen giggled again. She loved the way Roger talked, often a bit too loud and always cheerful.

Someone had sanded the street and the front walk which gave better footing to both the four-legged and the two-legged. The transfer of children and bags was quickly done, and Roger took his leave with a hearty, *"Frohes neues Jahr!"*

While John checked the fire in the basement furnace, Ida unbundled the children and herself. The house had been standing empty overnight, but the fire was in good shape from an earlier stoking – Roger again.

With the children tucked into bed, John flopped down on the davenport next to Ida. Their eyes met. He smiled. "How is Mama?"

"Mama is tired. And Papa?

Before answering, John glanced around the room with its sturdy walls and large front window looking out onto the wintery night. The Christmas tree was still up, and the room smelled of pine and wet wool, with just a hint of cooking smells from Ida's kitchen. "Well, Papa is glad we are all back here safely. I'm always lonely when you and the children are in Racine."

"I'm sorry. Maybe next time you can stay for the whole week instead of just taking us to Mama's and then coming back to retrieve us. Oma would love to have you all week if only to put you to work."

John smiled at the idea of his plump, sweet mother-in-law ordering him around. "Maybe. But it's sure good to have Mama back home." He leaned over and kissed her, his hand resting on her rounded belly. He pulled back slightly, leaving his hand in place. "How is my boy tonight?"

"I think he rather liked the train ride."

A quick punch under his hand took John by surprise. He jumped.

Ida laughed. "I think he's telling you himself that he is fine."

John was still looking at his hand. "Three more months?"

"Two and a half." Ida covered his hand with hers.

Off in the distance, church bells began to play the music of the arriving year. The peals echoed from the Catholic belfry at the end of the block and bounced across the village, joined by the two Lutheran bells, the Presbyterian bell, the Methodist bell, and the Congregational bell, all ringing the glad tidings of great expectations for the new year. The world had made it through once again. The distant booms of fireworks added syncopation to the tune, and the rat-a-tat-tat of fireworks, close by, kept the beat going for long moments before fading away.

"Happy New Year," they said almost as one and pecked a kiss in celebration.

John looked at Ida. "Did I ever tell you about the night that I knew I was going to marry you?"

"Mm. I don't believe so. I'd love to hear how you came to such a precipitous decision."

John chuckled. "Well, let's see…it was New Year's Eve and Ma threw a party."

Ida pulled back so she could look him in the eye. "Your mother?"

"Yes, my mother. It was the beginning of the new century, and the town was not going to be celebrated until the end of 1900. Ma was not about to be left out. So, she enlisted Al, Bob and me in throwing a shindig at her little house – a real old-country Sylvester celebration."

The Pouring
(New Year's Eve 1899)

John Wienke raised his cup and called out, *"Frohes neues Jahr!"* And those gathered responded in a shout, "Frohes neues Jahr!!" John imagined all the citizens of Woodstock, Illinois, gathered in groups like this one counting down the 1800s and welcoming 1900 with a shout of "Happy New Year.". He watched as couples came together for the first kiss of the new year. No kiss for him again this year – his twenty-ninth – because he was not yet coupled.

The gathering was a small one, about twenty family and friends. The Woodstock fathers had bowed to the national scholars who said that the 1900s started at midnight at the end of the year 1900 not at its beginning. They announced in *The Woodstock Sentinel* that city-wide celebrations of the new century would not commence until December 31, 1900, and so everyone was left to celebrate in private or church watches.

Protesting the decision of the authorities, John's mother, Sophia, gathered this company to her parlor to ring in the 1900s. John and two of his seven brothers still dwelt in his mother's house, and they had been put to work while she cooked the morning away.

By eight o'clock that evening when the first guest arrived, the buffet was laden with all the good things for Silvester. How silly it was to call New Year's Eve "Silvester" after a 4th Century Pope who died on this day in the year 335, but the Germans in town did just so, even if they were Lutherans. John was the designated keeper of the *Glühwein*, red wine warmed all day with cinnamon sticks, orange and other fruit, and then theatrically set on fire just after the first guests arrived, ensuring people would be prompt.

Al, Sophia's third youngest son, was assigned the duty of overseeing the lead pouring. This prophetic enterprise required old teaspoons, a candle, pea-sized chunks of lead, and a bowl of water.

Bob, second youngest of the eight Wienke brothers, was handling the pyrotechnics. The intent of loud fireworks at the dawn of the new year was to scare evil spirits away and keep them away for the whole year to come. Sophia insisted that they continue these old traditions that had been brought over the seas from Germany.

Most of the guests were attired in formal Edwardian style with high collars and ties for both men and women. The women wore long skirts in dark colors of gray, forest green, burgundy or dark blue reaching the floor with tight, white or cream bodices covered by short jackets. The bustle, which John had thought was going out of style, was part of several of the ensembles. Top hats filled the hat racks, and the cold evening had necessitated capes and topcoats, which were piled on his mother's bed down a short hallway.

A tremendous, earth-shaking ***BOOM!*** knocked John back on his heels. The windows rattled, and the china cups tinkled on their saucers. And then another one…***BOOM!*** The seated guest immediately rose and went to look out the east windows.

Outside the showers of white sparks twinkled against the black sky and sent light shimmering across the room overwhelming the light from the three meager oil lamps.

John looked at himself in the dark window glass between explosions of light. His face was pleasant, but far from handsome. His hair, what was left of it, was cut short. He was not ashamed of his bald pate, but he wished that it didn't make his head so pear-shaped. He was strong and tall, second tallest in the family at six feet; only Frank stood taller. His greatest strength was the color of his eyes. His father had had the same striking Prussian blue eyes, as did his mother and brothers. He would take no awards at the county fair with his looks, that's for sure, but he wasn't half bad. Tonight, he wore a stylish high-collared white shirt with a black waistcoat and continental cross tie. In the breast pocket of the waistcoat, he had placed a red handkerchief, to add just the right dash of color.

Al Wienke walked over to where John was looking out the front window and laughed. "I think Bob has finally found his calling—fireworks." **BOOM**…*sparkle, sparkle, sparkle.* The guests peered around each other to try to see out. Several men grabbed coats and went out on the side porch to watch the show.

John looked at his kid brother. Al had grown into a fine-looking man of twenty-five years. He was still sporting quite a bit of wavy hair. Maybe it was the styling. Al had allowed it to grow longer and then combed it forward to cover his high brow. It looked good. No wonder the girls noticed him. Al's eyes were an azure blue, not the paler blue of the older brothers, and tonight, they were attractively accented by his festive blue, single breasted waistcoat with cloth covered buttons over a white shirt. His au courant bow tie was black and floppier than the kind John would wear, but it looked modern and smart on Al. Both he and John were sans formal jackets, a bow to their 'positions' as hired help for the party.

John looked at the crowd craning their necks but said to his brother. "You look pretty good, cleaned up."

Al chuckled. "You, too, brother. Too bad Ma didn't invite any young women tonight. You look ready to pounce."

John had just taken a sip from his glass, and almost spit it out at the pounce suggestion. "I think you are the one who is about to pounce." He switched back to the subject of fireworks. "I'm glad there is room between here and the cemetery to set the fireworks off. It's safer than many places being used tonight. I had considered going out to help Bob but decided that it was my duty to stay here and guard the wine."

BOOM…*sparkle sparkle sparkle,* some red this time. "Oh-h-h-h-h-h-h," the crowd sighed.

"Ja, me too." Al shivered. "This cold snap doesn't seem to want to end, and I spend enough time out in the cold."

John laughed, "You aren't painting outside this time of year, are you? What a *Kätzchen* you are!"

Al tapped him lightly on the shoulder with his fist, careful not to spill the wine. "I'm no kitten! You are the one who works inside all day, you are the *Kätzchen!*" They chuckled together for a moment. "So, what are you up to these days at the typewriter factory, brother?"

BOOM! Those gathered sighed with pleasure, "A-a-a-a-a-h-h-h-h-h."

"We were on furlough last week, so I went over to see what trouble I could get into in Rockford. I'm still looking for a girl like yours." They both smiled thinking about pretty Lena from Wisconsin. "Speaking of Lena," said John, "I thought you'd be in Beloit tonight."

"Ah, well. Ma needed me for the pouring, and I must work tomorrow. We are completely engaged at city hall, don't cha know, and now Wienke and Davis have a new contract to re-paper the rooms at the Hotel Woodstock starting in only a few weeks."

"Goodness. That and the Opera House are going to overlap, aina? Need help? I'm free tomorrow."

BOOM BOOM BOOM BOOM!

"Ah the finale!" John finished off his drink.

The commotion in the side yard ceased, and the crowd clapped their appreciation and moved away from the windows and back to their seats and conversations.

"Albert?" his mother called out. "Mrs. Ohme vill da pourink do."

"Okay Ma, be right there," Al called. "Sure, come on over – wear old clothes. Have you done a pouring yet?'

"No…I suppose I should."

"Come on. You can pour after Mrs. Ohme."

John followed Al into the kitchen where the lead pouring was set up. Al put a small chunk of lead in the spoon.

"Be careful. Touch only the wooden handle," he said, handing it to Mrs. Ohme.

Mrs. Ohme put the spoon over the candle and watched as the lead quickly melted. She looked at Al who nodded that it was ready to be poured. She carefully transferred the spoon above the water and slowly poured the molten liquid into the water. While she was doing this, John had begun melting his own portion.

Al waited until the lead in the water was again solid and then using wooden tongs reached in and retrieved the piece of lead now in the form of….of what? The three examined the shape and Mrs. Ohme proclaimed, "A fish!" The others nodded. "A carp!" She modified her answer. Al looked up "carp" on a list that was as old as the old country… "*Karpfen. Unerwartete Gehaltserhogung,*" Al said in less than perfect German. Luckily, Mrs. Ohme was looking over his shoulder.

Mrs. Ohme laughed. "Unexpected raise in salary? Oh my, do you think Mr. Ohme is going to give me a ten-times raise? I get nuttin' now and ten times nuttin' is still nuttin'." They laughed with her.

"A windfall from an old uncle?" Al suggested.

"Maybe, but I only have old aunts." They laughed again.

John's lead was ready to be poured. He poured the melted liquid quickly in a glob. Al waited and then retrieved the lead.

"Oh my," said Mrs. Ohme.

"Wow!" said Al. A glob with gossamer wings.

"A bug," said John. "A beetle," said Al. "A bee," said Mrs. Ohme.

"Yes…a bee…let's see…," Al looked over the paper. "What is bee again, Mrs. Ohme?"

"*Beine.*" Mrs. Ohme shook her head as if disgusted by his ignorance.

"Ho, ho!" shouted Al. "*Perspektive der Ehe.* Good news, brother! This is the year! Did you hear that Ma? John's pouring is "Prospect of Marriage!"

The whole crowd burst into spontaneous applause. John reddened but stood and bowed low. He hoped so; he really hoped so! He raised his cup in salute! "Prost! Bring me your nieces," he called out to much hilarity.

Bob burst through the back door into the kitchen. His face was blackened with soot, and he smelled somewhat burnt. "What's all the clapping about?"

"You, my brother, and your fine fireworks display!" John raised his cup again. "To my brother, Bob. May he always have a way with fire."

The others responded, "To Bob!" and broke into applause, which Bob kindly accepted with a click of the heels, a slight bow, and a wide smile on his handsome face.

His bright blue eyes sparkled like the exploding caps he had provided for entertainment. His hair was black and thick with no sign of thinning. As he removed his overcoat, John wasn't surprised at the roguish paisley waistcoat he wore with a matching satin tie in reds and golds. Around his upper arm was the gold garter of the player that he was. His perfect white teeth glinted in the gaslight each time he broke into a smile, which was often.

"Any of that Silvester wine left? Or did you drink it all John?" Bob made his way to the buffet and eyed the food and immediately found the *Erbspüree* – Split Pea Soup – another good luck charm for the new year. "Ah soup! I'm freezing!" He ladled a bowl and tore up some Silvester bread into it and then examined the rest of the laid-out food. Sauerkraut and schnitzel and several kinds of oysters. The traditional smoked carp, with the scales removed and displayed nearby for guests to pocket for good luck before leaving, stared up at him with one eye. He loaded up a plate with oysters—good for virility!—and added pretzels, which surrounded a *kuchen* wreath symbolizing togetherness. He helped himself to portions of each dish and took a seat at the kitchen table near the lead pouring. A large stein of hot wine had been set at his place.

Bob held up the stein in a toast to his benefactor, John. "Looks like you brought the food."

John nodded. He was known to have an eye for quality when it came to foodstuffs. "Looks like you brought the wine."

Bob's turn to nod. "You should open your own grocery." Bob smiled at his big brother. "Then we'd always eat like this."

John smiled. "You just love oysters."

"I admit it, I've never met an oyster or a girl I didn't like." Bob took a large scoop of bread and soup.

John snorted. "Well, I imagine you meet quite a few down at your establishment, girls, not oysters."

"Ja, ve got *Madchen und Austern*. Aber, I hem not sure vhich ich love *mehr*," Bob said with a mock German accent that had a Norwegian lilt.

John had to laugh. The oysters were quite good at Wienke and Schneider's saloon. John changed the subject. "We haven't crossed paths at the Pleasure Club recently. You still working on the weights like a madman?"

Bob dropped his fork, stretched out his arms and made a muscle with each. "You bet I am! What do you think?"

John looked at the bulging sleeves of his twenty-three-year-old brother and took in the slim build, and the handsome face under the mop of dark hair. He was without a doubt the best looking of all the brothers and knew it. The Wienke boys all had tall slim bodies except for Emil whose body was more compact and athletic. At Nineteen years, Emil was the shortest at five foot nine, but with those piercing blue eyes, he was fine looking on his own account, especially in a baseball uniform. Bob's good looks were rakish even with soot smeared on his face.

"Hm…better work harder, I'd say." John was sober faced.

Bob lowered his arms and did his best to look hurt. "Wow, and I thought I was surely making progress."

John laughed and shook his head. "You are such a Mensch. How is business?" John didn't really approve of the saloon business, but Bob seemed happily committed to it.

"Not great, but not bad either. Enough to keep the place running with a bit of cash for the proprietors. I love the hours and the freedom with both of us serving. Albert Schneider is easy to work with, and we both try to be flexible. So, I'm happy enough. I might have to change professions if I meet the oyster of my dreams."

John laughed. "You do have a way with words, Bob Wienke. No wonder people like to drop in for a snort at your place."

"You should come down some time, on a day I'm serving. I'll give you a snort on the house."

John shook his head. "I'm not much for the hard stuff. A little wine is about all I take. Well, and beer, of course."

"Unt ve got wine unt bier!" Bob practically shouted this declaration. He stood up, raised his cup, and called out, "To *Glühwein und Bier*! Happy New Year!" And the crowd raised their cups saying, "Happy New Year."

Bob continued, used to being the center of attention, "Here's to the 1900s. May we spend it in as good company as this night finds us. May our house always be too small to hold all our friends."

"*Zum Wohl*!" called out those gathered, the German equivalent of 'Here, here!' It seemed an appropriate end to a good evening.

Later, after the last hug had happened, after that last sleigh had slid away into the darkness, after the booming of the fireworks across town had diminished into a few rifle shots in the air, after the food had been packed up and stored in the back-porch locker where it would freeze for another day, after Ma and his brothers had headed to bed, John sat at the kitchen table and thought about the coming year.

He had always looked forward to 1900. He would be 30 years old this year, and it was time to settle down. He was making good money at the Typewriter factory. With his salary and investments, it was time to start thinking about opening a business, most probably a grocery or a café or a bakery. But most of all he needed a wife! Not quite yet, but soon he would begin looking in earnest. He hoped this would be a year filled with *Wohlstand und Liebe*...with prosperity and love.

***

Personal Mention

John Wienke visited friends in Rockford last week.

Woodstock Sentinel, January 6, 1900.

***

Personal Mention

John Wienke visited friends at Madison last week.

Woodstock Sentinel, January 11, 1900.

***

Distinguished Visitors

The Woodstock "city dads," comprising Alderman Emil Arnold, Ben. Stupfel, F. W. Buell, C. W. Hill A. Dwight Osborn and Fred Walters were visitors here (Harvard), Wednesday. They were accompanied by City Engineer Wm. Wienke, City Marshal John Bolger and Policeman A. E. Rathbun. The delegation came here to inspect the new air compressor at the city pumping station and were so much impressed with the way it did its work that they will recommend the purchase of one exactly like it for the Woodstock plant.—Harvard Independent.

Woodstock Sentinel, January 18, 1900.

***

LOCAL INTELLIGENCE

Firemen's ball, Feb. 22.

Next horse sale, Feb. 14.

Oysters in bulk or in cans at Conklin's

The New Waverly house has a phone. It is No. 131.

Good lunch at all hours, day or night, at Huntzinger's restaurant.

Silk and satin waists, most any color, prices cut nearly ½ at Choate's.

The earth was covered with a mantle of white the first of the week, but not enough for sleighing.

If all the money in the world were divided equally among the people each would get about $30.

And here comes Prof. Cox, of the weather bureau, with the statement that the ground hog is unreliable as a weather prophet.

An elegant new cup case, the result of the labors of Carl Hanell, now hangs in Rowe & Nail's barber shop. It is a beauty and is already well filled with cups.

Report of the Woodstock public library for the week ending Feb. 6, 1900: Number of visitors, 515; number of books loaned, 183.

MRS. C. M. CURTISS, Librarian.

Wienke & Davis have been engaged for the past few weeks in repapering the rooms of Hotel Woodstock, putting them in first-class condition. Landlord Flint is a hotel man of wide experience, and nothing but the best will do for his patrons.

Woodstock Sentinel, February 8, 1900.

February 15, 1900
936 Huron Street
Racine, Wisconsin

Dear Lena,

I was distressed to hear that you were not able to see Albert for New Year's Eve. Has he asked you yet? How long will you wait before you ask him? Have you thought about the wedding? Where you'll have it? When? Ha. So many questions and your answers not coming for weeks. You must write soon!

You say that Al has an eligible brother - even for an old maid like me. I know we are the same age, but you have all the looks and I have all the talent! Ha! That is if handiwork is a talent. At least I can embroider pillowcases for your nuptial bed. I like the thought of a nuptial bed, but I wonder if all couples share them. My papa and mama did—OH MY! I shouldn't tell secrets like that, should I? I am so naughty.

My 'just-friends' Julian said that he will take me to dances to meet a beau. Isn't that sweet of him? I wish I could get interested in him, but he's just not my type, too particular, too natty a dresser, kind of a dandy. My homely self cannot measure up to his standards. He says he doesn't mind that I'm homely – isn't that adorable – that he would still marry me. But no, he is not the one. I will know when I meet the one, just as you knew with Al, don't you agree?

Racine has also put their new Century celebration at the end of 1900. I don't quite understand. Why wouldn't the year 1900 be the first year of THE 1900s? I wonder where I'll be on January 1, 1901, when the new Century begins.

I'm making myself – in my leisure time – a new spring frock. Maybe it will entice the boys when they see what a good seamstress I am. I also crocheted hats for everyone in my family for Christmas, even Mr. Stoffel who has become a fixture in our house and who has escorted my mother out on the town several times now. I can't really see them in a nuptial bed, but...one never knows! Herman took to the hat right away, and I don't think it was just brotherly kindness but rather the cold temperatures. Clara didn't like the color of hers, which was a pretty lavender, so I will redo it in pink, and I will have the lavender. Emma, Frank and the little ones also got hats, and Emma says they love them. She has three children already; can you believe it? I'd be jealous, but I'm above it. Ha!

Mama and I have been working on a gown for Mabelle Horlick. Her father is the malted milk fellow here in Racine. Have you tried malted milk? It's wonderful, especially with ice cream added. The gown is for the Spring Fling. Mama is doing the petticoat, and I am working on the outer dress in blues and yellows. It will be gorgeous. We also have had a lot of darning to do this winter — socks mostly — and letting out of dresses. Too many malted milks? Ha!

Oh! I must report on a strange event that happened a few days ago. There were these two men who were building a chicken coop for our neighbor to the north. We were surprised by a knocking on the front door and the boy there said that Mr. Jones had been taken ill and could Mama come and see if she could nurse him? We ran out just in time to see the man, Mr. Jones, take his last breath. That was the first time I've seen a man die, breathing one moment and not breathing the next. There was nothing Mama could do for him. We waited in the cold until the authorities arrived, and they just picked him up and put him in the back of a paddy wagon and he was gone. It made the paper. I shall include the clipping. Shows how quickly any of us can just pass over. They said in the paper that Mr. Jones was fifty-two, which is younger than Mama. It makes me more other hand, if I found a nice boy to marry, I would be truly happy.

Well, back to the needle as they say, ha. I'm looking forward to seeing you soon, as I hear you and your mother will be visiting sometime after the snow melts. I will hold my breath!

Greetings to all,

Ida

***

SUDDEN DEATH

William Jones, an old and well-known resident of Racine, dropped dead about 5 o'clock yesterday afternoon, at the residence of Mrs. Louise Doering, No. 936 Huron street. Mr. Jones, with David Luker, was engaged in building a chicken coop for Mr. Luker adjoining the residence. Mr. Luker had occasion to carry some lumber from a short distance away and when he returned, he found Mr. Jones lying on the ground and groaning. He assisted the fallen man to a sidewalk and hurriedly sent a small boy after Mrs. Doering. When she arrived, Mr. Jones was still alive, but he died in a very few minutes. Dr. F. J. Pope was called and gave his opinion that death resulted from apoplexy. The police office was notified, and the body was removed in the patrol wagon to the undertaking parlors of Thronson-Hansen Furniture company and later to the home of Mr. Jones, No. 1637 Douglas avenue.

Coroner Stripple was on the scene early and empaneled the following jury: Jon Dixon, Matt Speich, E. J. Evans, Charles Christianson, Byron Blish, Len Gerhauser. The inquest was held at 10 o'clock this morning, and after the evidence was heard a verdict was rendered that apoplexy was the cause of death.

William Jones was 52 years and 2 months old, and he had been a resident of Racine forty-three years. On the north side of the river, he was well known and favorably known, in fact was known in all parts of the city. He was a good natured, honest and upright man, and everybody had a good word for him. A wife and two grown up children survive him.

Racine Journal Times, February 13, 1900.

***

Personal Mention

Paint and paper are being applied to the store of C. F. Thorne by Wienke & Davis, making a great improvement.

There will be a grand masquerade ball in this city on St. Patrick's Day, Mar. 17. The bills have already been issued.

If you want a really satisfactory smoke buy the Fontella at Austin's grocery.

Railway trains were run at a disadvantage yesterday, and most of them were late on account of the drifting snow. Extra engines were added and still the schedule could not be maintained.

Woodstock Sentinel, March 1, 1900.

***

Old Customs Resumed

The early-closing agreement expired by limitations last week on Wednesday evening, and the business houses are again open until any hour of the night they see fit. The clerks and some of the proprietors are anxious to close year around. Why not?

Woodstock Sentinel, March 8, 1900.

***

WILL FORM A UNITARIAN CHURCH

KENOSHA, Wis., March 14.—An effort is being made to form a society of the Unitarian church in this city. Rev. Mr. Southworth, secretary of the general convention of the church was in Kenosha Monday and met with many of the leading members of the church here. The society formerly had a church in Kenosha, and at one time the church numbered among its members many of the most influential people in the city. The old church building on Chicago street is still the property of the few surviving members, and it will be turned over to the new congregation as soon as it is formed.

Racine Journal Times, March 14, 1900.

***

"Clara! Did you hear? Lena is coming next weekend." Ida Doering was breathless with excitement as she read Lena's letter for the third time.

"How wonderful! What shall we do? And don't, please, say *'walk by the lake.'* I am so sick of walking by the lake. Besides now with the ice gone it is disgusting, fish and flotsam up on shore. One has to wear high boots just to stay out of the muck."

"Don't worry. Mama won't want to just go for a walk. Maybe we'll go shopping downtown. What would you think about that?"

"Oh, I would love that!" Clara's face was all smiles but then fell. "Unless we have no *Geld* to spend. I hate shopping and then finding something and not being able to buy it."

Ida shrugged. "Well, do you have any money?"

A small voice. "A little."

"We shall have to see what we see. Mama is pleased that they're coming. I might be able to get some luncheon Geld at the least."

"Oh!" Clara's smile was back. "Can we go to the Hotel Racine for lunch? Maybe Mama, Mr. Stoffel, and Mrs. Steinke will join us."

Ida was impressed. "That is a splendid idea. You are turning out to be quite a bright girl."

Clara flounced a bit. "Of course, I am a bright girl! I am seventeen and ready to find my beloved. Everyone else can see that, why can't you?"

Ida looked at her little sister. "Maybe because I live with you day in and day out. I guess I don't think that you are ready to go out into the world, quite yet."

"Don't expect me to be like you. If I am ever twenty-six and not married, I shall just kill myself."

Ida turned to her. "You will what?"

Oh heavens! Was Ida thinking about killing herself? Clara's mood shifted again, and she looked at her sister with concern.

Ida was, in Clara's opinion, the prettiest of the sisters. Their older sister, Emma, was round-faced and looked very much like a Wisconsin milkmaid. And my face, Clara glanced in the mirror, looks like a baby, too chubby to be pretty. But I have a personality.

Ida had their father's face with a shapely, if somewhat pointed, nose and just slightly too-thin lips. But when she smiled, the whole room lit up, and when she laughed with her merry hazel-green eyes, she was a sight to behold. That she hadn't landed a man was a mystery to Clara. Maybe she was too straitlaced for these modern times. Women were starting to stand up for themselves, but Ida was satisfied to sit down, sew, and wait.

Ida felt her sister's gaze and looked up. "What?"

Clara shrugged. "Nothing."

"WHAT?" Ida said more urgently.

"You aren't going to kill yourself over being an old maid, are you?"

Ida was taken aback, but then burst out laughing. "No, Clara, I'm not going to kill myself. I shall just wither away on the vine here in Racine."

Still chuckling, Ida went back to her sewing. Did women really kill themselves over not finding a suitable mate? No. That was absurd. She would find someone, and if not, she'd be the best seamstress in Racine.

***

Closing Notes

Electro-magnetic, hot air or steam baths at Mrs. Sherwood's.

The world-girdlers, H. Darwin McIlrath and "the little woman," at the City Hall, Monday evening, May 7.

F. B. Dudley has resigned his position as city electrician, and A. C. Adams has again taken up the work. Mr. Dudley has kept the plant in splendid condition.

Wm. Wienke, city engineer, fell down the cellar stairs at his home last Monday, and was laid up for a few days. James Sullivan took his place at the pumping station.

Woodstock Sentinel, April 19, 1900.

***

COURT HOUSE NOTES
Grand Jurors for May

Dorr.....................Guy Still, John Wienke

Woodstock Sentinel, April 26, 1900.

LOCAL INTELLIGENCE

The store in the John J. Murphy block formerly occupied by Geo. F. Mills, jeweler, has been leased to Brown & Co., of Chicago, who will occupy it as a distribution place for teas, coffees, spices, etc. Wienke & Davis have put it into condition for the occupancy of a new firm.

Woodstock Sentinel, April 26, 1900.

***

Over 15,000 on Strike

Chicago, May 2—More than 15,000 men went on strike Tuesday in various cities of the country, the demands in most instances being for an eight-hour day and higher wages. In some cases, recognition of unions is the issue. The building trades are most seriously affected particularly in the east, although the railroads centering in Buffalo are threatened with general strikes. A conference will be held in Buffalo today at which it is hoped a settlement can be reached. In some cities the demands of the labor unions are still pending while in others sympathy strikers are being discussed

Woodstock Sentinel, May 3, 1900.

***

May 31, 1900
936 Huron St.
Racine, Wisconsin

Dear Lena,

Thank you for the kind letter of gratitude – you are most welcome. We also had a wonderful time. It isn't often that we all

get to go out on the town and with Mr. Stoffel footing the bill! I think he may be getting close to asking for Mama's hand.

We were so glad to see you and your mother and to learn all the news from Beloit. I'm glad you took the new evening train between Beloit and Kenosha, so you had an extra night here. Herman was very happy to pick you up. The streetlights are such a boon — extending the day easily to eleven o'clock or even after. It was such a joy to see your face after all the months of only writing. You are such a good friend, and I was glad to have time to catch up with all the news of your engagement and hopes for the future.

Wasn't the lunch at the Hotel Racine marvelous!! I just loved the little sandwiches with tuna and salmon and cucumbers. And the cakes!! I'll never forget those cakes. If that is the only time I get to go out for luncheon, I will die a happy girl.

Your talk of marriage inspired my mother because as we walked to church last Sunday, she asked me what my plans were. I asked what plans she was talking about. She said that there are several eligible older men at church who might be potential mates. OLDER? I think the youngest is forty-five. Can you imagine? I asked if she was trying to marry me off to the highest bidder. I shouldn't have said that, of course, because she got a little miffed and said she was just thinking about my best interests. So, do you think my lot in life has come to this? Marrying an old bachelor to save myself? Bah.

I am, however, very interested in meeting your fiancé's brother, John. How nice it would be to find someone mature and about my age to make a life with. Let me know what Al finds out, and we can make plans.

I best be off before mother says that not only am I an old maid, but I'm a lazy old maid.

Regards to all,

Ida

***

"John?" Al called out as he burst in through the kitchen door. He remembered to wipe his feet and then continued into the parlor with his bowler in hand. "John?"

"Shhhh," John admonished looking up from the paper. "Ma's already abed. Well, look at that – a new bowler! Aren't you the dashing bachelor? At least for a while."

"You heard! Ma never could keep a secret."

"Yes, I heard," John rose and stretched out his hand. "Congratulations, brother."

"Thanks, I'm very glad. But that's not why I ran all the way from the train station."

"No?"

"No. I just got off the train from Beloit, and Lena's friend wants to take a look at you."

"What?" John sat back down and motioned for Al to take a seat also. "Take a look at me?"

Al sat down to catch his breath. "Sorry, I am so excited to tell you, it's all muddled. Let me start from the beginning. Lena has a friend that she met in the Wisconsin German community. This girl grew up in Whitewater. Ida is her name. Ida's father died a few years ago, and they moved to Racine where they all live."

"All?"

"Yes, her family, I mean. Anyway, she moved, and so Lena hasn't seen her much for a few years, but they write letters, and so she suggested, or I guess I suggested, that she suggest that my brother might want to meet her as they were both getting older and needed…um… company."

John laughed aloud. "Company?"

Al rushed on. "Yes, company and a family and comfort."

John was still chuckling. "Comfort?"

Al was now red in the face. "You know what I mean, *Wisenheimer*!"

"So, little Ida wants to meet big bad John."

"Oh, she's not so little…I mean…young. I don't mean she's fat. At least I don't think so. The picture I saw, she was…well…pretty. She's the same age as Lena, 26. And you need to be bad more often." Al stopped and smiled.

"Oh, I don't know, Al. I'm becoming rather set in my ways. I always thought I'd find a Woodstock girl through church or something. Racine is a long way off for courting."

"It's just a brief two-hour train ride. You can go up and back in one day if you must."

"Well, you've certainly pulled off courting long-distance to Beloit. How are Lena and her family?"

As Al lapsed into events of the weekend in Beloit, John's mind wandered. A girl wanted to meet him. Can it be true?

John interrupted Al mid-sentence. "So how are we going to make this happen?"

"Make what happen?" Al looked at him confused.

"Meeting this girl, Ida." John was looking down at the paper, the epitome of nonchalance.

"Oh-h-h-h…." Al drew the "oh" out with an understanding smirk on his face. "Lena said that you should just go up to Racine and visit her. She would write you a letter of introduction."

"I don't think so. I couldn't do that…too humiliating if she takes one look and leaves me on the doorstep. When will Lena be down here? Will she move before the wedding or after?"

"Did Ma tell you that we will tie the knot next February? In Beloit? I wanted it sooner, but some cousins are coming over from the fatherland around that time so our wedding will be the main attraction at the circus. Looks like they'll move her goods down sometime in the fall before the roads get impassable. We'll find a big enough place at that time, and I'll take up residence, and then she'll move down officially after the wedding. But I'm sure she'll be down during the fall. What are you thinking?"

"Let's wait until Lena will be here, and she can invite Ida down for the day, and we can get together, or I suppose, we could all go to Racine."

"OK, I'll write Lena tonight. Ma went to bed early, aina? Is she all right?"

"Ja, day of rest and all. I sure wish they would add an English service at church. I'm to the point that I can understand about one-fifth of what they are saying. If it weren't that so much of the service repeats every Sunday, I'd be totally lost. Ma has no trouble, but a lot of the younger people are not coming as often."

"Hm…you should talk to Frank about that." Al hadn't been going to church much lately. "Seems like adding an English service would be easy to do. Except for finding the English-speaking pastor who will work for a pittance."

"Ja, there's always that. You better go write that letter! I haven't a moment to waste!"

Al smiled knowingly, gathered himself up, and put on his bowler slightly askew. "Dashing, aina? Lena thought so."

John rubbed his forehead. "Ja, dashing catches the girl, rightly so. Not sure how I'm going to accomplish dashing, except that I can run pretty fast."

"Just so you are running toward her, not away, you'll be all right." Al patted John on the arm and took his leave.

***

July 10, 1900
205 Mill St.
Beloit, Wisconsin

Dear Ida,

He wants to meet you! John Wienke wants to meet you. I am so excited because if this would come true, we would be sisters-in-law. How fun! And probably both live in Woodstock. Can good Wisconsin girls stand it so close to Chicago? Of course, you are used to a large city, but I'm just a country maiden. Al and I will try to get a meeting set up later on in the fall if you can wait that long. I'll be going down to start preparing the house or apartment…I do hope it's a house…it will need cleaning, polishing, painting, and furniture. I'm not sure how much we will have. Al may have to make some of the furniture at least at first.

I will write when we have found an agreeable day. We might make it a bit more of a party with other friends, so it isn't so uncomfortable if you take one look and decide not to pursue him. He is, I know, a hard worker, has good common sense, and can fix anything, at least according to you know who. I'm not sure how that blends into a man you would want or not, but that's what I hear. So, from one friend to another, it's worth taking the chance.

I can't wait to see you. I will post a letter as soon as I know something for certain.

Love to your mother and Clara,
Lena

***

Clara Doering modeled a new gown being sewn for a Racine debutant's coming-out party. She posed in the middle of the room and then walked one way and back at times curtsying deeply and saying to an invisible gathering with a slightly mocking tone, "Well, thank you. Thank you so much for coming. For ME? Oh my; it's beautiful. You must have some champagne. Why, good evening, Mr. Mayor. So glad you could come. Do try the canapes—they are marvelous."

"OK, that's fine, Clara. Thank you for your great showmanship." Ida tried to stop the show before too many straight pins fell out. "It flows nicely and accentuates what needs to be accentuated."

"Accentuates? What these?" Clara cupped her bosom in both hands. "I don't believe these need accentuating."

"Clara!! Goodness. Do not let Mama hear you saying such things!" Ida tried to sound stern, but there was a bit of a smile on her face.

Ida unpinned the back of the dress and Clara stepped out of character and back into her own restless self, pulling on her blouse and long skirt. "Did I tell you that I met a boy?"

Ida busied herself with needle and thread. "Yes, you did."

"And that we danced every dance and did more than just dance."

"Yes, you did."

"Goodness, Ida. Does nothing ever shock you?"

"Well, yes. It shocks me that you are expecting to live here, have food on the table and a roof over your head, while you continue to be a lazy girl about work. Sit down and get busy. That petticoat isn't going to make itself."

"You sound just like, Mama."

"No, she would say, '*Dieser Petticoat wird sich nicht von selbst machen lassen.*'" This petticoat isn't going to make itself.

"And I would say, '*Ich bin nicht faul, ich bin gelangweilt.*'" I'm not lazy, I'm bored.

"You're bored?" Ida shook her head. "I've never been bored for a moment of my life. Tired, certainly, but never bored. Remember the stitching that hangs on the wall downstairs: 'Let not the setting sun find at your hand no worthy labor done.'"

"And again, you sound just like Mama. You will make a good wife someday."

"Well, thank you. I'll take that as a compliment. And Miss Nosey, just so you know, I'm going to meet the man of my dreams very soon. He will be kind and tall and handsome. He will want many children and be a good father. He will be a shopkeeper and a Christian leader in our church. He will be—"

Clara's eyes grew large. "What did you do? Did you go to a soothsayer?"

"No such nonsense. Lena is going to introduce me to her fiancé's brother."

"OH Ida!....what's his name!!?"

"John."

"John?" Clara wrinkled her nose. "But that is Mr. Stoffel's first name. He doesn't even like it; he uses J. Nicholas. You need someone with a more unique name. Like James or Joseph or Raymond. Something you can shorten into sweet names like Jimmy or Joey or Ray baby darling!"

"I'm sorry, but I cannot change the name of a man that I may admire. Nor do I have the luxury of rejecting a man simply based on his name. John is a perfectly good name. It is neither hated nor loved."

"I'm going to look for a man with a unique name, so he will always know when I am talking to him. He won't say, 'Are you talking to me or that John over there.'"

"If you can't get back to your sewing, I'm going to talk to Mama again. And you might not get out of this house for the next decade."

"All right. You are so pushy, Miss Ida. You just wait until you and *JOHN* have ten children and need a nanny. I will be nowhere to be found." She flounced down on the hassock and picked up the petticoat and began making fine small stitches. Someday, she thought, she'd wear dresses like this instead of making them. Yes, someday.

"I'm going to look for a real job soon." Clara made the announcement without looking up.

Ida smiled. "Sure, you are."

***

THE WOODSTOCK SENTINEL
SAILORS SING SONGS
On Board the Battleship "Iowa" at the City Hall

Under the general direction of Prof. John Carrol, the members of the Woodstock Pleasure club gave a grand refined operatic minstrel performance at City Hall last Friday evening before one of the largest audiences ever assembled in this city, and they gave splendid satisfaction.

The opening scene represented the deck of the battleship "Iowa," manned with blackface sailors and officers. All of the sailors and crew, who constituted the chorus were attired in white, while the "men behind the guns" (tambourines and bones) were dressed in army blue. The effect was very striking as well as unique.

Dr. G.A. Cutterridge officiated as captain (interlocutor), Harry Cross as boatswain, and T.O. Cowlin as lookout man. The "tamboes" were handled by A. J. Mullen, Dr. W.C. Beasley, Owen Corr, F.H. Belcher and Harry Brubaker, and the bones by G.L. Mullen, A. Stephenson, F.W. Kniebusch, C.C. Harting and E.J.

Field. The chorus was made up of Ed. Watson, Wm. Colbrerg, W.S. McConnell, W.C. Huntzinger, Robert Wienke, D. F. Quinlan, Fred Joorfetz, Harry McLaughlin, A.E. Rogers, C. L. Quinlan, John Wienke, E.A. Wyant, Fred Roe, E.H. Allen, J.C. Rowe, W.B. McHatton, Geo. J. Griffiths, W.T. Conn, W.J. Holtz, Chas. Joorfetz and Albert Wienke – as clever a combination of wit, beauty and talent as can be found within the city.

The program opened with a chorus entitled, "Santiago Bay" in which the "Maine" was well remembered, and mirth and jollity prevailed without restraint. Members of the crew did their stint in a very creditable style. A.J. Mullen sang about the "Kleptomania Season," Harry McLaughlin's number was entitled "Sing Me a Song of the South," Owen Coor's "Nigger, Nigger, Never Die," J.C Rowe's "Do You Ever Sit and Dream," Harry Brubaker's "You Don't Stop This World from Going Round," Ed. Watson's "I Must Go Home Tonight, Jack," and the first part concluded with a good musical comedy, in which there was a genuine coon and 'possum hunt and much merry musical melody.

The olio opened with an excellent selection by Brubaker's orchestra, which rendered all of the accompaniments in exquisite style. Then came the great troupe of performing animals which brought down the house and was one of the most laughable numbers of the program. Curtis and Wynkoop gave a cornet duet entitled "The Swiss Boy" that was a musical gem faultlessly rendered. Then came D.C. Akers in a dramatic monologue entitled "The Shadow of a Song," in which he demonstrated his ability as a recitationist and dramatic performer of no mean pretensions. It was as fine an effort as any Woodstock audience had ever listened to. The grand march and chorus of "The Upper Swell Coons," with A.E. Rogers as captain and O.G. Mead as drillmaster of the corps were precision itself, and reflected credit on those who participated, as well as those who did the drilling.

The program concluded with a roaring farce entitled "The Black Breach of Promise Case,".... It was productive of much fun.

The entire entertainment was arranged by C.A. Stone, Theo. Hamer, F.H. Belcher, Harry Cross, W.S. McConnell, W.T. Conn, C.C. Harting and Dr. W.C. Beasley, and the beautiful scenery was painted by Wienke & Davis, who are artists in their line.

The Pleasure club realized about $100 from the performance, and the boys certainly have abundant reason to be proud of the success they scored. Few of them pretend to be singers, yet their choruses were all excellent and their individual numbers very meritorious.

When it comes to home talent minstrel performances, or almost anything else, Woodstock leads the world.

Woodstock Sentinel, May 17, 1900.

***

Al held open the door for his brothers as the exited City Hall. "Well, that was quite a lot of fun!" Al, John, and Bob were heading home after helping to clean the theater after the Pleasure Club's Minstrel show. "I hope we do it again next year."

"Ja, it was fun." John nodded. "But a lot of work. I guess clearing a hundred dollars isn't bad for the first time. What do you think, Bob? What would you do for a crisp Benjamin?"

"Hm." Bob looked up at the dark sky. "Race someone across Wonder Lake!"

"Indeed. How about you, Al?"

"No question. Paint and paper a small house."

Bob looked at his brother. "Oh, you workaholic. I was thinking more as a wager."

Al laughed. "Of course, you were. How about you, John?"

Although he had proposed the original question, John had to think a minute. What would he do for $100? "Well…maybe…I'd ask a girl to a dance and kiss her on her stoop."

Bob snorted. "Oh heck, I'd do that for free. Although I would kiss her on her lips?"

They all laughed. Bob was curious. "But why, pray tell, would you need to get paid to do that?"

"Because he's scared of girls." Al elbowed Bob.

John was glad it was dark so they couldn't see him blushing. "Only a little. Certainly not in general, but the thought that….oh never mind."

Al and Bob burst out laughing. They both were aware that he was to meet Lena's friend soon and was a bit nervous about the whole arrangement. John felt his face take on even more heat thinking about it.

John did his best to keep his voice level. "Not to change the subject—"

"Right," Bob and Al said in unison.

"Where are you off to next, Bob. You are quickly becoming the most traveled person in Woodstock."

"I don't know. I sure like watching the ponies."

Al snapped his fingers. "That's right. You went down for the Derby at the beginning of the month, didn't you?"

"Yup, and I hit it big too. Bet my wad on a horse named Lieutenant Gibson to win, place or show, and he won the whole caboodle! He was favored so I didn't win as much as I might have, but it was a great day!"

They walked a few minutes in silence considering how much a caboodle was.

"Have you entered any horses in the Elkhorn or McHenry County Fairs this year?" John pulled three cigars from his shirt pocket and offered them around. Both men took the offered smoke, and they stopped in the light of a shop window to light them.

"No. I haven't seen one that could run since Marmaduke." Bob puffed to get the stogie going from the match John held.

Albert shook his head. "Yes, Marmaduke could really run. Has it only been two years since THE RACE? Seems longer ago."

Bob blew out a cloud of smoke, and the rich smell of fine Virginia tobacco filled the air. "Yes, I miss it, but then it's finding a jockey and the training and…."

John started moving up the street again. "Old Marmaduke was the better horse. He had twice the talent of that old Splendidad or whatever they called her."

Bob reached into his pocket. "You know, I keep that article about the race from the paper in my wallet along with the carp scale for good luck – the scale not the article. The article is there as a reminder. I really had faith in that horse."

He pulled the clipping out and opened it. It looked a lot older than two years, browning but not brittle and still readable. They gathered under the last lamp before the darkness of the cemetery hill. The date "September 8, 1898" was penciled at the top along with "The Sentinel."

"Just read it out loud, Bobby," said Al. He and John didn't have enough light to read it over Bob's shoulder.

"Okay. I'll try to read it without crying."

John and Al chuckled and sucked on their cigars.

Splendoline the Winner

For some time, a good-natured rivalry has existed between John Dennis, the liveryman, and the Wienke brothers as to the speed qualities of Splendoline and Marmaduke, their respective running horses. This rivalry culminated in a matched race at the Fair grounds last Saturday afternoon for a purse of $100 a side, and a large crowd watched "Jack's" horse gather in the "boodle," making the distance in 53 ½ seconds, fully two lengths ahead of his rival. Spendoline drew the pole, and Judge Donnelly acted as starter. The horses were nose-and-nose when the word was given, Splendoline taking the lead around the turn and holding it the entire distance. Martin Richardson piloted Splendoline and Geo. Mountain was astride of Marmaduke. It was a nice race, and "Jack" is jubilant over his victory.

"One hundred dollars! I had forgotten that's how much we lost," said Al. "So where is old Marmaduke now?"

"Sold him to Bill Quinlan in Elgin for a surrey horse. I see him now and again." Bob carefully folded the clipping and put it back in his wallet. "My almost claim to fame."

"We all thought he'd win." Al patted him on the shoulder. Bob really had gotten emotional during the reading.

They walked up the hill in silence, contemplating a hundred dollars gained and lost, and the running of the ponies. Marmaduke's race was the one time that John and Al had bet on a race, and for John, at least, it was the last time, but something had clicked with Bob, and now he was very willing to pursue a wager of almost any kind.

What would he do for $100? The only good answer John could come up with was work at the factory for two months. He was not a betting man.

Al again brought up a new topic as they reached the top of the hill and rounded the corner almost home. "Are you going to the first baseball game, a week from Thursday?"

"You bet," said Bob.

"Hadn't planned on it," John answered. "Why?"

"Woodstock is playing Beloit," Al and Bob replied in unison.

"I'll be there!" John snuffed out his cigar on the porch rail and led the way into the house.

***

> *Wednesday 6:05 a. m.*
> *Ma, I didn't want to wake you, so I am leaving this note. I forgot to tell you that Emil will be here for a baseball game tomorrow afternoon. If you want a ride down to the park, tell me at supper.*
>
> *Al*

***

"Hi, John! Good to see you here!" Bob slid onto the bench beside John. The bleachers were filling fast with Olivers from the typewriter company just getting off work.

"I have Woodstock, two to one over Beloit, and Beloit eight to one over Woodstock. If Emil can pull this off, I win big. You in?"

"In? Robert, how many times do I have to tell you, I am not a gambler! I am here to enjoy the game, and that's all." John tried to put a sting in his tone to try to get his point across once and for all.

"Oh, big brother, so serious. I withdraw the offer. Al should be coming soon, right?"

"Yes, he went to pick up Ma, so she didn't have to walk."

"What did he do, take a cart to work this morning."

"I'm not sure, but I think he must have taken off a bit early from work to accomplish it. He has a little more flexibility than I do. My assignment was to save good seats."

"Ma might want a piece of the action." Bob did not look at John but gazed off toward the north.

"Bob...."

"Okay, okay. I have to circulate." And off he went to find other fellows more likely to have money to waste.

John watched the cart pull up with Al and his mother. They waved that they saw where he had saved seats in the hometown bleachers. Al secured the horse and then gave his mother a hand down. Together Al and John lifted their sturdy mother up to the seats, high enough to see well.

Just as they settled in, the field umpire, Billy Magill, called out, "Play ball!"

The first two batters from Beloit struck out and then Emil came to the plate. He let the count go to three balls and two strikes and then swung away for a nice hit down the right line. Sophia and her boys jumped up for joy forgetting they were cheering for the visiting team.

A snide voice behind them said, "What do we got here, boys? Beloiter squatters? You best be moving to the other side of the field, if youse know what's good for you."

Sophia stood up slowly and turned around to face the man. He had a Bollman hat on his head, a cigar clenched in his teeth, and a smug smile on his face. Sophia looked him straight in the eye. "*Ich bin ein* Woodstocker, *aber dieser* Beloiter *ist mein sohn.*" I am a Woodstocker, but that Beloiter is my son. Sophia was not a tall woman and was dressed in a black walking dress that just skimmed the tops of her sturdy black shoes. She was hatless, and her hair was pulled back into a severe bun. She could have just stepped off the streets of Berlin. Her milky blue eyes blazed as she looked up at the man in a white shirt, a blue garter around one sleeve. His black waistcoat, gray and white striped pants and brimmed hat made him look like he had just stepped off the streets of Dodge City.

Al mumbled, "Ma." But John stood up, turned around, and faced the man. John was a foot taller than Sophia, so he was eye-to-eye with the man. His strength was obvious in his work clothes, but it was from Sophia that the man heard.

"*Ich habe acht Sohne!*"

"She has eight sons." John translated.

Sophia looked at John and nodded. Going back to the man she said, "*Ja. Acht Sohne, und dieser is mein jüngster.*"

"That batter is her youngest."

"*Ja, und ich werde ihn anfeuern, whenn ich ist wunsche! Und auch seine Bruder!*"

"She says she will cheer for him if she wants to and so will his brothers.'

"*Ja!*" said Sophia.

The man stared at her and then touched the brim of his gambler's hat and in a milder voice said, "Sorry ma'am. You go right ahead!"

John smiled at the man, who nodded to John in return. John nodded back, and then he and Sophia turned back to the field and sat down.

John leaned close to Al and whispered, "Never underestimate the power of the Mama!"

Al smiled. "You said it."

***

FIRST OF THE SEASON
Woodstockites Secure Their First Scalp for 1900.

The Woodstock Baseball club opened the season of 1900 at the new baseball park yesterday by administering a severe drubbing to a nine from Beloit. They unmercifully lambasted the boys from the little college town up the road and demonstrated that all they need is the proper encouragement to put up a game that is invincible.

It was nearly 4 o'clock when Umpire "Billy Magill" started the sphere a-moving by crying "Play ball," and the battle was over at 6 o'clock, each Woodstockite dangling a Beloit scalp from his belt as he proudly marched from the field.

Haeger and Peter were in the points for the local nine, while Smith and Wienke (two former Woodstock boys) formed the battery for the visitors. Up to the last half of the sixth inning it looked like defeat for the locals, who appeared to be unable to find the ball, the score standing at 3 to 0 against them, but in the that inning the guns were turned loose, Smith let up on his delivery on account of weariness, and the leather-covered sphere chased itself all over the pasture, eight tallies resulting. Five more pairs of nimble Woodstock legs crossed the rubber in the seventh and three in the eighth, while the Beloits had to satisfy themselves with the scores already made.

A feature of the game was the perfect work of Emil Wienke behind the bat for the Beloits. He is a ballplayer from the ground up, but his support was hardly up to the standard he set.

Woodstock Sentinel, May 31, 1900.

***

PERSONAL MENTION

Mr. and Mrs. J. H. Finch, A. T. Montgomery, Lester Nogle and lady, Mr. and Mrs. A. J. Olson, C. A. Stone, M. B. Marum, Charles Darrell and Robert Wienke were among those who took in the Woodman excursion to Madison, Tuesday.

Woodstock Sentinel, June 21, 1900.

***

LOCAL INTELLIGENCE

The Hoy block is in the hands of Wienke & Davis, the painters, assisted by Fred Eiklor, and will soon shine in a new dress of color.

The new addition to the city powerhouse, which will include the new well and pump, will be built by P. J. McCauley, who has secured the contract.

The Oliver Typewriter band gave its first summer concert in the park last Thursday evening, and there was a large crowd out, regardless of the coolness of the evening.

Woodstock Sentinel, June 21, 1900.

***

John was awakened by a sound. He lay quietly, listening. Then he heard a giggle…a giggle? And a "shhhhh," and then Bob's bedroom door opened and closed. He thought about what he should do. Should he go right now and throw her out on her ear or maybe throw both of them out? No, the ruckus would wake Ma and tomorrow was a workday. He needed his sleep also. But tomorrow, he would put a quick end to this. He rolled over and closed his eyes. A strange heat had come over him and a yearning that he hadn't experienced since his youth. No, this could not go on under Ma's roof.

At first light, John again awoke to the sounds of footfalls in the hall. He rose, washed up with the tepid water on the nightstand, relieved himself in the chamber pot and got dressed for work. That should have given them time to say their good-byes, he thought.

As he came into the kitchen, there sat Bob, eyes dazzling with the craziness of what he had just done.

"How often you do that?" John asked abruptly as he busied himself with stoking the wood stove and pumping water for the coffee pot, his back turned to Bob.

Bob's head jerked up, and he looked at John, but was silent.

John turned to look at Bob over his shoulder. "How often?" He allowed some anger to seep into his voice, but he went back to busying himself at the stove.

"First time," was Bob's soft answer.

"Last time." John turned and looked Bob straight in the eyes. "Last time, understand?"

"Who are you to—"

"I am the older brother who lives with his mother who is a good Christian woman. I am a good Christian man, and you are not going to be bringing in hussies and prostitutes under this roof."

"She's not a—"

"I don't care who she is or what she is to you. Not here! Understand?" John let silence ride out awhile, and then said, "If you need to do that kind of thing, go to her place or—"

"She lives at home."

John's voice was raised as he let his anger show. "Then find a place of your own. Use some of the money you are wagering away to stand up and be a man."

Bob's face was red whether from anger or embarrassment, John wasn't sure which. He meant his words to hurt. "I'd talk. You are still living with your mama."

John turned to face him. "I have never desecrated this house with debauchery." The words clicked off John's tongue like arrows toward the bull's eye.

Bob looked at the floor. "Okay. But we might be getting marr—"

"Married? Do it then and get a job that pays more than gambling money and get your own place!" John's disdain for his younger brother and his shiftlessness was palpable in the room.

Bob stood up fast, knocking over the chair. His blue eyes sparked with danger. John readied himself for a punch, but instead, Bob turned, stalked from the room, disappeared down the hall, and slammed his bedroom door.

John put the chair right and found the frypan. He placed it on the woodstove and broke two eggs into it. As the eggs turned from clear to white, he cut two slices of homemade bread, and after turning the eggs over, laid the bread atop them to warm.

His mother came into the room in her headscarf and housecoat. "What vas da yellink about."

John pulled out a chair. "Want some eggs?"

The coffee had started to boil and would be ready soon. He found two cups and placed them on the table along with sugar, milk, and butter.

"John?"

John dished the eggs and the warm bread onto a plate and put it down in front of her.

John finally made eye contact. "Bob needs to find a place of his own. His behavior is unseemly, and it will sully your reputation…and mine…if he continues to live here." He turned and began the egg preparation anew. He took the coffee off the stove and set it on the sideboard to settle.

"Vat happens?" Sophia asked. Appreciating the eggs, she picked up her knife to butter the bread before it cooled.

"I'd rather not tell you, but I asked him to stop his carousing till all hours of the night, coming home half in the bag, and waking up the whole house. Either that or out."

"Vhat didst he say 'bout dat?" Sophia asked, taking her first bite of breakfast.

John paused, fussing with the bread and eggs and then picked up the coffee pot and carefully poured the coffee from the top trying to avoid the grounds. If there were any, they would settle to the bottom of the cup. Still holding the pot, John looked Sophia in the eye, hoping she would understand without him explaining about the girl. "He said they might be getting married."

"*O meine*," Sophia's continence had been somewhat befuddled, but now had a more understanding look. John had gone back to nursing his eggs. She looked at his stiff, upright back.

"Vell den." Her gaze was back on her own plate. "Maybe movink out ist best."

John turned with his own breakfast and sat down across from his mother. "Yes, I think so unless he makes some promises about his behavior."

As they ate in silence, John thought about the many times the Wienke family had sat around this very table joking with each other. He remembered his father, dead now 15 years, saying grace before a meal in German. His death had been sudden and unexpected at the young age of fifty-three. John buttered the bread and put the hot egg onto the bread and folded it in half. He took a bite savoring the way the butter, egg, and bread enhanced each other's flavors. As he chewed, he looked out the window at the cemetery.

Pa's grave was not more than two hundred yards away, just over a small rise in Oakland Cemetery. His mother visited it often. He had heard her talking to Pa in German as she planted blue cornflowers. Pa loved the color blue.

When Carl Wienke died in January of 1885, their family was left in dire financial straits. His oldest brother, William at twenty-two and working as a butcher in Belvedere, came home to manage the farm with Ed who was twenty-one. They did what had to be done and bowed to the duty left by their father to support their mother and younger siblings.

Sophia had finished her eggs and pulled her coffee over in front of her. She added two scoops of sugar and got a milk bottle from the icebox on the porch.

"Sorry, Ma. I forgot the milk."

"No matter. Easy to fix."

A dollop of milk and a little warm up from the pot, and she found her way back to her chair and her own thoughts. John wondered if she too was thinking about how they had found their way to this breakfast.

John wiped the plate with the last bite of his fried egg sandwich and tucked it into his mouth. He wanted to talk to Sophia about those days, but today was not the day. He had to watch the time since his shift started at the factory at 7:00 a.m.

"You verk today" Sophia sipped her coffee and then added a bit more milk.

"Yes. No rest for the wicked. Will you talk to Bob so it's not just me saying something? I am not his Pa or his Ma." John tried for a serious expression.

"Uf course. I vill *sprechen mit* him. Don't vorry. Ve vill be fine. He ist my boy."

That's exactly what he was worried about.

"Oh my, look at the time. Can we talk more about this tonight?"

"Ja, dat be gut." Sophia sipped the coffee and sighed.

***

Personals

Messrs. F. N. Blakeslee, J. P. Brink, F. L. Kappier, Frank Kniebusch, L.W. Richards, Amos Stevenson, C.N. Wright and Albert and Robert Wienke were at Lake Geneva, Sunday, going and coming via the electric railway from Harvard.

Woodstock Sentinel, July 21, 1900.

***

Al was sitting at his mother's table eating breakfast and looking over the paper when he noticed the brief personal. Bob or one of the other boys must have dropped a note off at the paper. He said nonchalantly, "Did I tell you that Bob and I went to Lake Geneva last Sunday?"

"Saw you not in church." Sophia didn't look up from cutting up vegetables for *Deutsche Gemüsesuppe* (German vegetable soup) for supper. It would be ground beef, green beans, shredded cabbage, onions, carrots, potatoes, corn, and peas in a thin milk broth. Hearty enough for hungry boys.

Al looked up at his mother's back. "Partly. Also, because I can't understand the service anymore."

"Humph. *Deutsch sprechen* at church. *Gott Deutsch verstehen.*"

"I'm not worried about God understanding. I'm worried about me NOT understanding. Anyway, we went over to Harvard and up on that new electric railroad. So easy. It is getting easier and easier to get around, isn't it."

"Vat ist in Lake Geneva?"

"The lake, the beer, the girls." Al teased her.

"Ach, pshht." Sophia shook a drying towel in his general direction in a shooing motion but smiled just the same. "Dats all youse boys tink 'bout."

"Well, right now I am thinking about a special girl and finding her a house to live in."

He turned to the 'People's Column.' "Let's see…." He perused the offerings.

PEOPLE'S COLUMN

["Ads." in this Column, 25c per week for 5 lines or less; over 5 lines, 5c per line]

FOR RENT. – Six-room house. Inquire of A. F. Miller.

FOR RENT. – A 6-room house, $6 per month. Inquire of Emil Arnold.

FOR RENT. – A good house on Tryon Street. Inquire of Mrs. E.S. Austin.

MONEY TO LOAN. – Inquire E. H. Waite, P. J., office in Hoy block.

TEN FINE SHOATS FOR SALE. – Inquire at the office of Wm. H. Cowlin.

"Ma, are you in the market for a shoat?"

"*Ein* goat?"

"No, you know, a little pig. Spanferkel. Bill Cowlin has some for sale." Al's mouth watered just thinking about it. "You could throw another party. Won't be so crowded in this house."

"*Nein.* Ve haft nuttin' to celebrate." Chop, chop, chop.

Al again looked at her back. A bit more rounded than he remembered it. They should throw a party celebrating her.

"We could raise it until it's ready to be butchered for the meat."

"Ach, *keine Zeit*…no time."

"You sure?"

"Ja."

"Okay." Al relented and read on, looking for a house.

> **FOR RENT.** – The Cook house on Jackson street.   D. F. Quinlan
>
> **FOR SALE.** – Four good square dining tables, one extension table and an Otto buggy. Inquire at Conklin's restaurant.
>
> **FOR SALE.** – Some good choice real estate situated in the city of Woodstock. Give us a call.
> BLAKESLY, BRINE & COWLIS.
>
> **FOR SALE.** – Large list of farmlands and city property.
> EICHELBERGES & MURPHY.

Not many houses for sale. Some good land possibilities, but he really wanted to wait until Lena was here to build. He should buy the land and build a new house of Lena's dreams, but a wedding in the spring had thrown the brush in the paint on that idea.

> **ESTRAY NOTICE.** – Strayed into my enclosure about May 1, a yearling bull, black and

white, with slim tail. Owner can have same by
paying for this notice and costs.

W. M. SULLIVAN, Seneca.

FOR SALE. – 8-room modern house fitted
complete for furnace, city water and electric
light, large cellar and attic: high, desirable
lot. House will be finished about July 25. F. W.
Streets, Owner.

Oh, here is one. Nope. Too soon. What would he do with an eight-room house alone until next March? Al sighed.

FOR SALE. – Republican newspaper for
sale, in a thriving town of 800 inhabitants in
Illinois. The only paper in town. Good location
for wide-awake and up-to-date man. Will sell
cheap for cash. Address Printer, SENTINEL,
Woodstock, Ill.

Wait, a newspaper is for sale? Cheap? Hm…maybe he should go into the newspaper business instead of the wallpaper business. He laughed aloud.

"Vat?" Sophia had finished chopping vegetables and they were now in the pot simmering with the already fried ground beef. She now sat down at the table with two cups of black boiled coffee and kuchen left over from supper last night. Sun streamed in the large windows revealing dust motes floating in the air. The room smelled of schnitzel and kraut.

Al looked at his mother, hand poised to dunk her coffeecake into her cup. Here he was looking for a modern house, and Ma was still pumping water at the sink and carrying out chamber pots every day. It was time to talk to his brothers about a better house for Ma. She should be able to sell this one with the ten acres of land for a good penny.

"Vhy laughed?" The coffeecake went below the black slightly oily surface of the strong coffee and came up drenched. Sophia expertly slid it into her mouth and savored the combined flavors with a smile.

"Oh nothing," he answered. "A newspaper is for sale 'cheap.' Should I buy it and go into a different kind of paper business?"

"Ach, no," Sophia took him seriously. "No money in dat business. Du need a new business?"

"No, no, no. I like my business. I'm just looking at houses for rent, not a new business. There are quite a few available just now. I suppose I don't need to rush into anything. The wedding is still six months away. I wish I could buy land and build."

"Vell, if du must let da haus, do. Move you now into da let *haus unt finde der dauerhafes Haus* later vhen Lena with her mind ist here."

"That's a good idea. If we rent now, I could live there, and she'd have time to get it shipshape before the wedding. And then she and I could look for a more permanent situation after we are married. I'll go take a look at these and see if they have potential. Lena wants a house not a flat so what Lena wants, Lena gets."

"Dat's a gut husbant," his mother encouraged.

***

THE NEW CITY HALL

The improvements that have for many weeks been in progress in the City Hall are substantially completed, and it will be interesting for our readers to know to what extent these have been carried out by our city authorities. After nearly ten years of use the hall had become quite badly out of repair, the ceiling being disfigured by water soaking, patches of plaster being off, and the premises otherwise rendered dirty and uninviting. This has all been overcome, and the "new City Hall" will prove a source of delight to all who attend its reopening at the play next Monday evening.

In the first place, the old dirty ceiling has been covered with a substantial steel ceiling of handsome pattern, put on in a skillful manner by Whitson Bro., rendering it a job that is really permanent. Then Wienke & Davis, with a large force of men, have applied paint in green and mahogany tints, with gilt trimmings, all over the interior of the building, from the lower floor to the ceiling of the main audience room, making a transformation that must be seen to be appreciated.

The improvements on the stage are also many and marked. A new drop curtain has been painted by Wm. Minor, an expert scenic artist. It is a handsome piece of workmanship, being a Venetian scene representing a sunset on the Bay of Naples, draped with velvet curtains and surrounded with the neatly displayed advertisements of the business public. The old curtain and the old scenery have been retouched, and a new parlor scene has been added. In addition to this the decorations for the proscenium arch have been brightened up, and the gridiron over the stage has been raised six feet, which makes it possible to use drop scenery, which has often heretofore been brought here by companies with scenic productions and left at the freight depot because it could not be used. This will conduce to a higher and more enjoyable class of entertainments being brought here.

Woodstock Sentinel, July 26, 1900.

***

PERSONAL MENTION

John Wienke and Fred Joorfetz were calling on friends at Algonquin, Nunda and Crystal Lake last Sunday.

Woodstock Sentinel, August 16, 1900.

***

BRIEF MENTION

Emil Wienke is home from Beloit this week.

Woodstock Sentinel, August 31, 1900.

***

NORTHCOTT COMING
Will Speak in City Hall, Tuesday Evening, Sept. 18.

The Young Men's McKinley club held a business meeting last night, removed the age limit whereas to allow all Republicans to join, authorized Capt. Eichelberger to organize a flambeaux club, appointed a committee of five to solicit members, chose C. F. Renich, D. T. Smiley and John Wienke to arrange for a public meeting next Wednesday evening, and transacted other important business.

It was announced that a meeting with local speakers will be held next Wednesday evening, to which everybody is invited.

On Tuesday evening, Sept. 18, Lieut. Gov. Northcott will address a mass meeting at City Hall and give the campaign impetus in this city.

Those who desire to join the flambeaux club are requested to meet at the armory this (Thursday) evening and enroll themselves.

Woodstock Sentinel, September 6, 1900.

***

CITY COUNCIL
REGULAR MEETING
WOODSTOCK, ILL., Sept. 7, 1900.

E. C. Jewett, presiding.

Ald. Cannon, Hill, Osborn, Schuett, Stupfel and Walters answering to their names at roll-call, constituting a full board. ....

The following bills, approved by the finance committee were read:

Wienke & Davis......................$ 403.05

W. H. Lahman, grates................ 39.80

Sosman & Landis, stage braces, etc.. 11.25

J. C. Choate, matting and shades..... 57.00

A. R. Murphey, paint and colors...... 152.31

P. P. Woodard, labor in library....... .50

Funk & Wagnalls Co., books......... 18.00

C. Heine, drayage and freight......... 20.68

A. J. Olson, tile......................... 175.00

Wm. Wienke, engineer................. 50.00

Woodstock Sentinel, September 13, 1900.

***

October 1, 1900
936 Huron Street
Racine, Wisconsin

Dear Lena,

Just a quick note to say, YES, I would love to come to Woodstock on Sunday, October 16th to see your new house and meet your fiancé and your Woodstock friends. I will be able to catch the 7:00 a.m. which will get me there by ten, and then I will have to meet the 5:30 p.m. coming back, but that should be fine, right? It isn't a lot of time but should be enough for a good look…at Woodstock that is.

Got to hurry off. Today, I am sewing at the laundry. I'm doing that more nowadays than sewing at home.

Highest regards,
Ida

***

John strode into the parlor with a great big smile on his face. His hair was recently cut, and he had on his church suit and two-tone shoes. His wide tie had been carefully knotted so that it lay comfortably on the front of his white shirt with the stiff starched collar.

"*Meine, sehr gutaussehend*…handsome," his mother said as she looked up from her mending. "Vhere you go off to?"

"To meet the girl of my dreams!" John practically chortled his good news.

His mother simply said, "Haft a gut time. Brink her home to meet me."

"I will, Ma. I will when I know for sure."

John's excitement was palpable. It was like Christmas in October, only better. He loved the anticipation of the moment.

It was a glorious fall day. The large trees in the cemetery across the field were in full color with oranges, reds, yellows, and just a bit of green still showing. It was his favorite time of year because fall postponed the advent of winter. As he hurried along on the dirt track passing between the Protestant and Catholic cemeteries, he could smell and even taste the clay in the air, dust from a passing surrey.

Al and Lena's house was easy to find, just over the hill on Jackson Street about halfway to the square from Ma's. It had come up for rent in August, and Al had jumped at it. In the intervening months, he had papered and painted it inside and out and had added bits of furniture, but it still needed a woman's touch.

Al was a hard worker and a civic minded soul who was doing well with his business. He had been asked to paint and paper many of the new houses in Woodstock and a number of the churches. His crew had worked their magic on the City Hall renovation. He was exactly at the right place in his life to take a wife.

But was John? John slowed his pace—suddenly a bit more nervous. He had no house, no business, no great looks to bring to the table. Did he know what he was getting into? What if he disliked how Ida looked? Maybe he should have asked for a photograph? He shook himself and picked up his pace again. If anything, she was the one who would be put off by his looks. He was going to have to have a personality today because his looks were not going to carry him. He stopped. He was standing in front of the house. His stomach took a lurch, but his curiosity won the day. He walked up the dirt path, up onto the porch, wiped his feet and turned the knob.

"John!" Al greeted him with exaggerated joviality. "Glad you could make it."

John looked around the interior of the house. A good number of people were already in attendance; after all this was a 'housewarming' for Al and Lena not a 'meet Ida' party. He had furnished much of the food and drink for the party – his donation. The house was not totally bare. One huge square, expandable wooden table was covered with a good variety of beverages, sweets, and sandwiches. With about twenty people milling around, it looked like a good turn-out.

John sought something to say in this uncomfortable situation as his eyes took in the room. "When do the drapes go up?"

"Lena's brother and father will be bringing her goods in two weekends. She can't wait to start decorating."

"Excellent!" John felt too exuberant in his reply. He tried to calm himself. "Are you enjoying your last few months of bachelorhood?"

"Not much; I have made a pallet on the floor in the bedroom. Lena says she might get a bed from her family. So, I'm on the floor for now. It's okay, but a bed would ease my back after a day of painting."

"I haven't seen you down at the Pleasure Club for a while. Lots of work?"

"Yes, we've been busy mostly with houses now…trying to get the outside work done before it gets too cold."

"Good for you!" Out of character he clapped Al on the back. "Is Bob here?" he asked looking around at faces for the first time.

"He said he's coming but isn't here yet. You shouldn't be so hard on him, John. He's just young and feeling his oats. John?"

John's mind had stopped working. He was hearing the words, but the advice was not registering. He was looking at a striking young woman who was laughing with Lena and a few other women. She stood out in the crowd in a stylish dark green brocade travel suit and a Gibson girl blouse with a black cross tie. Her brown hair was upswept under a fashionable black hat with a few tastefully applied feathers and a bow that hung down the back. She looked up and locked eyes with him. A small smile played across her lips, but then as if she remembered that it was rude to stare, she dropped her eyes and returned to the group.

Al smiled.

"John?" Al's voice broke through the reverie. "Do you want to meet her?"

As John walked with Al across the room that would soon be the parlor, he tried to smile or at least look friendly.

"Excuse me, ladies." The women made the circle wider. Oh no, not in front of all these women, John shouted silently. "Miss Ida Doering of Racine, Wisconsin, I would like you to meet my brother Mr. John Wienke of Woodstock, Illinois. John, this is Lena's friend, Ida."

Ida was first to extend a hand, not like a real handshake, but in a palm-down way that left John not really knowing what to do with it. He clasped it in his much larger hand. And they both said, "How do you do" in unison. He didn't bow to the hand, nor did he kiss it, which he had heard was at times appropriate. He lowered his eyes and his head as he took her hand and then just held it, as his eyes slid back up to her pretty face. They held each other's eyes for a long moment. And then as if on cue, Al and Lena both started talking about the house, and the moment was gone, the gaze was broken, and the hand was dropped.

John stood there spent. He listened to Lena's plans and tried to relax. Without warning, Ida was at his elbow. "Would you like to buy me a drink, John."

He startled a bit and then smiled back at her smile, "Of course, I would, Ida." He held out his arm to her. She took it, and they moved across the room as one.

***

November 1, 1900
936 Huron Street
Racine, Wisconsin

Dear Lena,

Oh, what a day you gave me. I am destroyed having to come back here and to not be able to see all of you until…when…your wedding, I suppose!

I am now clerking five days a week at Fisher laundry. Nice of my brother-in-law to offer the job to family, although I imagine it saves him money also. I am also working on a quick baptismal outfit. They didn't want to order it before the little one arrived safe and sound. But now they want it within the week. So, I must apply myself, but I can hardly think about hems and stitches to say nothing about embroidery designs.

Have you heard anything about whether John would want to see me again? I know there's hardly been time for letters to be sent. I was encouraged that he wanted to walk me to the train. It was such a short time to get to know someone. I'm all sixes and sevens.

Please, please, write soon and let me know what Al said after the party.

Anxiously awaiting your reply,
Ida

Ida looked at the sewing in her lap. She had gotten Lena's letter to the box just as the postman was emptying it. The letter should make today's train. She had to concentrate and embroider this beautiful little dress. As she stared at her work, needle poised to dip through the material, her father's face seemed to appear on the white fabric. Oh, how she still missed him.

Strong and handsome, Heinrich Döring was a real Mensch. With black hair and hazel-green eyes, he had turned many a lady's head. Heinrich or Henry, as he would be known in the new world, brought his family to America when Ida was six years old. She remembered the day they had stood hand in hand on the top deck of the ship, feeling the salt breeze on their faces looking westward toward America.

"Amerika ist ein großartiges Land und wir werden dort so glücklich und frei sein." America is a great land, and we are going to be so happy and free there. When she heard her Papa, little Ida felt such joy.

Then they sailed into New York City harbor where a man changed the spelling of their name. Papa told them *"Wie sind jetzt die Doerings von Amerika."* We are now the Doerings from America.

New York was so much taller than other cities. Ida loved the street cars, horses in straw hats, and the men in black suits and hats bustling with clothes racks on wheels.

"Was für ein wonderbarer Ort, um Schneider zu sein." Mama had said. What a great place to be a tailor.

Too soon they were off again, this time on a train to Racine, and then fifty miles inland by cart to the small town of Whitewater in Wisconsin where her Uncle Karl, her mother's brother and his family awaited them. *"Willkommen in Ihrem neuen Hause,"* everyone said. Welcome to your new home.

Those days in Whitewater were so happy, she pictured herself and her friends dancing and running in the meadow behind their house. She remembered the feeling of a safe haven as she sat on her papa's lap listening to stories read from a big German story book. She could still hear his calm, deep voice speaking his native language.

"*Und sie lebten glücklich bis ans Ende ihrer Tage. Das Ende*" And they lived happily ever after. The end.

But it wasn't the end. Ida was in high school when Papa's employer, the Easterly Works Wheat Processing closed and moved to Minneapolis. The company claimed they were forced to close because Wisconsin was changing from growing wheat to milking dairy cows. Papa found a new job, and they moved to Beloit, and within a year, he was dead.

Tears sprung to Ida's eyes. Had it already been eight years since that fateful day? She had come home from church and discovered her beloved father sprawled on the plush rug of the living room with a teacup still in his hand. The paper was brief:

> Henry Dorring, aged 49 years, dropped dead at his home at Beloit, from heart disease last night, while his wife was attending church. He was supposed to be in general good health until he fell dead.
>
> *Janesville Daily Gazette*, July 18, 1893.

And that was it. Quite an obituary for such a wonderful man. All happiness drained from the world for a long while after the day that Papa died.

Ida sighed and wiped her eyes with her sleeve handkerchief.

Last year, J. Nicholas Stoffel, who had lost his wife just about the same time that they lost Papa, rented a room in their house to be closer to his work at the J. I. Case facility down Huron Street. Could it be that her mother would marry again before she would? Ida shook her head at the irony.

Emma had mentioned last Sunday that she was again expecting – number four. "Don't tell Mama yet," Emma had whispered.

And now Ida was looking at marriage and moving away. Ida whispered, "Don't tell Mama, yet."

Mr. Stoffel and Mama seemed a good match. They were kind and polite to each other. Maybe—

"Ida? Ida!" Mama's voice was more than a bit strident, and it brought her back from reverie. "*Was machen sie?*" What are you making?

"Nothing, Mama."

"*Ich sehe das! Wie kommt das Kleid?*"?" I see that. How is the dress coming?

"The dress is coming fine." Ida hedged just a bit. "Mama, what would you do if I got married?"

"*Ich wäre so glücklich!*" The dress was all but forgotten.

"You would be happy? I'm just worried that I would leave you in the lurch."

"'Lurch?' *Was bedeutet ist?*"

"It means I would leave you without much income if I wasn't here in Racine." She rubbed her thumb and two fingers together, a universal sign of money.

"Ve be fine. *Ich haben*, um, *Gottes willen*, Mr. Stoffel." Louisa crossed her fingers on both hands. "*Wohin würdest du gehen?*" I have, God willing, Mr. Stoffel. Where would you go?

"Woodstock. Woodstock, Illinois."

"*Der Mensch ist?*"

"Lena's fiancé's brother, John. Remember we talked about him when she was here?"

"Ja."

"*Ich bin nicht absolut sicher, aber* I think he might be the one." A little smile played on Ida's lips.

Louisa gripped one of Ida's hands tightly, looking into her eyes. *"Ich muss ihn erst treffen."*

"Of course, you'll meet him first. I promise. Now I must work on this dress." Ida smiled at her mother and received a smile in return. So much for 'don't tell Mama.' At least she hadn't revealed Emma's secret.

***

WOODSTOCK PLEASURE CLUB

The Woodstock Pleasure club held its annual meeting last evening, and elected the following named officers for the ensuing year:

President—Harry Cross.

Vice-President—A. J. Mullen.

Secretary—Geo. W. Lemmers.

Treasurer—C. S. Northrop.

Trustees—Albert Wienke, C. C. Harting, E. A. Wyant and Wm. Gritzbaugh.

The club is in a very prosperous condition, and its popularity is not waning one iota.

Woodstock Sentinel, November 15, 1900.

***

CITY COUNCIL
Regular Meeting
Woodstock, Ill., November 2, 1900.

E. C. Jewett, Mayor presiding.

Ald. Cannon, Hill, Osborn, Schuett, Stupfel and Walters answered to their names at roll-call, constituting a full board.

The following bills were read:

Gus Olson, ditching..................$	88.50
C. Heine, drayage, freight, sprinkling	22.62
Jas. Corr, police duty...................	6.00
W. C. Bates, meals for prisoners......	2.90

Woodstock Sentinel, Co., printing....	37.35
Geo. W. Lemmers, postage, etc.......	1.50
Henry Holmgren, labor on streets....	41.25
Chas. C. Snyder, gravel.................	47.17
Schneider & Clark, building shed......	33.17
Citizens Telephone Co., poles.........	25.25
General Electric, Co., wire...............	43.05
Gen. Elec., Lamps, transformers, etc..	179.01
C. J. Bodeker & Co., coal..............	387.85
C. & N.-W. Ry. Co., freight...........	476.41
Mrs. C. M. Curtis, librarian..........	15.00
Wm. Wienke, City engineer..........	50.00
John Bolger, Marshal and supt. w.w.	65.00
A. E. Rathbun, nightwatch............	50.00
Fred Sahs, trimmer....................	40.00
Geo. W. Lemmers, clerk..............	15.00

A petition signed by Lee Barr, John Asmus, F. H. Smith and H. Hanson asking that a sidewalk be built from the intersection of the east side of Madison street with the southerly side of McHenry road, thence north easterly to the northeastern side of Park street, thence southeasterly to the south side of Center street, thence east to the terminus of Center street, was presented and read.

Moved by Ald. Hill, second by Ald. Cannon, that the prayer of said petition be granted. Rollcall showed motion unanimously carried.

Woodstock Sentinel, November 8, 1900.

***

Woodstock Pleasure Club
## Hoy Block		Woodstock, Illinois

November 30, 1900

Dear Ida,

I hope that your quick trip did not wear you out too much and that this letter finds you well.

I very much enjoyed our time together and hope that we will see each other again soon. In fact, I just had the opportunity to talk to Al and he says that Lena is coming to Woodstock for New Year's Eve and staying at a friend's house. I was wondering if you might think about doing the same. I believe you met many nice people when you came down, and I'm sure I can find someone to give you lodging overnight which will be a necessity on New Year's Eve, unless we just stay up all night and I put you on the morning train back to Racine, ha. You will probably have to work on New Year's Eve day but could take the 4:30 train which would get you here in plenty of time to celebrate with your new friends, including me. I do hope you consider me one of your new friends.

There will be a dance at the Armory on New Year's Eve and fireworks all over town at midnight. We may be small, but we throw a good New Year's party.

I know this would be a lot to arrange in a short order, but if you could, I would be glad to take you a few turns around the dance floor, as long as you go easy on me.

Thank you for considering this invitation and let me know if you accept as I must quickly find lodging for you. All of Woodstock looks forward to your return, especially.

John Wienke

***

PERSONAL MENTION

Emil Wienke was home from Beloit for the Thanksgiving holiday.

Woodstock Sentinel, December 6, 1900.

***

"Come on, Herman. You simply must come with me!" Ida plied her brother with her most beseeching look. "I need you! Mama won't let me go overnight alone." They were standing in the kitchen of the house on Huron Street, Ida having made Herman a late-night sandwich as he claimed he had missed supper while working. She hoped she could persuade him with food.

"I don't know. I—"

"I do know. I must find a way. I am becoming an old maid, and at twenty-six, this might be my last chance! Once we're there, you can stay with Al and I with Lena. Or we can all stay with Al. Goodness, we aren't children. All it will cost you is the train ticket and entrance to the dance. I'll even pay for that! Do you have a date lined up for Silvester?"

"Maybe…." Herman's voice trailed off.

"Oh, never mind! I'll just turn into a dried-up old spinster taking in sewing in Racine, Wisconsin."

"So why don't you just go?"

"Mr. Stoffel does not believe in women traveling alone, especially at night. Women don't belong out in the world. They must be protected by strong virile men." She grasped Herman's biceps and squeezed.

"Ouch! Stop that! Since when does Mr. Stoffel make the rules in this house?"

"See, I'm as strong as you are, stronger even. Since Mama listens to him. But who has the right to stop me from going to see my beau?" Ida wailed.

"Oh, your beau. I didn't understand the question. Will I facilitate you seeing your beau? How in the world can I say 'no' to that? Does this beau have a name?"

"John Wienke from Woodstock, Illinois…born and raised. Good German stock. Member of the German Lutheran Church in Woodstock."

"High or Low?" The question was one that was often asked by parents, but it didn't reflect a social position…not really. High German was spoken in the southern part of Germany where the elevation was higher. It was also the older version of German. The Doerings were high German. Low German was what one might call a simplified German common to Bavaria.

"Low," Ida admitted. "But this is America, so that shouldn't matter."

Herman raised his eyebrows with a grim look. "Looks like you are doomed. Romeo and Juliet; John and Ida. How will you ever understand each other?" Then he broke into a smile.

"Oh you! We both speak English very well, thank you!"

"How long have you known him?" Herman was still rubbing his arm.

"Since October, but he sent me a very nice invitation to come and even offered to arrange lodging with one of his friends. If I can't see him, I'll simply have a broken heart." Ida fluttered her eyelashes at him with a coy little smile.

"*Ach meine Gotte!* You are such a little flirt! This man doesn't have a chance." Herman laughed, shaking his head.

***

John ran as fast as the frozen, rutted sleigh track would allow. Dressed in his best wool suit and overcoat, he had fallen only once….so far. His galoshes flapped against his legs as he ran. He had stopped to pull them on before bolting out of his mother's house, which was lucky because twice a sleigh had trotted past forcing him into the crusty snow along the side of the road. The New Year revelers could have at least offered him a ride down to the square, he thought. It was cold out here. Their hail-fellow-well-met greetings were fine, but a ride would have been much more appreciated.

His breath was coming in great puffs of steam as he rounded the corner onto the square which was alive with sleighs and couples scurrying here and there even in the cold weather. He skirted the park on the north side and then went north on Benton Street toward the armory, just a few blocks ahead. Light reflecting off the low hanging clouds guided the way. He slowed to catch his breath. He didn't want to show up huffing and puffing like an old man.

As he pulled open the door, Brubaker's orchestra was playing a waltz and nearly all the young people seemed to be standing along the sides of the room while most of the older couples were dancing. Did his thirty years make him old or young? He hurried to the men's cloakroom and removed his coat, tucking his cap and gloves into his galoshes. He would need them for sure for the mile-walk home. Emerging he scanned the crowd – where was she?

John smiled as he looked out across the crowd. His height allowed him several inches on most of the assembly. He acknowledged a few friends from afar. Ida and her brother Herman had taken the train down from Racine to be here for the celebration and were staying at Al and Lena's new house. Al must have gotten some new beds. John wondered how long they would be staying. Not that it mattered greatly. This night was what was important, but he better find her, or her dance card would be full. He wanted to feel her in his arms. Where the heck….?

There she was! Dancing with Bob's business partner, Albert Schneider. She looked like the belle of the ball, and he made his way through the crowd, greeting Lena and Al, being introduced to Herman. The music stopped, and Albert, always the gentleman, guided Ida back to the circle of friends. Her beautiful light blue gown, with a high collar and lace across the breast and around the sleeves, swirled delightfully around her ankles. Did she have golden slippers on?

As they approached the group, Ida and Albert were laughing. Then Albert spied John. "Well, it's about time, Wienke. You shouldn't leave your girl lollygagging around for the likes of me to take advantage of." Albert's attention turned toward Ida. "There you are, m'lady. Safe and sound. A few crushed toes, but who's counting."

Albert and Ida laughed again – and inside joke.

John reached over and took Ida's hand. "I hope you haven't bruised her beautiful feet, Schneider, or I'll have to take you out behind the building!" Albert looked appropriately chagrined. Then John said, "Say, Al, can you find a nice Woodstock girl for my friend, Herman, to dance with. He's come a long way to get stuck talking to my brother."

Without waiting for an answer, John led Ida out onto the floor. As long as they kept up the Waltzes, he'd be okay, but once the orchestra moved on to the Turkey Trot or the Bunny Hop or the newest one, he just heard about yesterday, what was it…ah yes, the Texas Tommy….

"Can you dance the Texas Tommy?" John asked.

"The WHAT?" Ida's wide eyes made her look incredulous or maybe even a bit miffed. John realized that he hadn't even said hello yet.

"I hope you cannot dance the Texas Tommy or the Turkey Trot. Because if you can, I'm a cooked goose…er…turkey." He smiled, feeling her small body following his every move.

"No, my good man. I'm from Wisconsin, not Texas. I do, however, dance a pretty fine polka." Ida's smile grew even bigger as his face fell, and his bravado disappeared. And then she laughed – a wonderful sound –

even at his expense. "Don't worry, I won't make you polka. Waltzing is just fine with me."

They danced – his arms full of this beautiful maiden. They stepped around the dance floor with John silently counting, 1 2 3, 1 2 3, as competent as any other couple, and for the first time, John enjoyed dancing.

The next dance was a quadrille. John led Ida off the floor, and they found the punch bowl and watched the dancers. The four couples squared up and followed the call of the leader. It was complicated. At times one of the couples missed a cue, and the first most experienced couple had to work the square back into the dance. Interesting, but John had no desire to participate. He noticed that Ida was tapping her toe to the music, and he wondered if he was holding her back from enjoying the evening festivities.

John leaned over near her ear, "Would you like for me to find you a partner for the next quadrille?"

Ida looked up at him. "You would do that? Shuffle me off to another partner?"

"Oh no." His answer was instantaneous. "I just want you to dance all that you want and not to be held back by my two left feet."

Ida looked down at his shoes. They were well worn, but she could tell that he had tried to shine their scratched surface for the occasion. She smiled. "They don't both look left to me." She looked back up at his blue eyes. "I perfectly happy to stand on the sidelines and drink punch with you until the next waltz."

John smiled. "Good. Me too."

"Don't the ladies look like they have no feet and float rather than dance."

John chuckled. They did look like they were floating while the men kicked up their heals beside their partners.

"The women look so graceful while the men are barely keeping up."

The quadrille ended. Ida looked at her dance card. The next dance was a mazurka. "How about a mazurka?"

John paled. "A what?"

"Mazurka. It's very easy. From Russia. Just watch how it's done."

Dancers took the floor, and the music began. Couples took three deliberate steps forward and then turned so they were facing the opposite way and repeated the three steps and again rearranged and took the steps forward again.

"It doesn't look too hard." John rubbed his forehead with his hand.

"Come on, we'll try it right here on the sidelines. Everyone is watching the dancers on the floor. No one will notice us.

John took Ida's proffered hand and put his other hand at her side. They followed the steps of the others and had almost mastered the steps when the orchestra sped up the music. There was no time to think between movements and they immediately got their feet tangled on the transition from front to back.

They stopped, laughed together, and steadied each other so they wouldn't trip and fall.

"Dog-gone-it! I was just getting the hang of it." John formally took Ida in his arms, got the beat, and tried the steps again at the faster clip.

The orchestra increased speed, and they held on to each other for dear life. Then the music stopped! And all the dancers collapse into each other, panting, laughing; the men congratulated each other, and the smiling women floated off back to their seats.

"Now you know two dances." Ida patted her hair feeling for loose strands and found none. "Next the polka."

"I feel like I can try any of them with you."

"Be careful. I might make a dancer of you yet. Do you have dance contests here in Woodstock?"

John's gaze shifted from the dance floor to Ida's face to judge her seriousness. "Not that I've noticed."

Ida hid her smile behind her gloved hand, but he saw it in her eyes.

"You are quite the joker aren't you, Ida Doering." John shook his head and looked down at the floor and his scuffed shoes.

When the orchestra played the opening strains of "Roll Out The Barrel," the omni-present German drinking song and Ida stood, curtsied to John and held out her hand to John. He finished his punch before reaching for her hand and bowing over it. Ida then explained that the polka, how could he not know how to polka, used the same exaggerated step at the beginning, but then followed it with a rocking hop. She demonstrated. John nodded and the tried a few steps.

"Good!" Ida practically shouted over the music. "No instead of just rocking back and forth, take another step and we'll turn a circle."

Before long, they were circling the dance floor with Ida leading. It wasn't long before John found the beat and began to lead. "This dancing is exhausting," he shouted into Ida's ear, and she nodded her agreement.

As they counted down the clock at midnight, John was at Ida's elbow.

"5…4…3…2…1! Happy New Year!"

The crowd went wild, and the band struck up 'Auld Lang Syne.' John leaned down and placed a proper kiss on Ida

Doering's lips. And then gave her a brief cheek-to-cheek hug, saying "Happy New Year, Ida."

"Happy New Year, John." Ida's lips were so close to his ear that he felt her breath on his perspiring neck.

They stood holding hands and drinking in the intoxication of the moment. "This is going to be a good year!" they said to each other in unison. Yes, a very good year.

Ida Doering
14-16 years old.
Circa 1890

John F. Wienke
20 years old
Circa 1890

Vas You Dar, John?
(1901)

John Wienke and Ida Doering sat, huddled from the cold north wind, on the leeward side of the depot, waiting for the train that would take Ida and her brother back to Racine. The typewriter factory had given the boys January 1st off, and for once John was glad to have a no-pay day if it meant he could sit here and talk with Ida for a few minutes more. Herman made himself scarce, walking down the platform, pretending to read notices and wanted posters. They sat in silence improperly close, John's knee touching hers.

John felt like he'd just been gut-punched. He didn't want to let her go. Say something, fool.

"It was pretty quiet here last night...I mean...for New Year's Eve. We usually have a lot more fireworks and parties.

"Mm. Maybe because last year was the people's new century, and this year was the government's new century."

John chuckled. "You're right. For the people, January 1, 1900, was the beginning of the Twentieth Century. The people used up their fireworks last year."

Ida inched a bit closer. "So, when can you come see me?"

He took a deep breath, cleared his throat, and began to tell Ida how many hours the factory was expecting from their crew in the months to come. He wanted to be honest about this long-distance relationship. It wasn't going to be easy.

"…six days a week and sometimes Sundays, too, they say, depending on the orders."

"Noooo!" Ida almost whined. "When will we see each other? And Mama wants to meet you."

"I'll do what I can, but I don't want you to get your hopes up too high for frequent visits. On the sunny side, I will be earning a lot of money which I am saving for my store."

"Well, it looks like I'm going to have to make a few visits to Lena's then. First visit will be the wedding of the century."

John smiled. Al and Lena's house was ready for the new couple to move in. Lena's things had been moved before the first snow. Al, Lena, Ida, and Herman had served as their own chaperones the night before – the girls in the marriage bed and the boys on pallets on the floor in the parlor. John had been invited to join them, but he bowed to formality and walked the few blocks home. But he was back early to join them for breakfast and the walk to the station.

The train whistled its approach, and Ida arose to gather her belongings. Herman came over to help. The men shook hands.

"Nice little town you have here, John." Herman emphasized the word, 'little.'

"Thanks, it is. I'm glad you came to the festivities," he paused and looked at Ida, "and brought this wonderful girl with you."

"You betcha. Far be it from me to keep her from her beau." Herman sent Ida a knowing smile, gathered up the cases, and climbed aboard, waiting at the top of the steps for Ida.

John turned Ida toward him and kissed her lightly on the lips. "Thank you for coming."

"You betcha!" Her response was a bit too loud. They both chuckled. She held his gaze for another long moment then turned and pulled herself up onto the first step, still clasping John's hand. The train began to move, and their hands slipped apart. She stayed on the step until the train was past the platform then waved her handkerchief at him, turned, and disappeared inside.

John watched the caboose until it disappeared – until he could no longer hear the whistles at the crossings – until he realized that he was standing on the platform as if he had missed the train. He looked down and chuckled at himself. "This is a train I do not want to miss," he declared aloud. And he turned and headed back up Main Street to the square, whistling, 'Auld Lang Syne.'

***

OPENING OF A CENTURY.
Evening Celebrated Without Unusual Noise in This City

The dual evening – the opening of a new year and of a new century simultaneously – did not create any unusual excitement in Woodstock. As soon as Father Time had indicated the hour of midnight, Monday night, the announcement of the new year's arrival was made by the ringing of the church bells and the blowing of the whistle at the city power house, the firing of guns and cannon crackers, but the noise was not nearly as bewildering or as long drawn out as we have known it on previous announcements of the birth of a new year.

Aside from the watch meeting services at the M.E. church and the celebration of midnight mass at St. Mary's, there were many cases of individual and family watchings of the old year out and the new year in, and the usual hearty expressions of good wishes on the part of the participants.

None of THE SENTINEL readers ever before witnessed the birth of a century, and it is highly improbable that any of them ever will again, hence it behooves all to make the most of the years of this century that may be vouchsafed to them, realizing our dependence on and our responsibility to a Higher Power, and our duties to our fellows.

THE SENTINEL wishes all great joy and prosperity in this century, which, if men realize the possibilities that stretch out before them, is destined to be the greatest in the history of the world.

We welcome the new century! May it treat us no worse than its predecessor has done, and may it witness a greater and grander appreciation of the fatherhood of God and the brotherhood of man.

Woodstock Sentinel, January 3, 1901.

***

Local Intelligence

You should endeavor to discover your natural tendencies and apply them, unless, indeed, your natural tendencies are all evil.

When women don't know what etiquette would demand, they kiss each other.

Boys are, of course, taught to rise and give a seat to any lady who enters a room, also to rise and remain standing till a woman is seated, but the rule is often in abeyance to their own mothers and sisters. You may enter it on your records as a rule without exceptions, that no one will ever be at ease in society who fails in the little daily amenities in the home.

Have you been vaccinated yet? Arm or –?

Beware, the tax collector will soon be abroad in the land.

Woodstock Sentinel, January 31, 1901.

***

February 17, 1901
936 Huron Street
Racine, Wisconsin

Dear John,

In a week's time, you will be enjoying the wedding festivities while I will be in Racine playing nursemaid to sick people. Mr. Stoffel was the first to come down with the grippe, and so is the first to feel better. He was completely down for two days and then rested for two more. He says he will return to work tomorrow, although Mama is trying to persuade him to go back on Monday. Then comes Clara home with it – did I tell you that she is clerking for a doctor's office now? She was told she must stay home a week so as to not spread it to the patients, but it would seem to me it is the other way around. The patients spread it to her – they should stay away. Ha! And lastly Mama is feeling poorly this morning.

I have chamber pots to empty, soup to make, and cool sponge baths to give…and I'm just waiting to begin to feel feverish any time. So, I am quarantined here and cannot come to the wedding!!! It's not fair! But I wouldn't want to have all of you sick also. At least this grippe isn't as hard on one as it might be. When Mr. Stoffel came home, we were all very afraid. But the doctor said with rest and plenty of pea soup, he should be fine. I do not look forward to my sick time and am doing my best to stave it off with garlic and camphor.

Mama is calling. Must go and give this to the postman who will pass in about an hour.

I remain truly yours,
Ida

***

ALMOST AN EPIDEMIC.
Grippe Has Many Victims in Its Tortuous Grasp.

Grippe, or influenza, is certainly storming Woodstock, as well as Chicago and neighboring cities. Many victims have been confined to the house for the past two weeks, and the doctors have been busy night and day. It is not causing a great number of deaths, but it has left its hundreds and thousands out of business for a time. The fact that it is of a mild form is something to be thankful for, however, and that it is on the decrease is also a cause for thanks.

According to an eminent Chicago physician, the disease is caused by a germ. The germ is most active at this season for several reasons. One is people huddle into warm rooms and give the germs a chance to breed. Then the several sorts of weather we have had has helped the germ to get to work. Influenza generally affects the air passages in the throat and chest, but it frequently goes to other parts of the body. It sometimes descends into the bowels. Persons who are suffering from any other disease are very likely to catch influenza and to suffer with it more than others. A rest of several days under a physician's care is the only sure cure. The man who tries to stay on his feet and fight the disease is making a mistake.

Influenza, or the grippe, was first known as such in this country in 1891. It started in Russia in 1890 and went around the world. There was an epidemic of it in Chicago in 1891.

Woodstock Sentinel, January 24, 1901.

***

Surprised on His Birthday

On Tuesday evening Frank Kniebush took the evening meal at the home of his father, Wm. Kniebusch, and he had hardly finished the repast ere he was pounced upon by a bunch of his male friends, who had learned that it was the 26th anniversary of his birthday. "Finnegan" stood the onslaught heroically, and as soon as he had somewhat recovered his composure, the spokesman of the party arose and in a few well-worded sentences presented him with a beautiful opal stud richly set. The boys had a royal good time until the first gray streaks of dawn began to chase each other over the eastern hills, when they scattered to their respective homes, wishing their young friend many happy returns of the day. Those present were:

John Wienke	C. C. Harting
Robert Wienke	John C. Rowe
Albert Wienke	Albert Schneider
E. A. Boyce	Joe Connors
Harry Cross	C. A. Stone
Frank Martin	Amos Stephenson
John L. Carroll	Malte Schwabe
James Sullivan	Walter Holtz
Charles Bachman	Charles Bier
Charles Joorfetz	Fred Joorfetz
Geo. W. Field	Charles Hayes

T. O. Cowlin	Gus Wagner
Geo J. Griffiths	F. N. Blakeslee
E. L. Hayhurst	

Woodstock Sentinel, February 14, 1901.

***

Woodstock Pleasure Club
Woodstock, Illinois

February 25, 1901

Dear Ida,

I am so sorry that you will not be here for the wedding, but I do understand your nursing assignment. I do hope you do not fall ill along with everyone else. I will miss your presence as I'm sure Lena and Al will. However, I would suggest that you come instead on Monday evening, March 4 for an inaugural dance the Republicans are putting on in the Armory. It is sure to please. I don't know if you can get away on a Monday afternoon and Tuesday morning, but if you can, Lena has said that you may stay at their house. She and Al will be in Beloit making the after the wedding rounds of family.

We had a great Woodstock-type birthday party for a buddy of ours, Finnegan Kniebusch, last Thursday. We sprung a surprise on him at his father's home. It was not quite a drunken night of entertainment, but close to it. All the town boys that we grew up with were there. Al, Bob and I staggered to our beds just as the sun was rising. No work for us on Friday.

If you can come, please let me know by return post so that I can make arrangements. It would be very nice to see you.

Sincerely,

John

***

Closing Notes

Now March.

Best oysters in town at Conklin's.

If you want a good suit of clothes for $7, $8 or $10, why, call on Buckley. He's got it.

Paint and paper are being applied to the store of C. F. Thorne by Wienke & Davis, making a great improvement.

There will be a grand masquerade ball in this city on St. Patrick's day—Mar. 17. The bills have already been issued.

Railway trains were run at a disadvantage yesterday, and most of them were late on account of the drifting snow.

Woodstock Sentinel, March 1, 1900.

***

March 1, 1901
936 Huron Street
Racine, Wisconsin

Dear John,

Thank you so much for your short invitation to the dance, but I will have to decline as the weather has been horrible here by the lake, and Mama, while much improved, is still unable to keep up with the housework and cooking. We have had feet of snow instead of inches, and the city is working hard to shovel out. I'm not sure how deep the drifts are in Woodstock. Probably the drifts all melt the next day in that blessed city, but here they are even disrupting train service now. I'm sure you will be able to fill your dance card without me, but just don't hold those ladies too tightly or I'll be jealous. I won't even have Lena to spy for me. Ha!

We've been busy this winter with many engagements for Clara and her instruments. I've told you that she plays piano and sings beautifully, but I don't think you know that she also plays the mandolin. She has joined with two friends, and they sing for their suppers at various gatherings, especially during breaks in cinch card parties. The reviews have been good with more invitations each day. The girls have even had to turn down some engagements due to conflicting dates. Today she is off to a St. David's Day celebration. It is a common Welsh celebration, although I have never heard of St. David, have you? Here in Racine, we have a St. David's Society which is sponsoring the day. Clara and her friends will sing two songs, as will a ladies' quartet and a men's quartet from the Methodist church, along with a few solos, recitations, and speeches. Clara had to learn the Welsh national song in Welsh, so she can sing it with gusto at the appropriate time. She is now sure that she wants to be an entertainer. Can't you just see the theater poster "Clara Doering and Her Mandolin singing The Welsh National Song!" Ha! Ah, the pipedreams of youth.

Finnegan's party sounds great. I wish I could have come with you.

This isn't going to be a long letter like I usually write because I'm punishing you for your short letter of last week. You can do better than five lines, can't you? Your life can't be that busy, can it? On the other hand, if it is that busy, maybe you don't have time for a girl. Or maybe life in wonderful Woodstock isn't all it is touted to be. What do you say to that, kind sir?

Have a fine time celebrating McKinley's win. Save a dance for me next time we see each other.

I remain your friend,
Ida.

***

Local Intelligence

Delightful sunshine and moderate temperatures greeted the people this morning.

If you want your organ or sewing machine repaired, call on E. B. Conklin. Leave orders at Hooker's grocery store.

John Wienke was a visitor at Beloit last Saturday.

Woodstock Sentinel, March 7, 1901.

***

Personals

The Wienke place west of Oakland cemetery has been sold to Wm. Corr, who will soon take possession, and the Wienke family will become residents of this city. They are the kind of people who make good citizens.

Woodstock Sentinel, March 7, 1901.

Personals

The Wienke Bros. have purchased the E.A. Stone residence property on Washington.

Woodstock Sentinel, March 7, 1901.

ALBERT WIENKE MARRIED

Married, at the home of the officiating clergyman, Rev. H. Dannenfeldt, in this city on Thursday, Feb. 28, 1901, Albert Wienke and Miss Lena Steinke. The happy couple left at once for a trip to Beloit, where they remained for several days, the guests of relatives of both bride and groom.

The groom to this happy affair is the well-known painter and decorator, who was born and reared near this city and has spent his entire life here. He is a young man of ability, who has a wide circle of friends to extend to him best wishes for a long and prosperous married life. The bride is a native of Beloit and is said to be an exceedingly sensible and worthy young lady, who bears the respect of all who know her.

The young couple will make their home in this city. THE SENTINEL, and their many friends wish for them the best that life affords.

Woodstock Sentinel, March 7, 1901.

***

THE DORR CAUCUS
Declared for Lumley and Was
Shortest on Record

Pursuant to call, the Republican voters of the town of Dorr met in caucus at the courthouse in Woodstock, Ill., on Saturday March 3, 1900, at 1:30 p. m. L. T. Hoy, chairman of the town committee, called the caucus to order and read the call.

On motion duly made and seconded, E. C. Jewett was elected chairman and C. A. Lemmers secretary.

The following resolutions were presented and on motion were unanimously adopted:

Resolved, that V. S. Lumley, with two others whom he is hereby authorized to select, be appointed as a committee to select thirty delegates to represent the town of Dorr in the Republican county convention to be held at Woodstock, Ill., Mar. 5, 1901, and the chairman and secretary of this caucus are hereby authorized to issue credentials to said delegates when selected.

Be it further resolved That the delegates so selected be and they hereby are instructed to vote for and use all honorable means to secure the nomination of Hon. V. S. Lumley as state's attorney.

In accordance with said resolutions, V. S. Lumley, E. C. Jewett and C. H. Donnelly were named to constitute said committee.

By virtue of the power conferred upon them, the committee named the following as delegates to the county convention:

C. H. Donnelly	A. K. Bunker
John M. Hoy	O. H. Gilmore
E. C. Jewett	Geo. Eckert
Geo. W. Field	Frank R. Jackman
L. T. Hoy	Fred A. Walters
C. T. Donovan	F. A. Eastman
Fred W. Hartman	C. A. Lemmers
R. H. Conant	F. E. Hanaford
Jas. F. Casey	C. F. Thorne
C. A. Stone	L. J. Young
Ben Stupfel	D. F. Quinlan
Albert Wienke	W. S. McConnell
Geo. L. Murphy	Marcellus L. Joslyn
H. W. Wright	C. F. Renich

On motion the caucus adjourned.

Woodstock Sentinel, March 8, 1900.

IT MADE HIM MANY FRIENDS

That was a refreshing sight at the county convention when, realizing that he was defeated for a renomination by the Republicans of McHenry county, States Attorney Lumley arose before those who had turned him down, and, after thanking his friends for their cordial support and the Republicans of the county for the favors they have bestowed on him in the past, declared: "I am a Republican and no kicker or bolter," and then grasping his successful opponent by the hand, pledged him his unqualified support and extended to him his heartiest good-wishes.

Mr. Lumley is a fit representative of the large majority of Republicans of the town of Dorr, who, while they work with a vim for the nomination of a favorite son, loyally support the ticket whether they succeed in their efforts or not, realizing and believing that the will of the majority should be obeyed at all times if a party organization is to be maintained strong and hearty.

THE SENTINEL honors Mr. Lumley for the stand he took and the spirit he displayed and commends it to any who may be prone to disloyalty when their candidate fails in his aspirations.

Woodstock Sentinel, March 8, 1901.

***

PERSONAL MENTION

John Wienke was a visitor to Beloit last Saturday.

Woodstock Sentinel, March 14, 1901.

***

Woodstock Pleasure Club
Woodstock, Illinois

March 15, 1901

Dear Friend,

I finally have time to send a note. My brothers and I have finished our move to town. It took some doing. Ma's house was small, but twenty-five years of living there were packed into every closet and cupboard. We easily found a buyer because housing is at a premium here. The fellow who bought it owns a lot of rentals and will probably do some renovations and then rent it to someone at the

Oliver factory. I was amazed as I walked through one last time how my parents were able to raise eight children in five rooms —three bedrooms, a parlor, and a kitchen. Luckily, we were spread out enough that the older boys were gone before the younger ones needed a bed. They made it work.

We bought a house on Washington Street which is a residential street going out of town toward Harvard. The house has been updated with a good coat of paint, concrete paths, and modern conveniences. We are most happy with the change, and Ma is also. It's a bigger house with five bedrooms upstairs and one down. Each of us can have a bedroom with two left over, plus a kitchen, parlor and a formal dining room. Best of all, it is fully modernized. It has city water and a modern septic system with indoor plumbing! Ma is so happy with that as you might expect. No more chamber pots!

The last two weekends have been spent going to Beloit to bring the rest of Lena's goods to Woodstock. Her folks brought a wagon load last Fall, but she had two more loads which she entrusted to us to bring unharmed the forty miles to their new home. Bob and I went up on Saturday by train, and it took eight hours on the road on Sunday and then unloading. And then we turned around and did it again last weekend except that we took the wagon up on Saturday, loaded it, then back on Sunday, and unloaded it. It sure was hard to get up Monday morning.

I missed you at the dance. I only danced two waltzes all night, and they were not fun at all. I'm sure it was more fun than being snowed in at Racine under five-foot drifts with a north wind howling, but mostly it was just a lot of cheering and beer drinking. I left early and was abed by midnight. I hope that does not make me a bore in your mind.

I am still hoping you will be able to come down for the minstrel show in March. Let me know so I can plan.

I had thought of coming to visit a few weeks ago, before the snow hit, because I had a Sunday respite. But then I got bogged down in the details. If I come on Saturday after work, I will arrive after

supper and will have no place to lay my head. If I wait until Sunday,
I will arrive while you are away at church and will have to leave on
the 4:30 p.m. train so we would still have very little time together. IF
I came on Saturday, I could go to church with you Sunday morning
and see you for a longer time…but I would have to make my bed in
a snowbank outside your house. (It is spring here in Woodstock, but
I assume you still have piles of snow in Wisconsin.) Such a dilemma.
Please advise.

Must close as I work early tomorrow. They have been
keeping us to a twelve-hour day, but I don't complain. More work,
more money saved.

Yours truly,
John

***

Ida sat at her writing desk and read and then re-read the letter. Yes, she would go to Woodstock for that show no matter what. Seeing John in a minstrel show would be so funny. She imagined his face corked black and him singing with his mouth in an O like a cigar smoker making smoke rings. Now that she thought about it, she was glad he wasn't a cigarette smoker. He must smoke cigars now and again because she had smelled it on his jacket when they danced.

And yes, a place for him to lay his head if he visited Racine was a dilemma. She would ask her mother and Mr. Stoffel if John could stay here, but that was a bit difficult with the number of people who lived in the house now. She and Clara shared a bedroom, and Mama, Herman and Mr. Stoffel occupied the other three. Maybe John could just bunk on the couch in the front room. Herman called it the best bed in the house. Besides, it sounded like John was used to close quarters.

Mama often said, *"Lass der, der kalt ist, sick rühren die Kohlen."* Let the one who is cold stir the coals. Ida was without a doubt going to stir the coals. Even if they'd known each other for only six months and seen each other but a few times, he was the one she wanted. She would ask Mama about him staying, and then she'd see if she could get those coals glowing.

***

In his favorite chair in the parlor of the new house, John paged through the paper starting with the last page looking for the story. He wasn't sure why he always started with the last page…maybe just low expectations. "Men never get too old to acquire experience," said a quote on the last page… isn't that the truth!

The next page had an ad that caught his eye, "Gold dust in the water makes your dishes come out perfectly clean and free from grease. It is almost a pleasure to wash dishes with Gold Dust Washing Powder."

"Ma," he called out to Sophia in the kitchen where she was washing the evening dishes. "It says by the paper that you can get cleaner dishes if you put gold dust in the dish powder."

"Ach, no!" Sophia appeared in the doorway wiping her hands on a dish towel. "Vhat meanst *du*? My dishes are not so clean *fur deine Hoheit*? Vhy dey try'n to get rid of *Golt*?"

John laughed. "Did you just call me 'Your Highness?' Me? Why yes, fair maiden, come here and look at this!"

She looked over his shoulder. "Well, what 'bout dat? Must have too much Golt in 'laska. Soon in everyting."

"Like gold underwear."

"*Und* Golt Korsetts."

"Gold in flour. Maybe that's the secret ingredient in Gold Bond Flour."

"And in *Zucker*…Sugar…Just a bit sweeter *mit* Golt," Sophia wrote the ad for the sugar company.

They laughed, and John began turning the pages. When he reached the front page, he said, "Well, what do you know! We are front page news!" and began reading the article aloud as Sophia sank onto the sofa.

ARTISTES IN BLACK
Pleasure Club Minstrels Score a Big Success.

The white 700 or more crowded the City Hall to the very doors last Friday evening to witness the performance of the black 40 in refined minstrelsy, and while the audience gave very little sign that it was pleased, we have since heard no one express himself in any different manner. ….

"Ja," John interrupted himself. "The audience was very quiet at first, but we pulled them in."

"Mmmm." Sophia picked up her tatting, and he read on.

The audience, which was one of the largest ever seen in the hall, crowded the building to the very door, not a seat being vacant, the total from the sale of seats aggregating about $310.

John's eyes grew large. "Three hundred and ten dollars! That's three times what we made last year. Of course, this year's performance was much better than last year's. I think we are getting the hang of it."

"Mmmm." Sophia's hands worked swiftly making a lace fringe around a pillowcase. John looked at her and went back to the paper.

> With Director John L. Carroll and the Brubaker orchestra occupying their accustomed places in front of the footlights, the curtain went up at 8:15, revealing a very beautiful tropical scene, with potted plants, trailing vines, and a profusion of colored lights. In the rear of the stage was a balcony scene that was quite realistic. As the curtain went up the chorus, or circle, broke out…

Sophia looked up from her handiwork. "Vhat dat…circle."
"That's just what they call the singers in a minstrel show."
"*Warum?*"
"Why? Well…because…I guess because they stand or sit in a semi-circle when they sing." John hurried on.

> [The] circle, broke out with the opening chorus, "Hail, Little Children, All Hail," and from the balcony came the end men, with a song appropriate and beautiful, who marched to the front of the stage and after a few minutes' work with the bones and tamboes, took their places.

"Vas ist da bones and tamboes?" Sophia left her tatting behind as the article seemed to catch her attention.
"There is an interlocutor who is the master of ceremonies…*Der Zeremonienmeister*… and the two 'end men' who do the comedy with the…um…'funnymen'…the tambo and the bones. Sometimes there are more than just two, but they make jokes and make fun of the interlocutor behind his back."
"Okay." Sophia seemed to really be trying to understand.
John cleared his throat and continued.…

> Then Interlocutor Geo. W. Field appeared on the balcony with a song that began, "Now tell me, little children, do you hear me calling you?" to which there was a prompt and unanimous response. He descended the stairs, and his pages, Masters Richard and Edsall McHatton, bright and winsome sons of Mr. and Mrs. W.B. McHatton, followed with his chair, which they placed at the center of the circle, winning the applause of the audience by their skill and their neat and attractive attire.

Sophia shook her head. " *Kleine Kinder* in dis. *Waren es Neger?*"

"Yes Ma, young'uns and no…none of the people were Negroes. The children were little white boys with their faces blackened with burnt cork so they would look like little *Negerjungen.*"

"Hmmm." Sophia scrunched her brows together. "Not sure about *Kinder. Es ist nicht gut, Kinder so es benutzen!*"

"We weren't using them. They were part of the play— *ein Spiel.* It is a very funny play. We all pretend to be Negroes and then horse around."

"Hmmm. *Warum nicht ihre weißen Gesichter verwenden.*"

"Come on, English please, Ma."

"Vhy not be funny *mit* own white faces?"

John looked at his little mother, perched on the edge of the couch. "It wouldn't be as funny." John went back to reading, not giving a chance for more questions.

> The Interlocutor and end men were attired in full evening dress and white gloves with sparkling "diamonds," while the makeup of the circle was suits of white duck, black gloves and

sashes and red neckties, the effect being very pleasing—

Sophia frowned. "Vhen you hoss 'round?"

John looked up. "I was in the chorus and in the third part of the play. Reading ahead, John skipped down to the third act of the show.

> The program concluded with a roaring farce entitled, "The Coonville County Fair," which the histrionic ability of several young men was shown to good advantage. The stage was set to represent the McHenry County Fair in full operation, and Secretary Arnold got in his work by having a banner suspended from the flies advertising the next annual exhibition. There was a ticket office, where many tried to gain admittance by reminding the secretary that "I voted for you," the pool-seller's box, the judge's stand on the racetrack, the "blind pig," the side-show with its bewildering array of attractions and many other scenes familiar to Fair attendants. As the keeper of the sideshow, G.L. Mullen fairly brought down the house, no one who knows him realizing for a moment that he was gifted with such a "gift of gab." F. W. Kniebusch, as Madam De Gambo G. Louison the wonderful snake charmer, was certainly a "peach"; Harry McLaughlin as Madam De Bruski, the operatic marvel, was strictly "all right"; John Wienke, as Prime Ursus, the strong man, acted as if he could lift almost anything, even to a pocket-book; Owen Corr, as Signor Owenierous, the wonderful pedestal clog dancer, convinced everyone that he certainly knows how to handle his feet; and the Cherry

Brothers, Wm. Colberg and J. B. Cronk, in there buck and wing dancing, demonstrated that they have missed their calling by confining themselves to manual labor.

Woodstock Sentinel, April 4, 1901.

Sophia slapped her knee. "What knowst *du*! *Mein Junge is beruhmt*…famous. Maybe he is too gut to dry dishes!" She said as she arose and returned to the kitchen.

"I'll be right there; just leave 'em. The best thing about that night was that Ida was there from Racine."

Sophia's head popped back into the parlor for a moment to say, "Ida?"

John smiled. Did he know his mother well or what? "Yes, Ida. When I was singing, I looked out and there she was in the second-row grinning at me. I almost stopped singing." John was so proud, and thus he had really hammed it up during the finale. Ida and he had only had time for a quick hug and a peck on the cheek and then she was off and away with Lena so as to be on the 6:00 A.M. train back to Racine the next morning. He sighed. Too quick.

Sophia came back into the room. "Vhen vill I meet her?"

"Soon. I only got to see her for a moment after the show. She had to work in Racine the next day."

"Vell, dat's gut she here. Up, I'm going," said Sophia. "Dishes stand in *dem Waschbecken*…um…sink."

"Okay." John was still lost in reverie.

Sophia paused at the parlor door. "Best be tending to das *Madchen* 'fore she forget *du*."

"*Ja du hast recht*! G'night, Ma. Sweet dreams."

She WAS right. He did need to tend to his girl.

***

LOCAL INTELLIGENCE

Next horse sale, Apr. 11.

Get your Easter bonnet at Misses Donnelly's.

Spectators' tickets for the Easter ball will be 25 cents.

For prompt service get your meals at the Main street restaurant. Mr. Schrank will see you properly served.

The Wienke family moved on Tuesday to their new home on Washington street, recently purchased from E. A. Stone.

The roads in the county are said to be the worst in many years, the mud being something awful, precluding the possibility of hauling any heavy loads for some time, unless heavy rain comes to beat them down.

The approach of spring weather brings to our doors the usual lot of representatives of the genus hobo. If you want to be free from the visitations of these gentry, don't feed one that comes to your door.

Woodstock Sentinel, April 4, 1901.

***

April 5, 1901
936 Huron Street
Racine, Wis.

Dear Prime U,

I am overcome by your manliness and strength. Please come rescue a damsel in distress in Racine Wisconsin. I have been captured and am being forced to sweat out a living by sewing my fingers to the bone every day. I beg you use your power to come to release me very soon from this tedium.

Your captive audience,
Ida Doering

***

CITY COUNCIL
REGULAR MEETING
Woodstock, ILL., April 5, 1901.

The following bills, approved by the finance committee, were read:

Oliver Typewriter Co, corporation tax. $ 44.75
Das Volksblatt, pub proceedings, etc.... 18.00
Woodstock Sentinel, same................. 65.70
Chas C Snyder, hauling ashes, etc. 6.75
Mrs. W E Soles, boarding well man...... 4.00
Fred Sahs, board for horse............... 10.00
Albert Wienke, painting standpipe...... 50.00
A C Adams, electrician................... 70.00
Wm. Wienke, engineer................... 50.00
Fred Sahs, trimmer....................... 40.00
John Bolger, marshal and supt. w w ... 65.00
A E Rathbun, nightwatch............... 50.00
E C Jewett, mayor....................... 45.00

Woodstock Sentinel, April 11, 1901.

***

Personals

Wm. Wienke, city engineer, fell down the cellar stairs at his home last Monday, and was laid up for a few days. James Sullivan took his place at the pumping station.

Woodstock Sentinel, April 19, 1901.

***

April 20, 1901
Woodstock, Ill.

Dear Captive Audience Member,

I am sorry that it has taken me so long to answer your request for salvation from the tedium of working in Racine. I have had no time to write since my great strength has been needed in moving lock, stock, and barrel from one house to another.

I am, however, very gratified that you have acknowledged my strength and ability to rescue you from the dungeons of Racine, but I have been very busy with work and other manly endeavors.

I would be very happy to see you in the next few months and maybe go for a picnic. I know some fine places around Woodstock where picnics are quite pleasant. Do you have the same near Racine? I must say that I have missed your company, but my days are so full, and I do not see an opportunity to travel to your fair city in the next while.

Please come see our beautiful Woodstock in the summer. You will love it. If you will, I will plan an outing with our friends. And we will be able to have a nice long walk and talk without the noise of the crowd.

My brother, William, was hurt falling down the basement stairs last week. It took three of us to get him back up the stairs so the doctor could take a look. He seems to be none the worse for wear except for a broken leg and a good bump on the head. I'm sure he'll be right back at work as soon as he masters the crutches.

I hope you can see clear to come down and that I will see you soon.

Your devoted,
Prime U

***

New Arrival

Born to Mr. and Mrs. Ed Wienke, on
Saturday, April 27, 1901, a son, Edwin.

Woodstock Sentinel, May 2, 1901.

***

Matrimonial

On Sunday last, C. J. Rietberger, a friend of John Wienke, came down from Madison, Wis, bringing a lady friend with him, and John immediately suspected there was a wedding in the air. John's suspicions proved correct, for they repaired to the M. E. parsonage where Rev. Sunderlin pronounced C. J. Rietberger and Miss Allie Manley, of LaCrosse, Kas., husband and wife. John says he doesn't fancy having these matrimonial affairs come upon him so sudden like, but he wishes his Madison friend all kinds of good luck.

Woodstock Sentinel, May 3, 1901.

***

THE MAYOR'S APPOINTMENTS

Last Friday evening Mayor Jewett announced to the city council his appointments of subordinate officers for the ensuing year, and the same were promptly confirmed by a unanimous vote. The policy pursued by the mayor, that of reappointing every officer whose fitness has been demonstrated by experience, will meet with the hearty approval of the people.

Wm. Wienke, as engineer at the powerhouse, has at all times filled the requirements of that exacting position, and, with the assistance of the electrician, has kept the city's plant in an admirable condition.

Fred Sahs was reappointed as trimmer, a position he has filled for the past year in a very creditable manner.

Woodstock Sentinel, May 9, 1901.

***

A New Automobile

Dr. Emil Windmueller returned a few days ago from Milwaukee, Wis., with his new steam automobile, making the trip overland, leaving Milwaukee at 2 p.m. and arriving home at 10:30 p.m. He purchased the new vehicle of the Milwaukee Automobile company, and it is one of the handsomest the company turns out.

It is of the carriage pattern and combines all the latest improvements of modern horseless vehicles. A speed of thirty miles per hour can be maintained on good roads if the operator so desires and the doctor now has the best and fastest machine in the northwest, outside of Chicago. He found his trip from Milwaukee a most delightful one and says that in Milwaukee and Racine counties he found good roads but as soon as he crossed the borders of McHenry county, he encountered horrible roads and is inclined to the belief that our roads are sadly deficient in comparison with those of our neighboring counties. The trouble seems to be that no pains are taken here to keep the loose stones off the roads.

It is a certain fact that the automobile has come to stay, and we expect ere long to see several more of them in this city. The cost of these machines has now been brought within reasonable limits and they will soon come into use quite generally in the country towns. The one owned by the doctor can be used on any road a horse can travel, can be operated slow or fast, as desired, and mud or steep hills are no hindrance to it, while cobble stones only serve to help "settle the operator's dinner" and prevent indigestion, while to scare horses they are a complete failure.

McHenry County Democrat, May 19, 1901.

***

May 31, 1901
936 Huron St.
Racine, Wis.

Dear John,

Oh, how I wish we were sitting on a blanket in the wilderness as we were at this time last week. Isn't this Spring weather just heavenly? I love to see blue eyes...er...blue skies looking down at me.

I loved just sitting and talking about your plans for a grocery. It's amazing, but Herman had been discussing the same thing with Mama and Mr. Stoffel the other night...you two must talk next time you come to Racine....and please do come to Racine when you can.

The story you told about your Madison friend, CJ, running away to Woodstock to get married was hilarious. Maybe you should run away to Madison and challenge HIM to find a preacher. Or maybe he just wanted Prime U as his best man.

Mama has set upon a goal to have the whole house cleaned and aired out by the Fourth of July, one room at a time. She believes that the grippe germs hide in the dust. Clara is gone at least twelve hours a day between work and her singing engagements and that leaves the furniture moving to me. But then, I am a big strong girl. Not as strong as U, of course.

Shall I complain some more? I dread the heat and humidity of summer in Racine, but I doubt it will be much better in Woodstock, maybe worse. Have you thought about starting your restaurant in Fond du Lac where the breezes are always cool? Or up the shore in Manitowoc where we would be snowed in for 6 months of the year. Let me know your decision so I will not anticipate melting away to nothingness.

I'm not sure if it made the papers in Woodstock, but Mr. Stoffel had an awful occurrence happen in May when his grandson killed himself at the family home. Mr. Stoffel, as you know, has been keeping a room with us here on Huron Street to be close to work, but his sons called him home when his grandson, who had lived with him at the family home for a number of years, did not come to work. Mr. Stoffel and his daughter went to the grandson's room, and there he lay with a hole in his head from a gunshot. He wasn't yet dead, so they called a doctor who told them there was no hope. It was quite a dark time. Since then, Mr. Stoffel has been lodging with us full time even on weekends. I feel so sorry for him, but what can one say to make things better? He and Mama have been having long talks in German which I am sure is helpful.

I suppose I had better go to bed; my eyes are forcing me to do so although I would rather write all night to you. I hope your dreams are filled with the selling of fresh tomatoes and sweet corn. Ha!

Truly yours,
Ida

***

MATRIMONIAL
Derring – Stoffel

J. Nicholas Stoffel, one of the best-known residents on the north side of the river, was united in marriage last evening to Mrs. Louisa Derring. The announcement created considerable surprise as it had not been intimated that Mr. Stoffel was to take unto himself a bride. Congratulations are in order.

Racine Journal Times, June 18, 1901.

***

Oliver Typewriter Factory Squibs.

Last Call. Will someone let us know why we can't celebrate the 4th of July in Woodstock? Have we forgotten how, or don't we want to get the streets littered up with firecrackers?

"Beware" of anybody who says they are not going to Madison, Saturday, on the O. T. train. They are making sport of you, and you will be the only one left in Woodstock.

Woodstock Sentinel, June 20, 1901.

***

They Come in Carriages

We could not help but notice Saturday last the large number of carriages that were hitched to the chain around the public park. The time was that it was the exception for a farmer to own a carriage. Now nearly all are able to come to town in carriages to do their trading, which indicates the changing conditions that have come over this portion of our population as a result of the great prosperity brought about by continued Republican administrations, and we know of no one who begrudges this comfort and thrift. We hope the time will come when they will be able to use automobiles.

Woodstock Sentinel, June 25, 1901.

***

Barnum's Monkeys

"All well – all happy – lots of fun." That is the regular report from the monkey cage of

Barnum's Circus ever since the keepers began dosing the monkeys with Scott's Emulsion. Consumption was carrying off two thirds of them every year and the circus had to buy new ones.

One day a keeper accidentally broke a bottle of Scott's Emulsion near the monkey cage and the monkeys eagerly lapped it up from the floor. This suggested the idea that it might do them good. Since then, the monkeys have received regular doses and the keepers report very few deaths from consumption. Of course, it's cheaper to buy Scott's Emulsion than new monkeys – and that suits the circus men.

Consumption in monkeys and in man is the same disease. If you have it or are threatened with it, can you take the hint?

Send for a free sample.

Scott & Bowne,

409 Pearl St., New York

Woodstock Sentinel, July 1, 1901.

***

July 10, 1901
936 Huron St.
Racine, Wis.

Dear John,

What a nice surprise to see you standing on our doorstep on Saturday morning. And you having the whole weekend to be idle. I was glad to see you although you might have warned me so I could warn Mama and Mr. Stoffel, or I suppose I should say Papa Stoffel. I was glad to see they took you in and didn't just dump you unceremoniously at the curb.

I quite enjoyed the fireworks at the park…I'm not sure why they were on Saturday instead of the fourth. Maybe this will be the modern way to keep us working all week…moving all celebrations to the weekends so men will not have an extra day off. But still, it was good that you were here to see them with us. Do you think the Racine fireworks were more beautiful than those that we would have seen in Woodstock? Thank you for giving me shelter from the lake breeze under your arm.

Oh, how I wish you could come to Racine in a month's time…August 16 to be exact. We are to have a motorcar race! Everyone is so excited to see it. Two motorcars, one a Locomobile and the other a Winton, will start downtown and race out into the country and then go back for fifteen miles ending back downtown. There are posters all over town. My disappointment is that it will be on a Thursday, and I doubt you will be able to come. I'm hoping to sneak away to see at least the end.

It is getting late. The boys and girls are all in tonight and everybody is abed, except this nighthawk. I guess it is time that I at least began to think about it. Usually, it takes some time before I can make up my mind whether it is best to retire or sit up all night. It does not make very much difference tonight as tomorrow I do not have to go to work and can sleep late, until about half past six. I never sleep later than that. Ha!

With regards to all,
Ida

***

Local Intelligence

Next horse sale, Aug. 14.

Glorious summer weather.

A Michigan man who is lecturing on 'What I Know of Hell,' exhibits four marriage certificates among his credentials.

Many arms are just as beautiful at the wash tub as they are hanging from the shoulders of an actress.

Music from a large graphophone now issues from the store of J. C. Choate to give enjoyment to passers-by.

Many of our people are planning to attend the Pan-American exposition in the coming few weeks.

102 in the Shade

That was the record made by the weather yesterday. A strong southwest wind, right off the oven, prevailed all day. Vegetation wilted and shriveled, and humanity sweltered and suffered. The people, who could, flocked to the park and stood around the mineral spring like bees around the bunghole of a molasses barrel. A little relief was brought in the afternoon by the sun becoming obscured by clouds.

Woodstock Sentinel, July 11, 1901.

***

Woodstock Pleasure Club
Woodstock, Illinois

July 24, 1901

My Dear Friend,

I would have very much liked to have seen the road race. Your description of the end of the race with the winner losing all the way until the last half mile was very exciting. I can hardly wait to try a motorcar.

Dr. Windmueller's Milwaukee car has set all the boys here dreaming. The city will surely have to do something about the dirt streets if we go to horseless carriages, they kick up a lot more dust than two horses plodding along. Dr. W's auto does help him to get to house calls faster although one of the boys at the Pleasure Club said that Doc has needed to be pushed out of the mud multiple times when it rains. Not enough HORSE power I guess, ha.

The weather here has been extremely hot here. Enough to melt the rubber to the road, I dare say. The temperature in the factory reached a sweltering 93 degrees and so they shut down for two days to let the wave pass. All I could do was sit in the shade with lemonade. I hope the lake kept you cooler.

Your little Clara is a real spitfire, isn't she? You best reign her in a little or she'll be off to climes unknown before you can say Jahn Jahnson. The concert she provided us with when I was there was pure vaudeville. Tell Herman, if she were my sister, I wouldn't let her out of my sight.

Time to quit for now. I so look forward to your letters…more so, I daresay, than you do to mine. Please write soon and tell me what is going on in modern Racine.

I remain as ever,
John.

***

COURT HOUSE NOTES
Real Estate Transfers
E. A. Stone to Sophia Wienke, pt of lt 42,
and pt, sec 5, Woodstock............$ 2150.00
Woodstock Sentinel, August 15, 1901.

***

PERSONAL MENTION
John Wienke and Fred Joorfetz were calling on friends at Algonquin, Nunda and Crystal Lake last Sunday.
Woodstock Sentinel. August 16, 1901.

***

BRIEF MENTION

The schoolhouse is being painted under a contract with Albert Wienke.

Woodstock Sentinel, August 28, 1901.

***

Special Edition
PRESIDENT M'KINLEY SHOT AT BUFFALO
WOUNDS ARE BELIEVED TO BE FATAL

A Chicago Telephone Co. special to THE SENTINEL says that President McKinley was shot by an assassin while attending a reception in Buffalo this afternoon, and that the president is in a precarious condition.

A special from the Inter Ocean says that a man approached the president to shake hands with him, and had a revolver concealed in a handkerchief in his hand. He shook the president's hand and then wheeled and fired two bullets into him, one taking effect in his breast and the other in his stomach. The bullet was extracted from his breast, but the bullet in the stomach could not be located at last report.

The special says that the president is conscious, but that there is little hope of his recovery.

The assassin is under arrest and is housed in the 13th Precinct station at Buffalo.

Great excitement prevails all over the land, and the wires are crowded for information.

In common with all patriotic people of the land, the people of Woodstock have anxiously waited for every item of news that should bear information as to the president's condition, and

the prayers of all have ascended that the nation's
beloved chief magistrate may be restored to full
health and vigor without great pain or suffering.
Woodstock Sentinel, September 6, 1901.

***

"Ma? Emil?" John called out as he came quickly through the door.

"Ve here." His mother's voice came from the parlor. Emil and Sophia sat together on the sofa holding hands. "Ve pray for da President."

John pulled up a chair close and sat down. "I will pray with you." They held hands and bowed their heads for two or three minutes and then released each other.

John looked at his youngest brother. "Are you okay? You weren't hurt. Looks like someone gave you a black eye."

"I've been better." Emil was pale, and dark circles under his eyes said that he hadn't slept much. His left eye was blackened and slightly closed.

"I'm glad they let you leave Buffalo. I had heard the tracks were closed so they could round up the accomplices. Were you questioned?"

"Yes, for several hours. I was less than thirty feet from President McKinley when it happened. They grabbed me right away and threw me to the ground, along with any other citizens in the courtyard, and the one guy hit me, so I'd stay down. I was trying to get to the President to help him. I don't blame them. It was chaos."

"Vhy *du* go dar by President?" Sophia's hand rested comfortingly on Emil's knee.

"I heard his speech the day before, and it was a great speech, and so when I heard a rumor that he was shaking hands with commoners at the Temple of Music, I ran right

over there and squirmed up near the front of the line —
sometimes it helps to be small. There were a lot of people
waiting to see him."

"They just let the people go in without guards? Was no
one searched? Sounds like an assassination waiting to
happen. Did we learn nothing from Lincoln?" John's brows
were drawn together, and his face had reddened slightly.

"They had it set up like a cattle chute…one person at a
time walked in, greeting the President, and then walked
out."

"Were there military guards around?" John still felt
angry. How could those idiots let this happen?

"I don't know if they were military or private, but there
were a number of men standing around in the courtyard. I
was focused on the man himself. No one seemed worried
and the crowd was very excited to shake hands with him."

John nodded.

Sophia patted his knee. "Go on. Tell story."

"I could hear orchestra music playing from behind the
wall, and when it was my turn, I went down the chute and
walked right up to President McKinley standing on the
steps of the temple. I gave him greetings from Woodstock
and Beloit. He shook my hand, said that he loved the
Midwest, and wished me the 'best of luck.' I wasn't even
on the ramp out of the Temple when I heard the shots. I
turned and tried to run back to the steps, but the guards
stopped me. All I could see were men being wrestled to the
ground and a crowd on the steps. I couldn't really tell at
that moment what had happened."

Sophia looked at John. "Dat must haf bin awful."

"Then even though the other boys wanted to stay
another few days, I just couldn't, and I took the train
home." Emil had tears trickling down his cheeks. He
brushed them away with his sleeve.

John handed him a handkerchief. "It's bad enough seeing someone shot right before your eyes even if it isn't the President of the United States." John reached over and patted his brother's knee. "None of us has had to serve in the military so far. We have not been hardened by seeing men die by guns."

Sophia shook her head hard. "*Du hast Richt.* Pa not allow."

"Probably not, but also there hasn't been a war with a draft for years. That's when the coal would hit the scuttle. I'm not sure even Pa could have stopped the government from taking all those sons."

They sat there in silence for a few moments thinking about bullets both dodged and not dodged.

"Who will den President be?" Sophia did not bring her eyes up from the patterned rug at her feet.

"Teddy Roosevelt. Remember him?"

Emil nodded. "Ya, the Rough Riders."

"America is in good hands with him until McKinley comes back."

Emil took both of their hands and squeezed them and then pushed himself up from the couch. "Well, I haven't slept much in the last forty-eight hours. I think I want to go to bed. I'll be heading to Beloit tomorrow."

"*Nicht vor einem gutes Frühstück.*" Sophia clinched his biceps.

Emil looked to John for translation. "Not before a good breakfast."

"Okay, Ma. I won't hurry off. Good night." Emil went to the second floor, and for the first time in his life, to a bedroom that was his alone.

Sophia watched him to the top of the stairs. "He be okay. *Starker Jungen.*"

John nodded. "Yes, he is a strong boy."

Sophia arose. "*Ich gehe auch ins Bett.*" I am also going to bed.

John decided not to remind her to speak English tonight. "Good night, Ma. Sleep well."

"*Ich werde versuchen.*" I will try.

John got up and gave his little mother a quick hug. "Everything will be all right."

After Sophia had retired to the back bedroom, John sat, wondering what the world was coming to. If an anarchist could just walk up to the President and shoot him with all those guards around, was anyone safe? He wished he could talk to Ida. Ida…and in that moment, he had an urge to pack up, catch the train to Racine so he could hold her in his arms and protect her from harm. Life was so fragile. He would ask her to marry him. As soon as he was making good money and could build a house, he would ask her.

***

PERSONAL MENTION

Emil Wienke returned on Monday to his duties at Beloit, after a visit to the Pan-American exposition.

Woodstock Sentinel, September 8, 1901.

***

Death's Victory
President McKinley's Gallant
Struggle for Life is Unsuccessful

Milburn House, Buffalo, N.Y., Sept. 14.— President McKinley died at 2:35 a. m. He had been unconscious since 7:30 p. m. His last conscious hour on earth was spent with the wife to whom he devoted a lifetime of care. He died unattended by a minister of the Gospel, but his last words were a humble submission to the will of God in whom he believed. He was reconciled to the cruel fate to which the assassin's bullet had condemned him, and faced death in the same spirit of calmness and poise which has marked his long and honorable career. His last conscious words, reduced to writing by Dr. Mann, who stood at his bedside when they were uttered, were as follows: Good-by, all. It is God's way. His will be done.

Woodstock Sentinel, September 9, 1901.

***

WE HAD A GREAT FAIR
Records in All Departments Were Smashed

It was a great McHenry County fair that we had in this city last week. To the officers, 1901 belongs the distinction of bringing to a successful conclusion the greatest Fair in the history of society, the total receipts of which will approximate $9,000. There was no disorder on the grounds. There was an entire absence of fake schemes and gambling devices to trap the unwary, and the program was of high order and successfully carried out.

News of the Fairs

A. J. Austin and Robt. Wienke attended the Fair at Milwaukee last week.

Robt. Wienke, F. G. Arnold, Ben Stupfel and A. J. Austin went to the Elkhorn fair yesterday.

Special trains to the Elkhorn Fair leave Woodstock on Wednesday, Thursday and Friday of this week at 8:07 a. m., Ridgefield at

7:55, Hartland at 8:15, and Harvard at 8:30, connecting with the St. Paul train in Clinton Junction at 9:30 and reaching Elkhorn at 10 o'clock. Returning, the trains leave Elkhorn at 6:45. A low fare has been made for the round trip and it will prove a fine opportunity for residents of this locality to attend the greatest Fair in the Northwest.

Woodstock Sentinel, September 19, 1901.

Personals

Albert Wienke did a bit of flagpole sitting last week as he attached the rope to the newly painted flagpole. He drew quite a crowd who cheered him on with good results.

Woodstock Sentinel, September 19, 1901.

***

"Hi Ma! Look what I won for you." Bob came through the door with a broad mischievous smile, carrying a bundle which he gave to Sophia to unwrap.

Sophia had just sat down at the yellow checkered oilskin-covered table with a cup of black coffee, an egg and corned beef sandwich made from the last night's leftovers.

She hefted the bundle. Heavy. She unwrapped the prize and examined it. "Vell. Is dat not sometink." It was made of chalkware and had been painted in red, yellow and white. The shape was catlike with large black eyes and whiskers. "You von it? Do vhat?"

"Pitching a baseball." Bob's back was turned as he rummaged in the larder for bread and butter. He sat down and started preparing a sandwich from the leftovers. "I had to knock over some ugly hairy dolls with a baseball. I won ten cigars and then traded five of them for this prize."

"I do not hear of dis. Vhere?"

"At the Elkhorn Fair up in Wisconsin. I went with some friends to watch the surrey races, and then we saw the rest of the fair. We were walking by, and this hawker yelled, 'Come on over and win yourself a prize!' You get three balls for five cents, and each time you win, you get a prize, and if you win more than once, you can trade those prizes in for bigger prizes. It's a modern approach to gambling on your own skill. This…um…doll was the top prize, and I knew just who to give it to. My Ma!" Bob took a big bite of his sandwich and smiled as he chewed.

"How much times must you play to get dis doll?"

"Oh, I don't know. I played thirty or so. I didn't win every time, but I won enough to keep moving up and when I got enough small prizes, I traded for this…um…cat?"

"Hm…intrestink." Sophia looked at the cat-doll. "Tank you." She set it on the table. She rarely got gifts, and this thing was not at all beautiful, but it was kind of ….interesting…maybe. She would have to find a place to display it that was a bit out of the way.

"And da racing?" Sophia picked up her sandwich.

"Oh, the races were great! I won more than I lost so came away the better man."

"Good fer you. And vas plan have you today?"

"Orphan's game! Catching the noon train. You know what I heard." Bob's voice dropped several decibels like he was telling her a huge secret.

"Vas?" Sophia managed the word around a substantial bite.

"Did you know that the Orphans are now being referred to as the 'Remnants?'"

"*Nein*! Not hear."

He leaned closer. "But I heard that the Remnants might change their name to the Cubs. Can you believe it? Baby bears."

Sophia chuckled. "Vhy?"

"Because this year they are rebuilding the team and next year most of the players will be rookies – you know, new players – like our Moriarty from the Olivers. They are like bear cubs, I guess. But I tell you what, they will without doubt grow from the Cubs into da Bears. I'm sure of it." Bob took the last bite of his sandwich and chewed.

"Vell, gut luck to dem! You take a samvich with you for trip." Sophia loved feeding her boys.

"I will!!" Bob gave her a broad and handsome smile.

***

REMNANTS IN GREAT GAME

The Chicago Remnants defeated the Boston Beaneaters yesterday by a score of 1 to 0, in one of the most sensational games in the history of the National League, a game won in the seventeenth inning, when "Petie" Childs, with his fourth single of the day, sent Dexter home from third with the only run secured by either team in more than three hours' play.

This contest ranks as one of the four most noted in the history of the professional sport since Pitcher Radbourn won an eighteen-inning game for Providence against Detroit in 1882 by a home run hit in the final inning.

The end yesterday came through a partial collapse of the visitors under the nerve-racking suspense and tense endeavor of many extra innings. It was Herman Long, who had cut off hit after hit and nailed runners at first when the feat seemed impossible, who allowed the entering wedge by messing Dexter's grounder at the beginning of the seventeenth.

This appeared to unsettle Dineen, who had just pitched himself out of a seemingly impossible hole the inning before, which had been caused by a muffed fly by Cooley, leaving men on second and third, with one out. The visiting pitcher plainly showed his pique at Long's error, and the incident unsettled him enough that he grazed the arm of Hickey, the next batter. Then Gannon sacrificed, which brought Hickey to second and landed Dexter at third. McCormick was then awarded a base on balls, Dineen's only gift. Childs, with three balls and two strikes called and the bases loaded, pushed a short fly safe into right field, and the game was over.

Chicago Tribune, September 22, 1901.

***

Personals

John Wienke and others accompanied the Oliver Typewriter band to Elgin last Saturday and enjoyed the street Fair.

Woodstock Sentinel, October 3, 1901.

***

THE NEW BANK
Long List of Stockholders Has Been Secured – Organizing Today

The following have been handed to us as the names of stockholders in the new McHenry County State bank, who are meeting this afternoon to elect directors and officers:

C.H. Donnelly	J. D. Donovan
O.S. Marron	A. J. Olson

Thos. W. Coffey
Jas. P. Brink
J. J. Carrol
E. C. Barnard
William Desmond
L. D. Lowell, Jr.
A. Morse
N. R. Buckley
M. H. Fitzsimmons
J. R. Forman
John M. Mullen
Chas. T. Forrest
Fred C. Page
W. H. Forrest
H. A. Stone
John W. Chewning
A. D. Kennedy
John F. Hallisy
William Thorne
John J. Cooney
A. J. Austin
W. N. Cooney
J. H. Foreman
J. Hendricks
John Wienke
Henry Gorham
W. T. Conn
John McManus
G. W. Frame
Ernest Fues
G. R. Conn

L. E. Menich
Wm. B. Sullivan
E. H. Thompson
Geo. L. Murphy
W. B. Given
James Deneen
J. C. Hallisy
Frank B. Thompson
D. F. Coakley
B. R. Morse
J. T. Bower
C. H. Ormsby
John Coakley
Estelle C. Austin
L. A. Stone
Mary C. Quinlan
Priscilla Forman
C. P. Barnes
T. R. Deneen
H. D. McLaughlin
James McCauley
Thomas Jacobs
William Haley
W. C. Eichelberger
F. H. Opfergelt
T. J. Walsh
Justus Lawn
John A. Dufield
N. A. Chandler
E. G. Westerman
E. M. Ingersoll

Woodstock Sentinel, October 3, 1901.

***

John walked briskly down the boardwalk, away from the new McHenry County State Bank. His investment in this institution would open doors that otherwise would only crack a bit even if he could find the perfect way to beg

…like money for a house. But now since he was a founding stockholder, he could expect to get a good interest rate. A house would be his number one priority now. Save up the down payment, get his own business, get money, build the house, ask Ida to marry him, move her here. His future was set. As he walked around the square, he tipped his hat or greeted everyone he met. He was building his reputation which would bode well if he opened a grocery here or ran for office.

A number of groceries and mercantile shops had already been founded in Woodstock so the competition would be brisk, but he had connections in Chicago with the wholesalers, and he was a good negotiator, so he was sure he could beat their prices and make a success of it. Today, he had taken the first step.

"Judge Donnelly, good afternoon." John stopped near a man who was gazing out at the plot of land in the middle of the square. The trees planted some years ago were reaching a good size now, and it was beginning to look like the park the fathers had envisioned. Boardwalks crisscrossed the green expanse.

"Why hello, John," the judge removed a cigar from his mouth to speak and now pointed with it at the park. "Don't you think this park could use some sprucing up? I'm going to talk to the mayor and get the tree trimmed while the leaves are down and maybe get some grass growing under the trees for next summer. And maybe put some cobblestone paths through from one side to the other and keep them shoveled in the winter so we don't have to go the long way around."

John chuckled. "I was just thinking how nice it was to see a natural park in the middle of the square."

"Well, yes, but we can do better. Do you think that they allow the parks to get so overgrown in Chicago or New

York? I don't think so. We can do better," and with that the judge put the cigar back between his lips, sucked in, and blew out a large billow of smoke. "Good to see you, John." He reached out for John's hand.

John took the proffered hand and securely shook it. "Same here, judge. I'll be watching for the changes."

As the judge walked away back toward the courthouse, John once again felt the urge to run for office. Mayor would be nice or maybe alderman. Then he could provide ideas to improve the town. He shook his head wondering if this part of his dream would ever come true.

***

PERSONAL MENTION

Mr. and Mrs. Albert Wienke spent Sunday with relatives and friends at Clinton Junction, Wis.

Woodstock Sentinel, October 10, 1901.

***

PERSONAL MENTION

Fred G. Arnold and Robert Wienke left on Monday evening for a trip to Memphis to take in the great races.

Dr. W. V. Hopf, the dentist, will keep his office open every evening in the week, except Sunday, from 6 to 9 o'clock for the benefit of those who cannot call during the day.

Local Intelligence

The public library will be closed on Sunday afternoons until further notice by order of the board of directors, who feel that six days of labor for the librarian should be enough.

The weather of the last week has been very Indian summer-like and has been greatly appreciated.

Woodstock Sentinel, October 24, 1901.

***

Woodstock Pleasure Club
Woodstock, Illinois

November 1, 1901

Dear Friend,

Talk about snow. It is snowing very hard here just now. It is not unlike the storm you talked about in your last letter. If it keeps up, we will have a foot of snow by morning. Does that sound like a big one?

I was planning two weeks ago to come up to see you yesterday, but we had to work Saturday afternoon and three nights this week besides. If they keep that up, I do not know when I will be able to come, for I do not get a chance to make up for my lost time which I have to do when I am off. If Oliver closes on Saturday afternoons (there are rumors), I could come every Saturday, but I'm sure you would not want to see me every Saturday, and I understand.

I will be up there two weeks from today and spend Sunday with you. If I leave here on the 12:30 train after morning work, I can get up there sometime around 4:00 o'clock on Saturday if I can have the couch. I know that you wouldn't want me to come every Sunday and wear out my welcome with Mr. and Mrs. Stoffel. So, I will stretch out my comings and goings and keep them guessing.

I would like a photo of you husking corn. I would be glad to have one of you even not husking corn. Lena has such a picture in her parlor. If you have any more, I would be pleased to have one. I will send you one of mine in exchange if you will do so.

If I were your sister, I would not play for you at all. When I come up, I guess I better tell her what you said about her music. You ought to hear Lena play. She has a piano now so when you come down again you can play for us.

I had a good time in Madison last weekend. Went up on Saturday to Sunday night. I enjoyed the game very much and am planning to go again on the ninth for the last home game against Iowa State. The Badgers have a good chance at the conference championship this year.

We are planning a smoker at the Pleasure Club next weekend. It will be the third one since the Fourth of July. We make about $30 on each one and it does help with the rent and other expenses.

Well, I better close. Hoping to hear from you again, I remain yours as ever,

John

***

LOCAL INTELLIGENCE

The usual capers were cut up by the young people last Thursday evening (Hallowe'en) with horse blocks being turned over and other minor offenses committed, but we have heard of no serious damage. Youngsters will be youngsters.

Woodstock Sentinel, November 1, 1901.

***

Phone Your Items

Woodstock people who have phones in their houses will confer a favor on THE SENTINEL by sending in short news items. If you have visitors or are going away, call us up and tell us about it. It doesn't cost one cent.

Woodstock Sentinel, November 7, 1901.

***

November 10, 1901
936 Huron St.
Racine, Wis.

Dear John,

Why do you say you know I don't want to see you every Sunday? Of course, you are right, but how did you know it? I would have been glad to see you last Sunday because I was so lonely. Went to church in the morning with my "Mudder" and "Fodder." In the afternoon they both slept, the Mr. on the lounge and Mama went to bed for the rest of the day as she was sick with a cold; everybody else had gone out and I spent my time in blissful solitude. In the evening it was the same. Mr. Stoffel went to church and the others were all away, Mama sleeping and myself keeping watch. Watching so no one would carry away all our money.

Don't flatter yourself and think I should have been glad to see you drop in and share my solitude. That would have been too bad, since I love to be all alone, because it is my opinion that I'm in good company when I'm alone. How is that for conceit? It almost equals yours, but not quite.

Do you mean that you have every Saturday afternoon off now? Dear me, what do you do with so much time to dispose of? You ought to be ashamed to spend all that time in idleness. What in the world will become of such a lazy fellow?

I expect the next time you write you'll say you can't come next week. That's all right. Put it off for another four weeks, then it won't make any difference.

Would you like to know what Lena wrote? You won't find out for I'll not tell you. Had a letter from Emma the same day Lena's letter came; will tell you what she said when I see you unless I forget before then.

Have I talked mean enough to you tonight? I'm very sorry, honestly, I am. It shall never happen again, not until the next time.

If you cannot come next Sunday then plan on the Sunday before Christmas, won't you? I promise I won't tease you so badly as I have in this letter. It's been so long a time since we've seen each other, but you must do what you must do. I will be fine whatever you decide.

Until then I remain lonely,
Ida

***

Current Gossip

Mrs. Elizabeth Cady Stanton celebrated her eighty-eighth birthday on Nov. 12 at her home in New York city. She is still in excellent health and spirits and retains all her zeal for her favorite reform, women's suffrage.

Racine Journal Times, November 19, 1901

***

PERSONAL MENTION

E. C. Jewett, Geo. W. Field, John and Albert Wienke, L. T. Hoy, C. T. Donovan, Geo. L. Murphy, Fred Joorfetz, W. P. Hoy, George W. Lemmers, Geo, B. Richards, B. C. Young, D. C. Akers, Harry Cross, John Whitwoth, L. E. Copeland and William Colberg were among the number from here who witnessed the great Wisconsin-Minnesota football game last Saturday.

Woodstock Sentinel, November 21, 1901.

***

"Oh, for pity's sake. I don't think he's coming." Ida threw the dishcloth into the water. She felt like crying.

It was Saturday evening after Thanksgiving. The family had just finished dinner which had started at the normal 5 o'clock. She had hoped, with John's train coming at 4 o'clock, he would arrive in time to eat with them, but that was not the case.

Now as she and Clara washed up in the warm kitchen, it was already 6:30 p. m. with no word and nobody. Ida practically threw the pot into the dishwater. She was hurt and mad and frustrated!

"I'm sorry, Ida." Clara for once sounded sympathetic. "Maybe it's time to do more of a push."

"He says he doesn't have the money to take the train and walking would take too long."

Clara snorted. "Well, at least, he's funny. Can't say that any of my beaus right now are funny."

"I don't want funny!" Ida's voice sounded like a petulant child. "I want married."

"He seems to like you quite a lot. Does Lena see him around with other girls?"

"No." Ida's eyes were intently examining the dish water.

"Well then, you'll just have to be patient. Didn't mama say the other day, '*Alles zu seiner Zeit*'? All in good time."

"I don't want it to be in good time! I want it now! By the time he gets around to even asking me, I'll be all shriveled up and barren."

"You are funny. You look ten years younger than you are. Babies take a toll on women. I don't think I'll have any. I want to stay young forever!" Clara threw her long hair back over her shoulder in defiance.

"Thank you for the compliment, but I DO want to have babies…lots of them…boys and girls. I'm just going to have to be more forward or let him know that it makes me angry when he says he's coming and then doesn't show up…or…oh…I don't know. I need to do something!"

"Why don't you write Lena about it. Maybe she'll have some ideas. She landed a Wienke. Lena always has good ideas. Or let's ask mama if we can go to Woodstock next weekend or in two weeks, if Lena says we can stay with her. Then he'd have to see you and maybe you could tell if he is serious or not. Maybe he's just shy."

"Shy, shmy. He wasn't so shy when he kissed me at last year's New Year's Eve Party. He wasn't so shy when he showed up at the door on the 4th of July. It's like hot and cold water. He's here and then I don't hear from him for weeks, months even, and then he's here. Anyway, Mama won't say 'yes' to going to Woodstock unless Herman goes with us, and he's so wrapped up with his own plans! And I'm sure Lena is tired of hearing me whine."

"Herman might go."

"It makes me so mad I could spit tacks! He has all the time and money in the world for his friends, football games in Madison, and smoking at the Pleasure Palace. But he can't even write me a letter every week. Once a month is what I get, the leftovers." Ida's voice broke. Murder! She hated it when she got so mad that she cried. And what good did crying do anyway.

Clara came over and gave Ida a hug. "Maybe he isn't the one."

"He has to be, Clara." Ida withdrew from the embrace. "I've wasted so much precious time already on him, over a year. Maybe it is time to cut my losses, but I do like him very much and when we are together, we seem perfect for each other."

"You could…." Clara let her voice trail off.

"Could what!" Ida glared at her sister.

"You could move to Woodstock."

"Oh, don't be a fool. I'm not going to degrade myself chasing after him like that. If he wants me, he knows where to find me."

"Oh, I'm the fool, huh? Well, I'll have you know that I have a date for Silvester, do you?"

"No." Ida looked miserable. "I had hoped...." Now it was she who trailed off.

"Just put him out of your mind. Cheer up! We must decorate and get ready for Christmas. What are you making for all of us this year?"

"Scarves," said Ida. "You get the lavender one."

***

LOCAL INTELLIGENCE

Were you among the number from here who witnessed the great Wisconsin-Iowa game at Madison last Saturday?

Personal

Will the lady, who fell in a swoon last Thursday in front of the post office, call our store? She suffers from biliousness. Dr. Calwell's Syrup Pepsin will surely cure her.

It avails little to the unfortunate to be brave.

Sure of Approval

A girl may not be able to write poetry or paint sunsets, but if she can bake a biscuit that is somewhat softer than flint and can crochet a section of weatherboarding on the gable end of a pair of pantaloons, she may be pretty sure of the approval of some good man.

Woodstock Sentinel, December 5, 1901.

******

AN ENJOYABLE SMOKER

The Woodstock Pleasure club gave one of its far-famed "smokers" in the club rooms in the Hoy block on Tuesday evening, which was largely attended. These smokers always bring out members of the club who are seldom seen in the rooms at other times, and they invariably have an enjoyable time. On this occasion, there were a number of visitors present from Marengo, who were royally entertained. Excellent music was furnished by the orchestra, and dainty refreshments were served. It was a gentlemanly affair conducted by gentlemen in a gentlemanly manner.

Woodstock Sentinel, December 12, 1901.

THEY CRUSH THE POWERS

Mid-October. The long, oppressive summer is quite gone. Fading leaf, withering tree, and the rustling corn in the fields are signs of the season. Fog, frost, rain, snow – they are coming. You remember last winter. The weather was cruel. Ah! the thousands killed, and the hundreds of thousands it maimed and crippled. Oh, the rough grasp it laid on men at work, women at home, and children in cribs and cradles. Coughs that began before Thanksgiving Day racked and tore them as Christmas approached and grew worse as they dug deeper into the poor, tired throat, and lungs. Many were cured by using Benson's Porous Plasters. For the soothing and healing power of these Plasters is wonderful. They conquer all complaints…

THAT ARE KILLING THE PEOPLE.

No other plaster, no other medicine or application can compare with them. Coughs, colds, backache, rheumatism, lumbago, kidney and liver troubles, asthma, influenza, -- they all go down before Benson's Plasters like a snow image in the sun. You can't throw money away on a Benson's Plaster. Everybody is going to use them this season. But make certain you get the genuine. All druggists have them, or we will prepay postage on any number ordered in the United States on receipt of 25 cents each. Seabury & Johnson, Mfg. Chemists, N.Y.

Woodstock Sentinel, December 12, 1901.

***

LOCAL INTELLIGENCE.

A lot of new ads in this issue; read them!

We have not had time to mention it, but say, wasn't it cold last week? Coal bins were relieved of a lot of their burdens.

There were several cases of malignant diphtheria in the Bull Valley community, which are being quarantined and properly treated by the physicians of this city.

The Eminent Ladies will give a charity ball, New Year's night, in Murphy's hall. Music by Brubaker's orchestra. Supper at Dirrenberger's extra.

Woodstock Sentinel, December 16, 1901

PAINTERS AND DECORATORS

The principal painters and decorators of this city are Albert Wienke, who keeps a large force of men at work and who has done most of the finest work in the city for several years, Henry Burdick, E. W. Ercaubrack, and A. P. Baker.

Woodstock Sentinel, December 16, 1901.

***

December 25, 1901
936 Huron St.
Racine, Wis.

Merry Christmas John,

The very cold weather has precluded any attempt that Clara and I could have made to come to Woodstock. I am very frustrated that we see so little of each other, but it is too cold to stand on the train platform in the wind awaiting the train and then riding in its unheated seats for hours…and Clara is just starting to feel better from a cold…and finally, Mama won't allow it. She says we will come down with consumption or worse. I don't know what is worse than consumption, but there you are. We will just have to see what happens in the New Year.

If you would like you can go to the ball alone and hope that the ladies of Woodstock have pity on your bachelor self. Or go visit Bob's saloon, maybe he'll let you drink for free, so you don't have to spend a precious penny. Or you can just stay home and read the paper or possibly a miracle will happen, and you'll write to me. If it is too cold for us to 'go gallivanting,' as Mama put it (she can barely speak English, but she knows 'gallivanting'), it is too cold for you to do the same. Or is the Pleasure Palace having an event? A football game perhaps or had baseball already started? Anyway, don't freeze your toes off.

I'm waiting for Clara to call us to dinner. We are having roast duck with apple and raisin stuffing, potato dumplings, red cabbage, and fruitcake for dinner. Aren't you jealous? I hope you are. I did the baking and Mama did the cooking. There Clara is.

All of us on Huron street hope all of you in Woodstock had a very Merry Christmas and have a fine New year!

Your friend, Ida

***

IN SOCIETY CIRCLES
Secret and Other Societies of Woodstock

It was our intention to publish in our Twentieth century the names of the officers of all the local secret and charitable societies, but on account of the lack of space and the fact that several of the recording officers failed to send in names, we were unable to do so. The societies of Woodstock are named as follows:

MASONS.

ORDER OF THE EASTERN STAR.

INDEPENDENT ORDER OF ODD FELLOWS.

REBEKAHS.

MODERN WOODMEN OF AMERICA.

MACCABERS.

LADIES' SOCIAL BENEVOLENT PENNY MITE SOCIETY.

PHILATHEA CLASS.

BARACA BIBLE CLASS.

CEMETARY AID SOCIETY.

FREE METHODIST CHURCH.

MODERN AMERICAN FRATERNAL.

WOMAN'S RELIEF CORPS.

EMINENT LADIES OF THE GLOBE.

COMPANY G, 3RD REGIMENT, I.N.G.

COURT OF HONOR.

KNIGHTS OF THE GLOBE.

UNITED WORKMEN WOODSTOCK.

WOODSTOCK PLEASURE CLUB.

Woodstock Sentinel, December 26, 1901.

IMPORTANT NEW LAW GOES INTO EFFECT NEXT WEDNESDAY

For the information of the public, physicians, town and city clerks and all concerned, County

Clerk Rushton asks us to publish the following extracts from the new law requiring reports of deaths and births to the county clerks and regulating the internment or other disposal of dead bodies and a penalty attached for non-compliance with the provisions thereof, all of which takes effect Jan. 1, 1902.

"It shall be the duty of every physician and midwife in the state of Illinois who attends the birth of a child to report said birth, within thirty days after its occurrence, to the county clerk of the county in which the birth takes place. .... When no physician or midwife has been in attendance, then it shall be the duty of the parent, or, in case of the disability of the parent, of the householder to make said report within the time and manner aforesaid. ....

"No person shall inter, cremate, deposit in a vault or otherwise dispose of any human body, until he has received a permit so to do, as hereinafter provided, which permit shall bear date when issued, shall state the name of the deceased, the date and cause of death, the manner in which the body shall be disposed of and the place of such disposal, the name of the person to whom the permit is issued, and the name of the attending physician, midwife or coroner, and shall be signed by the official by whom it is issued. ....

Woodstock Sentinel, December 26, 1901.

We wish all of our readers a most happy new year, may the sun of happiness and prosperity shine upon you during 1902 with even greater effulgence than during 1901.

Woodstock Sentinel, December 26, 1901

***

Ida was at her wits end. Not a word! Not a single word from him! Not at Thanksgiving. Not at Christmas. Now not on New Year's Eve. She would not be that woman who begged a man for his attention. She had made it abundantly clear that she was interested in furthering the relationship. Going down to Woodstock for the minstrel show, writing every week, going down for a picnic weekend last May, telling him how lonely she was. What more could she do? Obviously, he was not interested in furthering this courtship. She took pen in hand and began…

December 31, 1901
936 Huron St.
Racine, WI

Dear John,

How I hate to write to you with this news, but I feel that I must tell you that I have found another beau. He is someone here in Racine making it easier to call and attend various functions without the long distance between us. I have much appreciated your attention and thought that there might be a hope for a mutual understanding, but I do not see that happening nor has our mutual admiration progressed to a point that—.

"Ida!" Mama called up the stairs. "*Jemand ist an der Tür für Sie.*"

Someone at the door? Ida's hand went to her forehead. "Mama. I'm not fit for company. Tell them I'll see them tomorrow at church. *Ich werde sie in der Kirche sehen.*"

"Ida!" Mama's voice was sharper. "*Sie wollen diesen Anrufer nehmen.*" You *WILL* want to take *this* caller.

Good heavens! She did not want to see anyone right now. Not a moment's peace. Ida took a long breath and blew it out. "*Wer ist es?*" She listened…silence…then…

"It's me, Ida." A baritone voice came up the stairs.

Her heart skipped a beat. Her breath caught. She put down her pen and looked at the letter she had started, picked up the piece of stationery, and crumpled it into a ball.

John!

Ida ran from her room to the top of the stairs and looked down at him. "Vas you dare, Charlie?" She gave him the Racine colloquial greeting to cover her nervous excitement. The answer, of course, was, "I vas dare, and now I'm here."

John laughed. "I'm John not Charlie, remember me?"

Ida was not smiling. "Almost not at all. I guess you don't know how to be polite and let a family know when you are coming for a visit?" She came a few steps down and stood with arms akimbo, towering over him.

John chuckled, but Mama and Clara swiftly withdrew to the kitchen.

John took a step up and leaned on the newel post. "Aw, Ida. Don't be mad at me." He looked to her like a bashful little boy. Her heart thawed just a bit.

"Why in the world would you think I was angry with you? Did you do something naughty?"

John seemed to consider what to say…admit guilt or deny it. "I'm sorry that I didn't let you know I was coming. I just couldn't resist any longer."

Oh, well played. Ida stepped down a few more stairs. "I've missed you and your letters, and I had almost given up on you. I had just decided that you had lost interest."

John took a step up to the landing. "Lost interest? I'll never lose interest. I've just been busy, and you know how time goes so fast when you are busy. I've been——"

"Working hard. I know. But to what end? To make yourself rich and lonely, Mr. Scrooge? Maybe that is who you are, not Charlie. Is that the future you want?"

John looked a bit dismayed at this comparison, but he moved closer on the landing as if to be ready to catch her if she fell. "Of course not, but—"

"No buts! Do you want to keep this…friendship, or do you want to be filthy rich and alone?"

"Are those my only two choices?" John's lips formed a tiny smile. Where was this going? John thought about the letters he had written where he always said how much he missed her. He had told her that he wasn't going to have much free time to come to Racine, but he had come up around the Fourth of July. And he'd written…a number of times—

"Right now, yes!"

"Of course, I want to keep this friendship. How could you ever think otherwise? I told you I was going to have trouble getting away. I am trying to make sure I can provide for my family before I make one." John's cheeks turned pink, and a little heat sounded in his voice.

Was he embarrassed? Angry? Ida considered this excuse. They weren't betrothed. He sounded like they were, as if her acceptance were a given. "I'm not family yet."

John stepped up from the landing to the step just two below where she had lit. "I know that, but I was sure—"

"You were sure about what? That I would just sit here and wait for you months on end to give me the time of day?"

"No…I thought…I was sure that…." He paused. "That we had made permanent plans."

"Permanent plans?!" Ida's loud laugh was surely heard in the kitchen. "You are lucky, mister, that I don't slam the door in your face! I have gone the extra mile to get you off first base, but you have resisted me at every turn."

John took another step. He was within arm's reach now. His voice was soft and calm. "Aw, come on, Ida. You know how fond I am of you. If you don't, I'll say it now. I'm very fond of you. Don't be angry. Give me a chance to make it up to you."

Ida looked at his earnest face and the hand he was holding out to her. She looked down at her feet. She could feel the tears welling up. She did not want to cry, but she was not sure that she could stop the emotional waterfall inside her. She reached out and took his hand, and her other one went to her face. She took a step down. They were still one step apart now, but eye to eye. His arms encircled her and lifted her off the step and into his embrace. Then she was crying, wetting his wool-covered breast.

He held her and let her cry for a few minutes, mumbling to the top of her head. "I'm so sorry. I didn't mean to hurt you. I hate to see you sad. I do care for you."

After a bit, Ida got her tears in check and pushed back. John pulled out a clean handkerchief. She wiped her eyes and dabbed her nose. Then she smiled a real smile. "I'm glad to see you."

John laughed loudly and turned to descend the stairs with his arm still around her, and they came down the stairs together.

As if a cue had been given, Mama and Clara scurried out of the kitchen (stage left). Each took a turn for a hug and a kiss on the cheek, and Clara hung John's coat and hat, which had found rest on the back of the davenport. Mr. Stoffel appeared out of nowhere and gave John a hearty handshake and a clap on the back and welcomed him to sit down. John wasn't sure that he had ever in his life been greeted with such enthusiasm.

Ida stayed utmost in his thoughts throughout the greetings. They could not keep their eyes off each other. Ida took a seat on the sofa a respectable distance from her beau. She watched him talk easily with her family and took a deep breath, letting it out slowly. John gave her a look of concern. She returned a quick smile. They would talk later. Now was family time.

Later they sat together on the sofa, holding hands. Just having him here was a wonder, and he had said he could stay until tomorrow evening, because the typewriter factory was closed as a New Year holiday. She still wasn't sure where they stood long term, but she was sure that he wanted to be here with her as the year turned over. She was encouraged by his presence.

Mama and Papa Stoffel had made their way to bed, and Clara and Herman had taken their leave to go celebrate the new year out on the town. So, here they were…alone…together…a first. He smelled of wet wool, perspiration, and cigar smoke. He must have sat in the smoking car coming up. AND he had just brought her hand to his lips for a kiss.

"You know, Mr. Wienke, that I really had almost given up on you. Six months without a visit and only a few brief notes. I was sure you had met another."

"Well, Miss Doering, I'll have you know that I thought about you every day of those months. I even thought about sitting with you on this very comfortable sofa, holding your hand. It has not been easy for me either."

Ida pulled back and dropped his hand and looked him straight in the eyes in mock astonishment. "I should say NOT with all the traveling to and fro, to Madison football games and street fairs and various other locations to curry the favor of your future customers, I assume, while I was left sitting here wondering about your intentions."

John blushed. He had told her of all his comings and goings in his letters, but he never expected that she would feel that he didn't have her still in his thoughts on those occasions. His brow furrowed in concern. "Well…I…was just trying…I'm sorry…I can see now that I should probably have made one of those trips to Racine. I apologize."

"Probably?" Her lips made a little pout.

"I surely should have."

She left him hanging for a bit, just so the lesson would make an impression. "You know it would be pretty easy for me to find a fine union factory man here in Racine to marry. I could do that. There are plenty of anarchists to go around."

John looked somewhat stunned. "Do you know anarchists? Has one of them been pursuing you? I thought…." His voice trailed away. Maybe she did not like him as he thought she did.

His face had turned so glum that she couldn't hold the ruse any longer. "Oh, John. At present, I only have eyes for you. I'm just expecting a bit more…." Her eyes went to the ceiling as she searched for a word. "A bit more attentiveness from someone I admire so much and who, I think, admires me."

John reclaimed her hand. "I am so sorry I caused you to question my desire to continue this courtship." He looked directly into her eyes, as one must when coming to an agreement of great consequence. "I thought my intentions were clear. That I expressed them in every letter and always when we were together."

Ida didn't break the gaze. "I'm worried that you are saying that, and believe it, but then expect me to just sit here in

Racine and wait. I know you have plans and aims for your life, and I want to be a part of those if we are to form a family someday. I believe that actions speak louder than words."

John was quiet. At a loss for words. Was he such a catch that a girl would be glad to wait for HIM to be ready? His eyes had softened, and now they wandered around her face landing on her lips. He cleared his throat. "I do greatly admire you Miss Doering, and I would like nothing better than to show you my admiration with a kiss."

Oh, for heaven's sake, stop talking about it and just do it! Ida smiled, "Well, Mr. Wienke, what are you waiting for? It's about time we get serious about this pairing or give this courtship up, wouldn't you say?"

"I WOULD say." And John gathered her into his arms, and the embers were glowing again.

And that's how Herman, and then Clara, found them when they returned from their New Year Celebration, long after the clock struck twelve. Fast asleep in each other's arms, fully clothed, mind you, but very content, nonetheless.

The Wienke Brothers at John and Ida's Wedding
R to L: William, Frank, Albert, John, and Bob

Two Cities
(1902)

Yule's come and yule's gone,
And we hae feasted weel;
Sae Jock mann to his flail again,
And Jenny to her wheel.

***

A Four Days' Vacation

The employees of the Oliver typewriter factory are enjoying a four days' vacation. The factory has shut down on Tuesday evening until next Monday, in order to allow time for annual inventory. The employees of the factory appreciate the rest, for they have been given a taste of the strenuous life in real earnest the past few months.

Woodstock Sentinel, January 2, 1902.

***

Sophia Wienke sat in her comfortable chair in the generous parlor of the house on Washington Street. She had pulled her hair back into a bun at the nape of her neck as she did every morning. She wore a drab-brown ankle length house dress and sturdy shoes of black leather, but no jewelry or other adornments, as this was not the way of a German Lutheran lady. Her hands moved swiftly as she tatted a doily that she would add to her gift bag. Sophia liked giving handmade gifts, especially food.

She had spent the night before, New Year's Eve, and most of this morning alone with all her boys off on their own business, and she was a bit at a loss for things that needed to be done. Charles and Emil had been with her overnight, coming home in the wee hours and slipping out just after dawn. They each, smelling of beer and smoke from Bob's Saloon, gave her a quick kiss on the cheek before they caught the early train back to Beloit.

She had planned to cook the lamb shank out in the icebox, but who would eat it? She had eaten a bowl of oatmeal, a piece of kuchen, and fresh coffee for breakfast and was getting hungry at a bit past noon.

Sophia dropped her tatting to her lap and looked around the room. She was happy in this new house, she supposed. The rooms were sizeable, and she could easily fit everyone around the dining room table, even the grandchildren. She sighed. Here she had gotten the larger house with five bedrooms just in time to be alone. She needed only three rooms – a kitchen, a parlor, and a bedroom. Oh yes, and a privy or should she say, 'water closet' since hers was now inside the house. She loved the indoor necessary room. Four rooms then were all she really needed.

She got up and made her way to the kitchen. She had woken up stiff and sore this morning and needed to move around. Winter was the worst time for joints. They couldn't be eased by a brisk walk uptown.

Another complaint. She must shake this feeling. This was a lovely house, and she had such wonderful sons to have moved her from her tiny house to this lavish one. As she stood at the sink looking out at the railroad track which ran along Washington Street, a train approached from the north, its whistle wailing, a lonely sound to her ear. She took a New Year's Day inventory.

Two girls lost in Germany. Tears welled in her eyes blurring the green of the outside world. Those girls would have loved America.

A husband lost in America, buried on a bitter cold day where they had to use a pickaxe to dig the grave. Two tears trickled down her wrinkled cheeks picturing the box being lowered into the hole as she shivered against the cold.

The shiver broke the spell. She looked down into the sink, with its silver faucets bringing her fresh water, and wiped her cheeks with the back of her hand. She had nothing to cry about. Look at all the luck and joy this new land had brought her.

Eight strong, healthy boys. Five married to good women.

Nine grandchildren and another on the way.

Of the three unmarried sons, John would soon be married, she was sure.

Bob might never marry, although he was quite a catch – handsome and fun.

And little Emil, a real worker, dedicated, and an athlete. He would meet a girl in Beloit, she prophesied.

Sophia turned from the window and looked around her kitchen with the many cupboards, heavy wooden table, running water, and new cookstove. Yes, she had fine sons. Out of the blue it came to her, and she knew what she would do. She would make a German New Year's cake for each family, at least the ones in Woodstock, and one for the house. A generous New Year's gift. And then she'd invite her sons to pick them up, and she'd get to see them. It was a wonderful idea.

She went to the cupboard and found the fillings for the three layers. Poppy seeds for the first layer for good luck in the new year. Almonds for the second layer for good health. And for the top layer, cinnamon apples, canned last fall, to add sweetness to life. She laid out the ingredients along with milk, eggs, and clabbered cream from her new icebox and set to work.

Sophia worked the dough and set aside four portions in the icebox to chill while she prepared the fillings for the layers, quadrupling the amounts to provide for four cakes.

The first layer. Into the pot went poppy seed, butter, sugar, raisins, milk, honey, and nearly a cup of rum for flavor. The mixture slowly came to a boil and then was removed to rest.

She shelled and chopped the almonds and mixed them with sugar, milk, cinnamon and crushed cloves. The spicy fragrance tickled her nose, and she sneezed. She chuckled and said aloud, *"Gesundheit."* To health.

Sophia opened the first mason jar of apples, using her apron to grip the cap, and poured the contents into a bowl. They looked fresh and delicious. It was everything she could do not to eat them right there. Two jars for four cakes.

The fillings were complete, so she retrieved the first dough ball and cut it into four pieces. She rolled out each into a thin layer and using a ten-inch spring-form cake pan like a cookie cutter, she cut out four identical circles of dough. She greased and floured the pan and then placed the first circle of dough at the bottom. She added enough of the poppy seed mixture to just more than cover the bottom…not thin…not thick…just right, and then added another circle of dough. The nut mixture, her favorite, went in the pan next. The layer was just a bit thicker than the poppy seed, bringing the next circle of dough to within a half inch of the top rim. On the very top she added a single layer of apples and covered it with the fourth round of dough. Her mouth watered, and she stole one of the apple pieces from the jar.

Sophia broke an egg into a small bowl and beat it thoroughly, but not enough to foam. With a sharp knife, she slit the dough in eight places and brushed the egg over the entire cake letting the golden liquid soak down through the holes to the layers below.

She replenished the water pan and placed it in the oven next to the firebox to absorb some of the heat from the hot spot to assure a more constant temperature. Then, carefully, she placed the cake into the hot oven and closed the door. She had not baked very much with this stove, so she would have to watch this cake closely and then adjust the fire and time based on this first experience. It should take about three-quarters of an hour or maybe an hour to bake. Sophia turned over the hourglass, so she would not lose track of time.

With a satisfied smile on her face, she started the process again for the second cake. She had only two ten-inch pans so she would make the second and get it in the oven and wait for the first to cool very well before releasing the spring to remove the sides, deploying the cake onto a plate, and sprinkling powdered sugar in a thick layer on top. And then she would move on to the third and fourth cakes. It would be an all-afternoon endeavor.

Ideally, the cakes should sit in a cool place overnight before removing them from the pan, but two cakes would have to jell overnight without the pan. She hoped they would not slide apart before jelling.

The next challenge was where she could set them to jell. She would put them out on the enclosed porch off the kitchen for a while, but it was too cold for overnight. They would freeze rather than jell. She decided it would have to be the icebox to keep them cold, but not frozen. She would have to make room for four cakes in the already well stocked icebox. Not an easy task.

Sophia was glad she had thought about this gift. She would call the boys tonight on the infernal telephone to pick them up in the morning. How surprised Minnie, Anna, and Lena would be to have a wonderful New Year cake for dinner tomorrow. And how surprised John and Bobby would be upon their return home. If they came back today, the cake might not make it to tomorrow.

Her stomach growled. In her enthusiasm for the cakes, she had forgotten to eat. She went to the icebox and began pulling sandwich fixings out. She'd have time to eat while the cake baked. She took her time removing foodstuffs and looking each over carefully. She threw away some less than desirable items thereby making room for the cakes. Two birds with one stone. Cakes and a clean icebox. It was a wonderful New Year's Day.

***

January 8, 1902
936 Huron Street
Racine, Wisconsin

Dearest John,

How I miss you and wish you were here in Racine rather than there in Illinois. I can barely stand going to work, traveling through the drifts and ice only to sweat in the laundry for hour upon hour and then get a chill walking home. If you were here by my side, I would be warmer, and you would be colder, I'm sure.

I'll have you know that Mama and Papa Stoffel and even Clara had nothing but good to say about you after you left on New Year's Day. It was John this and John that and wasn't it nice of

John until I told them to desist. I told them that I like you just fine now, and they shouldn't worry. I must agree that you were most generous with your good nature during our short time together. I know I appreciated it, and I guess they did too.

Did you catch your death on the cold train on the way home? We certainly have had a cold spell since you were here. Some nights the stoves must be stoked halfway through the night so there will still be embers in the morning. It's snowing again now so we can expect drifts in the morning and boots full of water by the time we get anywhere. Oh, wait! Tomorrow is Saturday! I can just stay home and sew. What a lucky ducky am I.

I suppose you will not be able to be lazy tomorrow. I can hardly believe what that factory expects from you boys. Days, nights, Saturdays. You better not be working yourself to death. I will be very upset with you and will punish you for not writing. Ha.

I must start thinking about heading to bed even with the day off tomorrow. I will have to get up and feed the boys before they go off to work and then I'm sure Mama will have chores for me before I can settle down to sew. Such is the life of the handmaiden. I will be thinking about you slaving away at your station. That will warm me up.

When will I see you again, Mr. Blue Eyes?

Soon I hope,

Ida

***

Personal Mention

Robert Wienke visited with friends at McHenry, New Year's night.

Chas. Wienke, of Beloit, was in the city for a few days visiting with relatives and friends.

Mrs. Linda Wienke [Steinke] of Beloit is a guest at the home of Albert Wienke this week.

Emil Wienke was home from Beloit for the holidays, the guest of his mother and brothers.

Woodstock Sentinel, January 9, 1902.

***

An Addition Being Made to the Oliver Typewriter Factory

The predicted addition to the Oliver typewriter factory is well under way. This addition, which is being made on the north end of the factory building, is 40 X 60 feet, and we understand that it will be two stories high and built to conform to the character of the main building. More room has been badly needed for a long time, and the officers of the company being progressive men, are determined not to be cramped for room in turning out the best and most popular typewriter on the market. The factory force is again working three nights a week and the forces downstairs work every night, and even then, it is a difficult task to keep up with the demand for the machines.

Woodstock Sentinel, January 16, 1902.

***

FOR PLEASURE ONLY

Several years ago, some of our citizens conceived the idea that it would be a good thing, on account of the large number of young men drawn to this city by the Oliver typewriter factory, to form a club and secure quarters for its maintenance, the same to be organized purely on social lines and maintained for the benefit of its members. Such a club was soon organized, and quarters were secured in the third story of the Hoy block. The first quarters were the rooms for many years occupied by Medlar's photography gallery, but as soon as the Odd Fellows vacated the adjoining hall a doorway was cut through the brick wall and these rooms were added to the club's quarters, giving plenty of room for carrying out the plan at first contemplated, so that the Woodstock Pleasure club now occupies all of the third floor of the Hoy block except that portion used by the SENTINEL office.

The west portion of the club rooms is used as a reading and card room. In it is a piano, which is always kept well-tuned, a fine roll-top writing desk, in which is sheltered one of the latest Oliver typewriters, a library for the accommodation of the collection of books that the club is getting together, four round-top card tables, and an abundant supply of high-back and easy rocking chairs. Recently a telephone has also been hung on the walls. To the rear of this room is a bootblack's outfit for the accommodation of club members, as well as water closets and washroom, plenty of soap and clean towels being always on hand. Here the club members gather after their day's work to read the Chicago daily papers and the leading magazines and periodicals of the day, the club subscribing for several of the best of them. Here also who desire while away the moments playing cards, whilst being the ruling favorite at the present time and for many months past. Others occupy the easy chairs and discuss the leading events prominent in the public mind. In the east room is located a fine new billiard table received last week from the Brunswick-Balke-Collender Co., of Chicago, at an expense of $275, and a good pool table, with an abundance of cues placed in racks suspended on the walls. Those who use the tables are expected to drop a nickel in a box provided for that purpose after they have ceased playing, and no member is allowed to use the tables longer than the prescribed limit if others are waiting for a chance to play.

To the rear of this room is a gymnasium, in which is a punching bag, a lifting machine, Indian clubs, dumb-bells, and exerciser, swinging rings, and other apparatus for exercise, and these are generally well patronized.

Both of the main rooms are hung with beautiful pictures in attractive frames, making them pleasant places for the young men to congregate.

The members of the club are subject to rules that are cheerfully respected, one of which says:

"Gambling or drinking of intoxicating liquors in the rooms of the club are strictly prohibited and any member or members who shall violate the provisions of this article shall, for the first offense, be suspended for a period of one month, and for the second offense shall be expelled permanently."

This rule has never been violated and even on occasions when the club has given a "smoker" or other social function there has been no thought of disregarding it.

Membership in the club is open to all who are residents of this city or vicinity, the fee being $10, and in the securing of this membership the by-laws make an exacting process of acceptance by the entire club for each new member.

Each member upon acceptance is required to pay monthly dues of 50 cents in advance which entitles him to all the privileges of the club.

The present officers of the club are:

President – Harry Cross.

Vice-President – Arthur J. Mullen.

Secretary – George Lemmers.

Treasurer – Chas S. Northrop.

Directors – The above and E. A. Wyant, C. C. Harting, Albert Wienke and William Gritzbaugh.

The rooms are cared for and kept clean by Lee Parker, who is paid a salary for his services.

The membership of the club has shown a steady increase since its organization, and even since the entrance fee was doubled there has been a steady increase of membership, the applicants realizing that in this institution is provided a means for harmless amusement that is possessed of much merit. The officers of the club are men who are respected in the community, and they, as well as the individual members, take a lively interest in its welfare. The Pleasure club has a membership of over 100 men listed below (among them John Wienke, Robert Wienke, Albert Wienke, Dr. Emil Windmueller, Lynn W. Richards, Chas. L. Quinlan, Chas. F. Renich, H. B. Medlar, Geo. W. Lemmers, C. A. Lemmers, David R. Joslyn, Marcellus L. Joslyn, Theo. Hamer, George Eckert, J. J. Cooney, C. H. Donnelly, Walter H. Eckert, Harry Cross, Joe Connors, and Albert Schneider).

Woodstock Sentinel, January 30, 1902.

***

Ida pulled open the front door of 936 Huron Street after a loud knock, and her mouth fell open. "What are you doing here?"

"Is that any way to greet a person you admire?" John stood there as big as life on the stoop on a Monday afternoon.

Ida pulled him in from the cold and threw her arms around him. He acknowledged her admiration by holding her tight and kissing her cheek.

"Here give me your wet coat and hat. What are you doing here?"

John took off his hat and unwound his scarf. "Well, it's this way. The Union boys pushed a little too hard at good old Oliver, and so they closed the shop for three days so we could all consider our sins against the company, the management, and Woodstock itself. I decided that, if you'll have me, I could consider my transgressions in Racine as well as in Woodstock." He smiled.

Ida hung the wet things on the rack and pointed at his galoshes. "What do you mean pushed too hard?"

John bent to unhook them. "Three-quarters of the shop decided to start a local trade union to negotiate better hours with the management." He pulled off the boots and stood them on the entry rug side-by-side. "The management, however, was having none of it and so has closed down the shop rather than let it unionize."

"Good grief." Ida motioned him into the kitchen. They settled at the kitchen table where Ida could keep track of supper while they talked. Mama had gone up to dress and the other workers would be home soon and be hungry. "May I ask which side you took?"

The kitchen was overly warm, but it felt good on John's half-frozen feet. "It was a hard decision. Oliver has been very good to Woodstock in so many ways. We have almost no unemployed and the housing and other markets are booming because the workers have money to spend. On the other hand, I would love to see you more often. Did I tell you we won't be called back until Thursday?"

"Indeed!" Ida's heart took a little jump. Three days!

John smiled at her reaction. "On Thursday, when they reopen, everyone has to either drop their union membership or they are fired. Those who didn't sign on with the union will be welcomed back with no extra requirements."

Ida got up to stir something on the stove. "So, you didn't join." Her back was to John, and he didn't know how to read the comment.

"Would you have wanted me to?" He hedged a bit.

"Sixty or more hours a week seems a lot for a man…and for his family. I don't know. I would just want you home more than that if we were married." She continued to toil at the stove.

"But just think what sixty-some hours a week will buy. A grand house, a business, a fine horse and coach. Housewives often have sixty or even eighty-hour weeks – maybe more – for no pay. Should they unionize?"

Ida turned to look at him smiling. "Even if we say that each has one employer and each have ways to negotiate. But a woman does her work in the home with the family around her, except, of course, for her husband who is working sixty hours a week at the typewriter factory. It's not an apple-to-apple comparison."

John chuckled. How he loved to talk to this smart woman. "It's not all work at the factory either. The management does so much for their employees. They pay for extra trains to Madison for football games. They sponsor a band that plays at the park in summer and a baseball team good enough to send some players to the majors. They donate to causes like the hospital fund, and they keep building the factory to bring more people to Woodstock. It seems like a hand-shake relationship to me."

"But what is the cost of the sixty-hour week on your family or your fiancé?"

It was a blatant hint, but it seemed to go right over John's head or maybe he would have noticed, had Mama Stoffel not come bustling in and reacted with a screech of joy at seeing John sitting at the kitchen table causing them to drop the subject. They weren't quite on the same page John reflected the next day as he enjoyed his day off in Racine…but almost.

***

O. T. Shut Down

From Monday noon until Thursday morning of last week the works of the Oliver Typewriter Co. in this city were shut down. This move on the part of the management of the factory was made because a large number of employees had organized a local trade union. The management of the factory, while not opposed to organized labor as a principle or to union men working in a factory as individuals, did object to the local union, composed mostly of unskilled workmen, attempting to unionize the factory.

Soon after the shutdown, notices were posted stating that work would be resumed on Thursday morning and all former employees could return as individuals but not as members of the local union.

On Thursday morning the factory reopened. All of the former employees who had not affiliated themselves with the newly organized local union were on hand and took up their former positions. A large percentage of those who had joined the union, surrendered their membership and returned to work. The others, about sixty in number, stood pat and remained out, and are still out.

Woodstock Sentinel, February 10, 1902.

***

Woodstock Supports Oliver Management

About town the sentiment of the people of this city has in a large degree been opposed to the local union not because they are opposed to union labor but because of the laudable desire to actively support the Oliver Typewriter Co.

and the management of their factory in accordance with their best judgment. The citizens of Woodstock are justly proud of their factory, and they are extremely jealous of any movement which they fear may interfere with its successful operation.

THE SENTINEL has observed that a large number of its exchanges have contained garbled reports of the happenings here regarding the factory and of the conditions surrounding the closure. We regret that this is true and that our friends of the press in neighboring cities did not better inform themselves before they published long-winded articles under big scareheads.

Woodstock Sentinel, February 13, 1902.

LOCAL INTELLIGENCE

Next horse sale, Mar. 12.

Have you been buttonholed yet?

Brick ice cream to your order at Dirrenberger's

The air is full of politics, but there is no rancor in it.

Extra fine Heinz Sauer kraut at Conklin's market.

Ladies' Pleasure club will meet with Mrs. Davis, Friday afternoon, Feb. 14.

Report of Woodstock Public library for week ending Feb. 9, 1902: Number of visitors, 447; number of books loaned, 230.

Mrs. C. M. Curtis, Librarian.

The office of Dr. E. Windmueller has been greatly beautified by the sill of Albert Wienke in the paper hanging and painting line. "Doc" is never happy unless things are looking pretty sleek around him.

The factory employees have taken possession of the new addition to the factory, and all appreciate the added room given them for the prosecution of their labors. About sixty machines are turned out per day now, and 300 hands are employed.

Woodstock Sentinel, February 13, 1902.

***

Racine Situation Alarming

Racine Wis. Feb 15 –[Special]-State health officers were called here today and made an examination of three cases of smallpox. Dr. Wingate, secretary of the state board, at once ordered that the houses where the sick persons were found would be quarantined and that "Smallpox" signs be posted.

Local health officers were criticized by the State officer for allowing persons to enter or leave the houses as it was found that the cases were severe.

Chicago Tribune, February 16, 1902.

***

February 16, 1902
Woodstock, Ill

Dearest Ida,

I just put down the Tribune after reading about the smallpox outbreak in Racine. Please tell me that you and your family are being careful and staying away from the public squares that bring this sickness upon the unwary receiver. I want to come and snatch you from that vile city this instant, but I know that I cannot. If you want to escape to these healthy environs, please but come! Or maybe I should come there rather than you bringing the pox here with you…please write and tell me that you are healthy, and I will be so pleased.

I am working many hours and have a plan now for a house. Al has a lot on Lincoln Avenue, and I have one out a bit just off McHenry Avenue that I invested in a few years ago. I am going to talk to him about trading the two because I would want to be close to the square if I…or we…were to open a shop. We shall see what he says. Al and Lena seem happy. She is going to have a baby, which you probably know. Ma is so happy. Not that she doesn't have other grandchildren, but as she always says, the more the better.

Al has buttonholed me twice now about running for office this Spring. He always catches me at time when he knows I can't escape so I just make jokes. He is the one with all the admirers, not me. What do you think? Should I run? Maybe for dog catcher?

Please write and tell me that you and yours have not come down with any deadly diseases.

I remain truly yours,
John

***

AROUSED TO SMALLPOX DANGER
Adjoining States Heed Warning from Chicago Health Department

As a result of the crusade against smallpox conducted by the Chicago Health department the boards of health of adjoining States are taking negligent cities and towns into their own hands. Word was received yesterday that the Wisconsin board has threatened Racine with shotgun quarantine unless immediate steps are taken to stamp out the disease there.

Complaint against negligence in Des Moines and other Iowa cities has resulted in a movement in the Legislature of that State which is expected to result in most sweeping powers being conferred on the Board of Health.

Chicago Daily Tribune, February 20, 1902.

***

COUNTRY GOING MAD

Dr. R. B. Hoyt of Detroit has authority for the statement that by the year 2162, the world will be populated by madmen. He bases his belief on the statement that during the past fifty years insanity and fanaticism has increased 300 per cent, and that should the same pace continue for 100 years, it will absorb all the common sense and sanity there is left.

The doctor appears to be a pessimist of pronounced type. He is perfectly café in making this prediction because he will not be present to verify his claim. While the statement is extremely radical, it contains more than a grain of truth as far as fanaticism is concerned, and that fanaticism not unfrequently develops into a danger to the welfare of humanity as it lies close to the surface, requiring but a breath to fan a flame that is threatening.

The various political fads are constantly coming to the surface, under the alluring guise of report, are paralleled to the religious world by creeds that are loose and equally dangerous. The age is restless and unstable. There are more people chasing phantoms and riding hobbies than ever before. This is doubtless the danger to which the doctor alluded. What the world needs, especially this land of rapid progress, is stability.

Janesville Daily Gazette, Feb. 19. 1902.

***

February 21, 1902
932 Huron St.
Racine, Wis

Dear John,

 A quick reply to ease your mind. The paper has reported smallpox in another part of town where rooming houses are the rule rather than the exception and then only two actual cases. Most of the cases are varioloid which is a mild case of smallpox that someone gets after they have been vaccinated. We have not had a single case of the pox or varioloid that we know of here close to downtown and the lake. We are all as safe as we can be as we go about our usual business. I am careful about meeting people at the laundry when I work. I do not offer my hand and try to watch for blemishes which give away infected individuals. Besides, a few sniffles here or there we have all been healthy this winter. And now we can look forward to spring in the near future.

 I do hope that we may see each other soon. I so enjoyed our last meeting and would entertain any plan to meet again.

 You seem to have very negative feelings about Racine, calling it a "vile town." I will have you know that we have all the modern conveniences in Racine without the crowds of Milwaukee. Our streets and streetlights are very modern and along with our very good rail system both to Milwaukee and to Chicago it say nothing of points westward. We have the very finest stores and a grand hotel with high society luncheons. We have not just one theater, but two, where the best entertainments come to town, I daresay, long before they come to the Opera House in Woodstock. We also have access to all that the lake brings by boat and steamer. Our fresh fruit and meat are practically still on the vine and hoof. The opportunities for employment are vast. If someone wants to work, there is work to be had. The laundry is thriving, and we have not seen any downturn in the sewing business due to Mama's fine handiwork.

On the other side, I will concede that we have more Democrats and anarchists than Republicans which is sometimes troublesome as they make up most of the union members who are demanding additional benefits, marching in the streets, and so forth. But this just makes life more exciting, don't you agree? I know you do.

As for Wisconsin, it is very progressive. Why a proposition that a man could divorce his wife if she is insane for three years was just voted down in Madison. So, you would not be able to get rid of me so easily if we lived in Racine. Do you have such a law in Illinois?

All in all, I doubt that there is a more up-to-date or exciting city anywhere in the United States than Racine, Wisconsin. So much more cosmopolitan than the small village of Woodstock.

That said…I am sure we are as safe here as anywhere these days, as you will surely agree.

Must run! A seamstress' work is never sewed up. Ha!

Truly yours,

Ida

***

PERSONAL MENTION

Albert Wienke and Joe Connors were Chicago visitors one day last week.

Woodstock Sentinel, February 27, 1902

***

PERSONAL MENTION

Mrs. Sophia Wienke and Robert Wienke went to Dundee, on Monday, for a short visit with friends.

Woodstock Sentinel, March 6, 1902.

For Collector

The undersigned will be a candidate for collector of the town of Dorr at the approaching township election and invites support of the Republicans of the town.

ALBERT WIENKE

Woodstock Sentinel, March 6, 1902.

New Arrivals

Born to Mr. and Mrs. Albert Wienke, in this city, on Tuesday, Mar. 4, 1902, a daughter. The respected parents have the congratulations of their many friends.

Woodstock, Sentinel, March 6, 1902

***

Attend the Town Caucus

The Republican town caucus will be held at the courthouse in this city next Saturday, and it is hoped that there will be a large attendance. The only contest that appears is for the office of collector, for which Frank J. Hendricks and Albert Wienke are seeking the nomination. It is up to the Republicans of the township to say which one of these worthy young men they desire to have this office the coming year. Both are capable of filling it, and both have many friends who are urging their claims.

Woodstock Sentinel, March 13, 1902.

***

Election Results

The contest between Frank J. Henricks and Albert Wienke for the nomination for collector having developed considerable interest, the caucus voted, and the result was Hendricks, 307 and Wienke, 191.

Woodstock Sentinel, March 20, 1902.

Popular Vote

Madison, Wis., Feb. 13.—A joint resolution was introduced in the assembly today requesting congress to forthwith issue a call for a constitutional convention to pass an amendment related to the election of United States senators by popular vote.

Woodstock Sentinel, March 20, 1902.

To Increase Output

The Oliver Typewriter Co. has gradually increased the output of their factory in this city. Superintendent Whitworth was in Chicago a few days ago and purchased about $10,000 worth of new machinery to be placed in the works here, and they expect soon to be manufacturing seventy-five typewriters per day.

Woodstock Sentinel, March 20, 1902.

***

"Hello Al…and Lena! And Evie! Come, come in out of that wind." John held the door wide and inviting.

"Hi John. Evie, meet your Uncle John." And with that Lena placed the baby in his arms while she removed her coat and hat.

"Um…hi there Evie. Look! She's smiling at me."

"Gas," said Al.

"Albert!" Lena playfully slapped Al's arm, and then turned her attention back to John, "She might have smiled at you. You *are,* after all, her favorite uncle."

Lena took the baby and unwrapped her from the blanket. She is tiny, thought John. Are they all so tiny? Lena handed her back, now clothed in a one-piece flannel slip dress common to babies of both sexes. She felt so small in his big hands. Her eyes were open, but now her face crumpled, and she began to cry.

"John, you are holding her at arms-length like she is going to break, cuddle her in. She's probably just a little cold from taking off the blanket." John pulled her in and tucked her in his right arm as he would a football, and she quieted.

"Vat's dat I hear!" Sophia hurried into the kitchen. "Aw, da litl' one."

John without hesitation transferred Evie to Sophia who began to bounce and cluck like a mother hen. John smiled. That lady knew how to comfort a child.

Al and John retreated to the parlor leaving the women with the baby.

John took his usual chair motioning Al to the settee.

Al settled on the cranberry brocade with a rose motif of the couch. "How are you, brother? How's your love life?"

"Never better. Sorry about the caucus vote. Maybe next time."

"I should have put more effort into campaigning, but with the baby and all the painting jobs, I just didn't have time. Yes, maybe next time." Al took a seat in John's favorite chair making John have to look around the parlor for a place to sit.

"Your work is getting you pretty well known around town, so you'll have a better chance next time." John sank into the end of the sofa.

"You know you should run, John. You are the one who is on a first name basis with the politico. Me, I'm just John Wienke's brother, the painter."

John chuckled. "Maybe. I've been thinking about it. I have a lot on my plate right now trying to get ready to ask for Ida's hand and—"

"What? Excellent!" Al interrupted. "Did…" he began to call out to Lena.

"No, wait," John shushed him. "I don't want Lena to know yet because she'll break the surprise before I do."

"No, she won't."

"Yes, she might…without meaning to, of course. Let's just keep it between you and me. I'll let you know when you can tell her…I've still got a long row to hoe. I've been trying to figure out how we can get married before we have a house. I just don't have enough money saved yet. My money is tied up in real estate and in the bank. I suppose I can sell a lot for a down payment and borrow the rest or I could buy an old house and fix it up or—"

"Whoa, slow down," said Al. "Sounds like you have a lot on your mind besides politics."

"Ja, I guess I do," John admitted.

"Lena and I got married before we had a house," Al reminded him. "And you know, we are still living in the rental and will, just now, start looking for something more permanent."

"But that was because of timing, not money."

"True, and also, wanting Lena to have a say in the new house. So, one thing at a time. If you feel you want or need to ask Ida, do it. Then work it out between the two of you when you'll marry and when you'll buy a house, and when you'll open a business. It's much more fun to make plans with a helpmate, I assure you."

John sighed. The task just seemed overwhelming.

Al leaned forward in the chair. "John don't let your conservative ways stand in your path to happiness. There is a lot more to life than having money. You are going to need Ida's help, in all the ways a wife can, as you go forward. Don't push it off until she has given up on you. Neither of you is getting younger and I assume you want children. If so, you better get cracking." Al's eyes were intense.

John looked at his feet. "I want children. I never thought about that being an issue."

"Okay, go, talk to her, and if everything seems right, ask her. Maybe she'll say 'no,' and you can stop worrying."

"What?" John looked up in alarm. "She'll says no?"

Al laughed, "I'm just kidding, but you don't know until you pop the question! Oh, here they come, my darlings."

Sophia came in with Evie in her arms followed by Lena with a tray with coffee and *Marmorkuchen* (marble cake) fresh from the oven. The smell of it had permeated the air and now the sight of it sent all their mouths to desire.

"Get it while it's hot," Lena said, as she began cutting the cake and sliding healthy pieces onto the dessert plates.

***

600 Converts in Four Weeks

Rev. William A. Sunday, known as the baseball evangelist, has closed a series of meetings at Fairmont, Ind., securing in all 600 converts in four weeks. A large tabernacle was erected for the use of the evangelist and at least 1,200 people heard him every afternoon and evening. The evangelist is not paid a regular salary for his work but is given the collections taken up on the last day. Mr. Sunday received $1,600 for his work at Fairmont.

Woodstock Sentinel, April 3, 1902

***

The Annual Tramp Crop

The keeper of the tramp house, Charles Roth, states that the number of knights of the road who are sheltered at his resort is not decreasing. This army of those who have fallen behind in life's struggle for supremacy begin to put in their appearance at nightfall and before 9 p. m. the register often shows fifteen signatures. While there is nothing luxurious about the local quarters, it is a paradise in comparison to other towns along the line. Kenosha, especially, where there is nothing but a dingy, cold room. The boys who hit this town find comfortable quarters with good anthracite coal at ten dollars a ton to toast their shins. They claim to represent men from all lines of industry, mechanics, and now and then, a professional man. The other evening, a patron claiming his home in the east registered for the night. He claimed to be an M. D., but the crowded condition of the profession coupled together with a strenuous life made it necessary for him to drop out, and while his present existence was not a matter of choice, it was nevertheless compulsory for the time being, at least. Still, he hoped to see better days.

Racine Journal Times, April 8, 1902.

***

RACINE FEARS MOB RULE AS RESULT OF LABOR WAR.

Racine, Wis., April 12 –[Special]—Attacks on the jail and the J.I. Case plow works by a mob are feared as the result of the shooting of a union molder by a non-union employee this afternoon. Both places are guarded by special deputies and the police.

The shooting was the outcome of the lockout by Case company of its union molders, and union men of all trades are aroused over the affair. Should the wounded man die it is promised the jail doors will be battered in and the prisoner lynched.

Howard Fristo of Bourbon, Ind., aged 25 years, and a non-union molder employed at the Case works, when returning home from work this afternoon, was followed by August Reiman and August Kall, union molders who were locked out. Fristo turned upon the men and without drawing his revolver from his coat pocket, fired six times, three of the bullets striking Reiman, the fourth the tire of the bicycle Reiman was leading, and the other bullets went wide of the mark.

When Reiman fell to the ground, Fristo started to run away and an angry mob followed him, hurling rocks and stones at the assailant, who while running, emptied the spent shells from the revolver and reloaded it, turning upon his followers and threatening to shoot them. He was followed to his boarding-house, and the police were notified, Fristo was found locked in his room, where he had hidden the revolver and changed his clothing.

Chicago Tribune, April 12, 1902.

***

April 15, 1902
Woodstock, IL

Dearest Ida,

I hope this finds you well and safe inside the confines of your home, away from the anarchists and union thugs. The Tribune says that Racine is just short of mob rule. If you and your family need to escape, we can find a respite in Woodstock for all of you.

You are of the opinion that Racine is superior to Woodstock. My what a sheltered life you have led in the big city. One major way that Woodstock is better is that we don't have armed marauders traveling the streets at night. We do sometimes have young boys with firecrackers who set them off under windows and then run away. We also have the best crime fighters for a town our size and the county courthouse and jail where hoodlums, if we have any, pay their dues. These jailbirds are most often from Chicago or other crime centers. Woodstock has not had an outbreak of the grippe this winter as you have in Racine, nor have the pox taken any lives or even been reported. We have had a few cases of consumption, but no more than any other municipality of this size?

Everything in Woodstock is within walking distance of everything else eliminating the need for street cars and taxis. If you walked 18 or 19 blocks in Woodstock, you would have walked across the whole town. We do have, as does Racine, trains that run through town and bring danger in their crossing of the public thoroughfare. But we do not have street cars killing people or unions revolting and shooting guns at people. We do have people who celebrate by shooting guns in the air, but we have not had a murder. Everything in Woodstock is fairly new…mostly thanks to the destruction of the old by fire. As the wooden structures burnt down, we replaced them with brick and stone, so we are somewhat fireproof at least downtown around the square. Each year we see new buildings being put up and wonderful new commercial spaces being let to entrepreneurs, like me, hopefully soon.

Everyone in Woodstock, basically, knows everyone else. How many of your neighbors and fellow citizens do you know? Only a handful, I would guess. I know your friends are precious to you, but it seems that they are few and mostly from church. I cannot count the number of my friends and acquaintances, and while some are from church, most I have met in the day-to-day life of the citizenry.

I know that I am totally besotted with my town, and if you lived here, I'm sure that you would be also. I am coming next weekend if you agree to see me.

As ever,

John

***

LOCAL INTELLIGENCE

The interior of the German Lutheran church is being repainted and repapered by Albert Wienke and his helpers, and it will look beautiful when the job is finished, for Mr. Wienke is an expert in his field.

Woodstock Sentinel, April 17, 1902.

***

Ida smiled up at John who had just come through the door. The broad grin he sported said that he was glad to see her. He took her in his arms and kissed her. Now *that* was a greeting any girl would swoon over.

John sighed. "How I have missed you."

"And I, you." Ida let her hands rest on his chest, not backing out of his embrace. "Your defense of Woodstock's values was very…um…moving."

He laughed and swung her around. "It's all true!!" He kissed her again.

"*Ahem!*" Mr. Stoffel cleared his throat. They separated, and John quickly crossed to shake hands with him as Ida's mother hurried into the room wiping her hands on her apron. John realized that there was a wonderful aroma of baking bread or strudel.   His mouth began to water. He hugged Louisa, kissing her on each cheek.

"Something sure smells good." John sniffed the air like a dog would. "*Es riecht gut.*"

Louisa covered a small smile with a hand. "*Wir haben etwas Besonderes für du gemacht.*"

"Something special?" John looked at Ida who just smiled and nodded.

"*Bienenstich.*"

Now John's mouth was really watering….the smell and the memory of the Bee Sting Cake, the semi-sweet cake filled with sweet creamy custard. This cake was not easy to make and so was only made on the most special occasions.

"What is the occasion?" John asked.

"You being here." Ida slipped her hand into his.

John thought back to that New Years Eve when his pouring had been a *beine* – a bee – and its prediction of the prospect of marriage. He smiled. This was an occasion.

After the dinner of bratwurst and *schmorkohl* (cabbage), and of course, the *Bienenstich*, Mama and Clara insisted that they would wash up. John and Ida adjourned to the parlor and sat close on the davenport facing slightly inward so they could see each other's smile.

"I feel like a celebrity. It was an absolutely wonderful meal and fantastic company."

"*Schau, ich habe es der gesagt, Mama.*" Ida raised her voice so the kitchen crew could hear. "*Er ist ein gutter Essen.* I told her that you are—"

"A good eater." John wanted to show his ability in German.

"You understand more than I think you do." Ida's look was curious.

"*Ein Bisschen.* Only a little. Although your accent is difficult at times." John was still smiling.

"Our accent? We don't have an accent."

"In German you do. Wait until you are struggling with Ma's German. You'll see what I mean. As for me, I suppose I understand better than I speak. I caught your mother wanting to laugh at my attempts earlier."

It was Ida's turn to smile. She nodded. "I did too."

John settled back into the davenport and took one of Ida's hands. "We are having a bit of a struggle at our church right now because the first generation and even some of the second generation want to keep everything in German. *Alle auf Deutsch!* But some of us want at least one service in English so that we can understand the sermon better. My brothers and I have talked about adding a service, but the church *Väter* are not in favor of that. And you know, church *Mütter* can't vote, even in German."

"Yes, but do the church mothers want to vote?" Ida's question was a good one.

"I'm not sure, but I would think that women would want some part in the running of the church, wouldn't they?" John's fingers gently massaged the soft skin of Ida's hand.

"M-a-y-b-e." Ida drew the word out considering. "I suppose that women should have a voice, but we don't even have a vote in political elections. How is it right then that we have a vote in the church?"

"It is right because…." He hesitated. "It is right because it is right!" John's voice was certain. "You are no less God's child than I am. You have every right to have a vote in what happens in our church."

"Okay. I agree, but I doubt you'll convince the church fathers of that."

"Don't just agree. Say that you will take a part in making sure our church will accept our daughters as total equals with our sons."

"Our church?" Ida smiled coyly.

"Yes, our church," John said. He reached into his breast pocket and took out a small box. He opened it and showed it to her.

"This is how the boys do it today." He slid off the couch onto one knee and said, "Ida Doering, will you marry me?"

She smiled down at him. Her eyes were filled with tears. Finally, it was her turn!

"Yes, John Wienke, I will marry you!"

He slipped the ring on her finger, and she kissed him in a way that left him breathless.

Clara and her mother had been as quiet as church mice cleaning up the dishes after dinner. Each was keeping an ear open toward the two in the parlor. Every now and then Clara would venture into the dining room and peek in to see what was happening. She didn't expect much in the way of amour, but things seemed different this visit.

Clara tiptoed back to the kitchen and filled in Louisa in a whisper. "They are just sitting there looking at each other. I think I heard the word *'Kirche'*."

"*Kirche? Warm eine Kirche?*" Louisa answered, also in a whisper.

Clara shrugged. "I don't know why. Maybe for the wedding?" She slipped back to the dining room and dared to risk another peek around the corner but quickly pulled back. She beckoned for her mother to join her and whispered directly into her ear. "He's down on one knee!"

Louisa's brows drew together, and she shook her head. *He is what?*

"Down on one knee…it means…he is proposing." Her excited voice came out in a hiss, and she clapped a hand over her mouth to stifle the giggles.

Louisa did the same thing, although a tiny squeak managed to escape.

Clara peeked again. They were embracing. Clara turned back to her mother, "I think she said yes!"

Louisa lost herself in joy and clapped her hands once and then covered her quickly reddening face.

Ida's voice, full of amusement, floated out of the parlor. "Okay, you two. You can come in."

Louisa and Clara looked at each other with big eyes.

"Oh, nein, nein, nein. Du musst allein sein." Louisa turned toward the stairs. *Gute Nacht, wir sind auf dem Weg ins Bett. Komm Clara."* No, no, no. You must be alone. Good Night. We are on our way to bed. Come, Clara.

Clara took her hand from her mouth and went after her. "Come back, Mama. Ida said, it's okay. Come. let's congratulate them, and then we can go upstairs," she whispered.

Louisa halted her escape, smiling broadly. "Ja."

John and Ida arose from the couch and came into the dining room with Ida holding out her hand so they could see the ring.

Clara took her hand and looked at the ring. An intricately lacy millwork covered the sides of the platinum ring, and a beautiful sparkling sapphire graced the setting. Clara gasped. A ring fit for a queen. It may take this man a while to act, but he didn't do things halfway when he did.

"Oh, it's beautiful." Clara hugged Ida, and partly to make room for her mother to admire the ring, she went to John. She had to stand on tiptoe to hug him and place a kiss on his cheek. "Congratulations, almost brother-in-law."

She turned back to her mother to see her pull a hankie out of her sleeve to catch tears. Ida took her into her arms and cooed "Mama. Mama, it's all right. Don't cry."

John leaned down to Clara. "I didn't mean to make everyone cry."

Clara flashed him a smile. "It means we are happy."

John shook his head, looking at mother and daughter both with tears streaming down their faces. "I don't think I'll ever understand."

Clara put her hand through his arm. "You'll get it. I have faith."

John patted her hand. "I certainly hope so."

***

Spell Iowa Out

The post office department has issued a bulletin asking that the name of the state of Iowa should never be abbreviated as Ia. It is explained that the abbreviation, Ia., might be mistaken for Idaho, this abbreviation being used in that state as it is in Iowa. No one ever gained anything by the use of abbreviations. The suggestions are well worth heeding and practicing.

Harvard Herald, April 29, 1902.

***

GOOD ADVICE ABOUT TELEPHONING
Which May Be of Advantage to All Users of Telephones

Marshall Field & Company have a printed card reading as follows on each of their telephones:

"The manner in which a person uses a telephone indicates his character to a great extent and makes either a good or bad impression. And this impression is reflected directly upon the establishment from which such a message comes.

"It is a pleasure doing business with a house which performs every detail in a clean-cut, satisfactory manner, but it leaves a sting to be answered abruptly or discourteously over telephone. It is folly to lose one's temper because one does not get immediate connection. This is rarely ever the fault of the telephone operators, who are nearly always courteous and prompt.

"When one is called to the telephone, he should respond quickly, and the person calling should not be left to hold the wire too long — something decidedly irritating, and often unnecessary.

"Let us throughout the house strive to excel in satisfactory telephoning."

If all users of telephones were guided by the above, the service would be greatly improved. It should also be remembered that "Central" cannot make the party called answer in case they are not in hearing distance of the bell.

Chicago Daily Tribune, March 16, 1902.

***

"Hello, is anyone there?" John's frustration was beginning to grow, and his purse was beginning to shrink. "Hello?"

He had decided to call Ida to see how everyone was, but for some reason the call had gotten stuck. He clicked the hook a couple times, and the "Hello Girl" came on the line.

"Number please?"

"I was calling Racine and the call got stuck."

"I'm sorry. Number?"

John repeated the number and the girl said, "Racine, Wisconsin, you say?"

"Yes."

"One moment please."

The receiver proceeded with clicks and clacks and static and then he heard the phone ringing at the other end and a small voice said, "Hello?"

"Clara, is that you? It's John Wienke."

He heard a small gasp followed by a loud bump. He pictured the receiver being dropped and bouncing off the wall. In his mind, it swayed now at the end of the cord. He heard, "Ida, Ida, Ida" the sound far away and in a cave. "It's John."

Then another voice, "What do you mean it's John. Did something happen? A letter?" He heard quick footfalls and then close-by, "No, Ida. On the telephone."

"What? Oh dear! How do I do this?"

The first voice said, "Listen with this and talk in here."

Ida's shout of "HELLO! JOHN?" almost broke his eardrum.

"You don't need to shout Ida. Hello, it's John Wienke." He heard some scrabbling around.

"SAY THAT AGAIN JOHN….I can't hear him."

"Oh, for heaven's sake, hold it this way." Now John was laughing.

"I hear him laughing," said Ida. And that set Clara off and soon they had spent twenty or thirty seconds of precious time laughing together.

"Good afternoon, Ida, how are you?" John fought to recover his composure.

"Good afternoon, John, I am fine. How are you?"

"Ida," whispered Clara, "Just talk like normal, like he's standing right here."

"Ouch! That hurt, Ida. Keep your elbows to yourself!" Clara's voice, and John began laughing again.

"He's laughing again," said Ida.

"Here give me that. Hi John. Clara here. Sorry, this is Ida's first talk on the telephone, and she's a bit flustered."

"I guessed. Put her back on. Thanks, Clara."

"Ida."

"Yes, John."

"I love you.' His voice was still alive with mirth.

***

PERSONAL MENTION

Clayton Harting, Harry Cross, John Carroll,
Frank Martin, and Robert Wienke drove to
Pistaqua Bay, Sunday.

Woodstock Sentinel, May 1, 1902.

***

THE MAYOR'S APPOINTMENTS

By the council proceedings published in these columns last week you will observe that the mayor made an announcement of his appointive officers for the ensuing year, and that the same were promptly confirmed by the council, without a dissenting vote. The officers thus appointed are:

Marshal—John Bolger.
Nightwatch—J. F. Eckert.
Electrician—A. C. Adams.
Engineer—William Wienke.
Trimmer—Fred Sahs

It is a marked compliment to the efficiency and worth of the officers thus selected that their reappointment and confirmation should be thus unanimously made. All have served the city well during the incumbency of their respective offices and all deserved the mark of favor bestowed upon them by Mayor Jewett in their reappointment. The may evidently does not believe in changing horses and does believe that a faithful and conscientious city officer should be kept in his place as long as he performs his duties satisfactorily. On these officers, in large measure, depends the peace of this city and the care of its valuable water and light property, and the work they have done in the past is a guarantee that these will be well looked after in the coming year.

Woodstock Sentinel, May 15, 1902.

***

WILL VACCINATE ALL RACINE
Authorities Decide to Invade Every
House in City to Search for Smallpox
Patients.

Racine, Wis., May 26 –[Special]—Every resident of the city will be vaccinated at once at the expense of the treasury and every building will be inspected by competent physicians as a result of the alarm over the smallpox situation.

The disease continues to spread, there being at present 400 cases in the city.

The Board of Health and the Common Council at a special meeting tonight decided to engage physicians to visit every house in the city. If people are found afflicted with smallpox, houses will be quarantined. Special watchmen will be engaged to see that no one leaves these houses and if any attempt is made to do so arrests and prosecutions are to follow.

Chicago Tribune, May 27, 1902.

***

Exercises of the Grammar Room

The commencement exercises of the grammar room were held in the City Hall on Thursday evening, when a most excellent program was rendered, it being as follows:

Chorus..School
Essay-"Growth of our Nation"....Harley Gill
Recitation-"Gettysburg".......Bertha Bourne
Solo-"Dear Little Heart".............Lelia Brooks
Recitation-"Grandma Keeler"....Josie Begley
Drill by twenty-four boys and girls representing Cubans, Spaniards and Americans
Instrumental Solo-"Bonnie Doon"...Blanche Tyron
Essay-"Fall of Spanish Empire"...Glenn Richards
Dialogue-"Trial of Fing Wing...............
by Seven Boys and One Girl
Solo- "Japanese Love Song"...Marguerite Smith
Recitation-"Flying Jim's Last Leap"...Emma Pfeiffer

Dialogue-"Donation Party…by Seven Girls and Five Boys
Solo-"The Swallow"……..Florence M. Poley
Presentation of Diplomas…President Arnold
Forty-three graduates including Frank C. Wienke, William Wienke's son.

Woodstock Sentinel, June 19, 1902

***

PERSONAL MENTION

C. C. Harting, Albert and Robert Wienke and Charles H. Sanford enjoyed a trip to Lake Geneva via the trolley line from Harvard last Sunday.

Woodstock Sentinel, June 18, 1902.

***

TWENTY-FIVE WOMEN FOR HOURS IN PERIL ON LAKE

Steam Launch Blown Far from Shore and Party from Racine Becomes Panic Stricken

Racine, Wis., --[Special]—With a strong west wind blowing, a steam launch, in charge of B. Larson and Bert Russell, and having on board a party of twenty-five women, was blown out on the lake today and only rescued after hours of work. The engine of the launch was disabled and the craft rapidly drifted three miles out into Lake Michigan. The party on board became frightened and attempted to signal the people on shore. Two smaller launches made an effort to tow the disabled boat to port but failed. The Racine lifesaving crew went out and after two hours of hard work landed the party.

Chicago Tribune, July 3, 1902.

***

"Clara! Clar-r-ra! Clara, where are you?" Ida dashed along the dock in the gathering gloom looking from face to face. Where *was* she? Other people were getting off the boat, but she couldn't find her sister among them. What if she had been swept overboard, and they didn't realize it? Did they know for sure that everyone was still on board after the rescue? And then she heard her sister's voice through a megaphone no less. Ida came to an abrupt halt and slowly turned around looking at the disabled launch.

"Okay, that's good! That's the last of them, boys. Let's give a round of appreciation for the crew and captain of this ship for keeping us safe even in the dire straits of the middle of Lake Michigan. We have not succumbed but are safe and sound on God's green earth again."

The crowd hooted approval and several men let loose whistles appreciating not only the boys who saved them, but of the pretty girl broadcasting the news.

Oh boy, thought Ida, she's not merely safe, but she's running the show, as usual.

"Clara!" Ida waved up to the deck and caught Clara's eye and Clara sent back an enthusiastic wave, like this was the greatest adventure on earth. Ida beckoned and mouthed 'come down.' Reluctantly, Clara gave up the megaphone and made her way to the gangplank. Then she rushed down into Ida's embrace.

"Are you OK?" Ida pushed Clara back so she could get a good look at her.

"Oh yes, fantastic! It was great fun. A lot of the girls were scared, but not me. I figured I could swim back to shore if I needed to."

"Do you know how to swim?" asked Ida.

"You betcha. I learned at the beach. It's just floating and paddling." Clara assured Ida as they turned back toward the main street and home.

"But the wind would have been blowing you away from shore And the water is very cold."

"Hmph…I hadn't thought of that, but no matter. The brave men of our life-saving squad came and rescued us. Weren't they handsome? I was their special mascot because I didn't faint or run to my cabin or act like a scared little girl. They put me in charge of all the fainters, and I got to nurse them back to health before we docked."

Ida looked at her young sister. "You are such a strange girl, Clara Doering."

"Why am I strange? I knew the men would come to rescue the damsels in distress. They always come to rescue the damsels in distress." Clara flicked her hair in the general direction of the docks.

"When we heard that a boat was in distress, you should have heard Mama. We knew it was yours, just knew it! Mama straightaway went to bed and possibly pulled the covers over her head, and I headed down here to wait. I hope you are impressed with how much we care about you."

"Oh, thank you, kind sister, for your concern, but I am fine. Never better."

"Well, let's get on home before Mama dies of dread." They began walking toward Huron Street.

Clara was practically skipping along, overflowing with energy. "Maybe I should be a reporter. Reporters get sucked into this kind of thing all the time. I loved it." She twirled around and skipped up the block ahead of Ida.

"Watch out for the mud in the street," Ida called after her. "It rained to—"

Clara took a mighty leap into the street at the end of the boardwalk and went ankle deep into the mud.

And thus falls the queen from her steed, thought Ida, as she worked her way carefully across the street with her skirts held high, while Clara unscathed by her dangerous hours at sea, stomped and jumped and most likely ruined her shoes, her petticoat, and her dress crossing just one street.

As they came back together on the other side of the street, Ida was shaking her head. "Now Clara, tell me truthfully…did you sabotage that boat?"

Clara's face took on a mischievous grin. "I'll never tell."

***

Cyclone Sweeps Wisconsin

Racine, Wis., July 2 –[Special]- One man was killed, and several persons injured, houses and trees blown down, and stock killed in a strip ten miles long and half a mile wide by a cyclone which swept the country from the town of Raymond to the village of Washer this afternoon. Crops were ruined and great damage done.

The storm first struck the house of William Cook, just west of Raymond, a new structure, and blew it into pieces. J.J. Laing's house was wrecked, and Mr. Laing was badly hurt, but his family escaped. The only fatality reported is at the home of G. Thysen of Caledonia. His house was demolished and also the barns. Thysen was about 50 years old. A wife and seven children survive.

Reports on the district state that there are many other barns and houses blown away and that it is hard to estimate an exact number. Telephone lines are down throughout the country.

Chicago Tribune, July 3, 1902.

***

PITTSBURGH OUSTS ANARCHISTS

Pittsburg, Pa., July 2.—[Special]—Because President Roosevelt is to spend the fourth of July in Pittsburgh all known anarchists have been ordered to leave the city this week and to stay away for a week. Detectives have just finished the rounds of their haunts and told them that if they did not obey the order they would be arrested as suspicious persons and locked up for the week. The detectives also visited the coal mining towns where there are groups of anarchists and notified them that if they came to Pittsburgh any day this week they would be arrested. Allegheny anarchists have received similar warnings.

Chicago Tribune, July 3, 1902.

***

July 5, 1902
936 Huron Street
Racine, WI

Dearest John,

Oh, how frightening the past few days have been. First of all, there was a storm that narrowly missed carrying me away, across the lake. It was headed right for Racine, and we watched the sky grow darker and darker until it was black as midnight. Of course, we didn't know how bad it really was until reading about it the next day.

That day, that same day, mind you, Clara and her friends decide to go out on the lake, and the storm overwhelmed the motoring ability of the launch, and they were blown out to the middle of the lake where they couldn't even signal for help because they couldn't see the shore. Eventually someone on shore noticed that they had not returned from their voyage and sent out the life rescue squad who pulled them back in, and there was Clara, unhurt, up on the top deck with a megaphone bossing everyone around. Now she wants to be a newspaper reporter so that she can have such adventures daily.

AND we all got smallpox vaccinations which hurt like the dickens and festered all up like they were royally infected. The scabs soon dried up and just fell off. I guess we are safe from the disease, you will be glad to know.

That's all the mundane news from here. When will I see you again, Mr. Blue Eyes?

Yours always,
Ida

***

Lena threw down the rolled-up newspaper with such force that it hit the tabletop, sprang up, and fell, fluttering to the kitchen floor.

"Why!" she asked aloud to no one in the room. "Why is it always the woman's fault?"

She took a deep breath, bent over, and retrieved the paper. She had read only the headline, 'Tried Thrice for Insanity was This Lady.' Maybe there was more to the story.

> After three trials by a jury in the county court covering a period of nearly a year, Mrs. Julia Jaap, wife of Arthur Jaap of Harvard, was declared insane Tuesday afternoon. The first trial occurred Nov. 4, 1901, and returned a

> verdict of not insane from the jury. The second
> trial occurred, Friday, July 3 of this year, and the
> jury was unable to agree. That there was a close
> question as to the woman's sanity is shown by
> the three different trials.

Three trials? What kind of man would put his wife through three trials to prove she is insane? What had she done to make this man want to have her 'put away' as Lena had heard it phrased?

> Mrs. Jaap appears to be sane on every
> question except one, a peculiarity found in the
> majority of insane cases. Her hallucination takes
> an unusual turn, however. She believes her
> husband is in love with other women, and his
> attentions are so pronounced that she is
> neglected. With this hallucination in her mind,
> she becomes so irrational at times that she must
> be restrained.

Aren't we all irrational at times? Surely, we are. And men often took a lover when the wife was not bending to their desires. She believes he is disloyal, and he denies it. Who will the jury believe?

Lena could see herself in the position of Mrs. Jaap, making claims without proof but just a feeling. With as much as Al was gone, who knew? He always came back at some point during the night. Women used feelings quite a lot to decide such dilemmas. But no one in this fine and perfect city would believe the charge of unfaithfulness toward their favorite son if Lena did question Al's loyalties.

Lena had taken, of late, to smelling Al's shirts to see if she could find a whiff of perfume, but all they smelled like was cigar smoke which covered up any other odor. She could, therefore, do nothing but trust that he was being loyal. But then why should he be when she was acting like a shrew? They fought more than they kissed. He hated the tears of both mother and child, so he left for work early and came home from…what did Ida call it? Ah yes…came home from the Pleasure Palace late. She couldn't go with him to the lake with a tiny baby, but that didn't stop him from going. She knew that girls of all types were available there. She took a deep breath which turned into a long sigh and turned back to the newspaper and the story of poor Mrs. Jaap.

> Judge Gillmore has not yet issued the order that will send the woman to Elgin hospital for treatment. The jury was so late in reaching a verdict, Tuesday evening, the court decided to send the woman to her home in the care of Sheriff Lake, who resides at Harvard. Later, if the woman's mental aberration continues to be displayed, she will be taken to the hospital at once. This action is taken by the court because of the fact that Mrs. Jaap has a little baby of only a few weeks old in her arms, and he feels it would be unwise to separate them at the present time and then only under the most extreme circumstances. The judge believes that the woman is not so mentally weak, but now that she realizes her condition that she will make an effort to restrain herself.
>
> *Woodstock Sentinel.*

What? In the midst of this ordeal, this woman was pregnant! "Yes, crazy pregnant woman! Restrain thyself!!" Lena shrieked to no one listening.

A good chance existed that her 'loving' husband had found some comfort during her pregnancy in the arms of another woman. They would put her in Elgin for being sensitive to her husband's needs and desires. And while she was with child?

Mein Gott! Disgusting! Lena ripped the page from the paper and tore it into small pieces, tears streaming down her pretty face. She buried her face in her arms on the tabletop and sobbed for the injustice Mrs. Jaap had endured.

As the waves of grief and anger subsided, Lena raised her head and looked around. She looked at the paper torn to shreds. What had she done? Al would want to read the paper in the morning with breakfast. He would ask where the missing pages were, and she wouldn't be able to explain. And he would accuse her of being crazy again. She tried to gather up all the torn pieces from the floor and spread them on the tabletop. She began arranging and rearranging the pieces into a mosaic. Here…no…there…no…okay…start from the top…she sank into a chair and put her head back on her arms and began sobbing. Woman, restrain thyself! She mentally slapped herself to try to regain composure, but she couldn't. The tears continued in great gales of despair.

Bit by bit, she became aware of a baby crying. She was not alone as she had imagined. Another voice was wailing along with hers. A baby…that woman's baby was crying hard. She looked up. Where was it? She followed the sound into the parlor and found the baby in a cradle. Shhh…quiet baby, she rocked the cradle, but the sound continued.

"OH, PLEASE STOP!" Lena screamed, her hands over her ears. She sat down hard on the floor beside the cradle. "STOP CRYING!" But the little one seemed to only cry harder, louder. Where was the child's mother? Now she remembered. They had locked her up in Elgin hospital. Poor child. No wonder it was crying.

Lena reached in and lifted the child and blanket into her arms and held it rocking back and forth. The child quieted and began pushing its face into her chest. Lena pushed the little face away, but then felt her milk let down, staining through her bodice. What was going on? She looked down at the hungry child. Could she feed an insane woman's child?

She watched as the little hands clenched and unclenched in anger and the little face contorted as it attempted to find purchase on an unseen nipple. Light dawned as she recognized the little girl. This wasn't a strange baby of an unknown woman. This was Evie. The baby's eyes were dark, her face red, her hands punched the air as she looked up into her mother's face. My baby.

She brought the baby to her shoulder and held her tightly. Evie squeaked, unable to get enough air to cry out. Oh, Evie! How could I not know you? My own flesh and blood. She squeezed more tightly. I can never let you go. Evie squeaked again. Lena attempted to loosen her grip. It seemed impossible. The squeezing had stopped the crying.

A voice, which seemed to come from everywhere and nowhere, roared in her ears: "STOP! You're killing her! Restrain yourself!"

Lena loosened her embrace instantly, almost dropping Evie to the floor. She caught the tiny body awkwardly, and Evie began to scream. Taking the baby to a rocking chair, she ripped open her bodice, unconcerned with the propriety of nursing in the parlor, several small white buttons flew through the air and ricocheted off the wooden floor. She brought the baby's mouth to her nipple. The screaming stopped, and Evie began to suckle even before she made contact. Lena leaned her head back against the chair and tried to relax so the milk would flow easily.

She closed her eyes. Tears continued to run down her cheeks. She rocked and hummed a familiar tune, and then looking down at her baby, she began to sing softly. Evie's eyes popped open in surprise – had she never sung to the child? *"Schlaf, Kindlein, schlaf. Dein Vater bewacht de schafe; deine Mutter schüttelt die Bäume, und ein kleiner Traum fällt heab. Schlaf, kindlein, schlaf!"* Sleep, baby, sleep. Thy father guards the sheep; thy mother shakes the trees, and a little dream falls down. Sleep, baby, sleep.

How often had she heard her mother sing those words? Without warning, the anguish overwhelmed her. She missed her mother! Hot tears again rolled down her cheeks. "Mama!" She sobbed. "I must go home." Yes, that was it! She must go home and see her mother and then all would be well. Her mother would know what to do.

She took a deep breath. The resolution to return to Beloit calmed her, and she sang the lullaby again and then bits and pieces she remembered from other stanzas. And as she sang, the world fell back into place.

***

IN WOODSTOCK

Albert Wienke purchased the Northrop house,
corner of Judd and Tryon streets in Woodstock.

McHenry Plaindealer, July 10, 1902.

***

Seventy Followers of Dowie Arrived
Yesterday in Racine

One of Zion's Seventies, or in other words, seventy followers of Alexander Dowie of Zion City, arrived in this city yesterday morning and assembled on the green plat just east of the Chicago & Northwestern depot. They were loaded down with literature touching upon the teachings of Dowie.

During the day there was preaching, and the town was flooded with tracts. In the afternoon

Rev. O. Jacobsen of the Trinity M. E. church happened to pass along State street. One of the Dowieites accosted him and offered a circular and invited him to the meeting. Rev. Jacobsen politely refused the invitation and discussed the nature of Dowie's teachings with the man. The discussion was animated and a crowd of several hundred gathered and applauded the Racine minister, who completely floored the follower of Dowie.

Racine Journal Times, August 18, 1902.

***

BRIEF MENTION

Mr. and Mrs. William Wienke and family returned last Saturday evening from a visit of a few days with his brother at Beloit, Wisc.

Woodstock Sentinel, August 26, 1902

***

Local Intelligence

And still it rains.

Next horse sale, Oct. 8.

A husband in hand is worth two that are beyond control.

The heavy wind of the last few days has worked havoc on the standing corn, and the farmer who has his cut is indeed a lucky fellow.

Woodstock Sentinel, September 15, 1902.

Personal Mention

Frank Wienke [the younger] went to Dundee last Saturday to visit friends for a day or two.

Woodstock Sentinel, September 15, 1902.

***

IN WOODSTOCK

Albert Wienke and his force of painters are engaged in beautifying the German Presbyterian church on Washington, giving the entire structure two new coats of paint.

McHenry Plaindealer, September 18, 1902.

***

September 25, 1902
936 Huron Street
Racine, Wisconsin

Dearest John,

I hope this finds you fit as a fiddle. We are fine here, also. No diseases to speak of. The unbelievably good weather of this Fall has fallen to the wet cold rains of the coming winter. The leaves are still beautiful, maybe even more beautiful wet. The heavy rain is removing them from the trees, so one must look smartly before they are gone.

Shall I see you in the near future? I did appreciate, I think, the telephone call. I liked it more than the last time when we laughed through the whole call. I would like to see you tomorrow or the next, but I know that is impossible with the work they have you doing at the factory. You said that they were going to hire some people so that your long hours would cease. Is that happening? I hate to think how little I will see you once we are married, and I will be in a town where I only know one other person. I suppose I will quickly make friends through church, right?

Speaking of church, Clara has stopped going to the Lutheran Church. Mama is having a fit, but Clara says she needs to explore other religions and then she'll be back. She has gone to the Universalist church with a friend the last few weeks. She says it is so relaxing to hear a sermon in English, although she misses the formality of the Lutheran service. That church doesn't believe in hell, can you believe it? I said, 'What keeps people from doing dastardly deeds?" She couldn't answer. Like most of her endeavors, I'm sure this will be short-lived. I sympathize with wanting to speak English in church, but I'm not sure about completely changing one's religion for it. She says that the Universalists don't require a change of religion – that it is Christian but just more forgiving. It gives responsibility to the believers. What do you think?

I must move on to my next project now. The sewing has been slow this fall so I've been working more at the laundry and even doing some desk sitting at the YMCA. Trying to put aside a nest egg like my betrothed is doing. Write and tell me when I will see you. Soon, I hope.

Sincerely yours,
Ida

***

LOCAL INTELLIGENCE

And it still rains.

Theodore Roosevelt can truly be called the great protector of the rights of the American people.

Do your clothes look yellow? Maple City Self-Washing Soap washes them snow white.

The city authorities have repaired a lot of dilapidated sidewalks in the past few weeks and put them into shape for winter.

The heavy wind of the past few days has worked havoc with standing corn, and the farmer who has his cut is indeed a lucky fellow.

The German church on Washington street is being beautified by liberal applications of paint administered by Albert Wienke and his helpers.

Woodstock Sentinel, September 25, 1902.

***

Woodstock Pleasure Club
Woodstock, Illinois

October 1, 1902

My Dearest Ida,

I wish we were together this evening to just sit and watch the rain. It was a very warm day, but the rain tonight bodes a cooling down to autumnal temperatures. I'm sorry I have not gotten up to your tempting city for well over a month or has it been two? I am a very bad beau, but we will see each other soon, I promise. The factory hired fifty new people in the last month, so our hours are going back to normal this week. So soon, my girl.

You write of Clara's change of faith. Here we have faith all around us and all good choices except maybe the Catholics and their questionable ways. My brother Emil has been drawn into the revivals of the Methodist since his high school days here and thereafter in Beloit. I've gone a few times but find it more emotional than substantive. Our papers are filled with news of the churches and each week a sermon is published in the paper by a pastor far afield from Woodstock for shut ins. These are usually based on the Bible stories or the clerical season. It is in fact hard to escape the message of the good news, even if one would want to.

We did have a Universalist church here in Woodstock, but it was shuttered last year. It was very much in line with the Congregationalist with their bottom-up leadership. Myself, I believe in a strong minister who guides the church for the parishioners, not the other way around. Also, Unitarians are different from Trinitarians like Lutherans. They believe in one God, but not the three in one God. All in all, I would not want our children to become Unitarians. That said, I do believe in freedom of religion as guaranteed to us as citizens. It's difficult to know which should take precedence.

I think I've used up my words for now, and I shall get this in the mail to you tomorrow. I hope your evening has been as delightfully rainy as mine. I send you my undying devotion.

Sincerely yours,

John

***

Personals

Miss Clara Doering entertained the L'Cameas at cinch.

Racine Journal Times, October 8, 1902.

Stretching Things

What is the sense of some evangelists in stretching things so? It has gone so far that women have been charged with being immoral who have danced or played cards and the men charged with committing wrongs they never even thought of.

Racine Journal Times, October 8, 1902.

***

John bounded up the steps to 936 Huron Street in Racine. Before he could throw up a hand to knock, the door flew open, and Ida jumped into his arms. Their kiss lasted a little too long for standing out on the stoop.

"There you are." John's voice was husky as he smoothed back her hair which had started to unravel from its bun. "There you are," John repeated.

"Yes, here I am," Ida's voice purred.

John felt a wonderful urgency in his britches, and her hands guided him into the house and closed the door. He had taken a day off to come visit her. They didn't get many days off at the factory, but he had found that the supervisors were understanding about such things as doctor's visits or other family emergencies, so he had claimed an emergency just so he could see Ida.

"I've never seen your hair down." He reached up and began to unpin her bun. She was beautiful…but wait…what was he doing? He stopped. "I'm sorry…I…I…I'm sorry."

Ida laughed. "It's okay. It's a mess. I need to re-pin it anyway." She reached up and pulled the rest of the pins out and allowed her hair to fall around her shoulders. Then she put her arms around his neck and allowed him to pull her close for another kiss. Her hand caressed the back of his neck. As the kiss stretched longer, the urge to allow his hands to roam a bit down her back to her waist was overwhelming, and then below— He abruptly broke off the kiss and pulled away looking around. "I am so sorry. I don't know what's gotten into me."

"A little bit of the devil, I'd say." Ida paused looking at him, but then went on. "You know, John, I truly don't mind at all." She drew him over to the sofa and they sat much too close. She kissed him again with great enthusiasm.

John was trying not to give in to the impulse to touch her everywhere. He pulled back. "Where is everyone?"

"Gone." Ida kissed him and then said with her lips still touching his.

"Gone to work." Kiss.

"Gone to ladies' aid." Kiss.

"Gone for at least two hours." Kiss.

"We are all alone." The next kiss became deep and long, and John felt like he was quickly reaching a point where he would not want to pull back.

"Ida, this isn't a good idea." He spoke into her neck and did not try to pull away.

"Why isn't it a good idea?" Ida swung her leg over his lap so it touched places it shouldn't.

"How about we go for a walk downtown, and…and…I'll buy you a new hat." He was breathing hard, and it was difficult to think.

Ida looked him up and down and smiled. "Okay." She pushed away from him.

Oh no! What had he done? Was she giving up so easily? She reached down and took his hand and pulled him to his feet. Yes, a walk was the best thing. They'd go for a walk and….

Ida led him to the stairs. She kissed him again and he brought his hands to her hips. She turned in his grasp and proceeded up the stairs holding his hands steady on her hips.

They reached the upper hallway, and she drew him into her room and closed the door. After two years of yearning, they could not wait one minute longer. She turned away from him, reaching behind herself to uncouple button loops. He moved to help. His fingers were tentative and clumsy, but he disengaged each one until her dress fell to the floor and she stepped out of it. Turning around, she removed his jacket, and slid her hands over his muscular shoulders and down his arms. Then she put her hands on either side of the row of buttons running down the shirt and ripped the lapels apart. Buttons popped and flew. John stood wide-eyed and open-mouthed at what she had done.

"I'll fix those later." Ida's hand caressed his cheek during another prolonged kiss.

She pulled down his suspenders, undid the three-button fly and pushed his wool suit pants down around his ankles. Noticing the bulge under his white cotton underwear, she casually brushed against it while turning away. She pulled her slip up over her head and flung it toward the closed door.

John attempted to rid himself of his underdrawers by pulling them and his pants off over his boots. In frustration, he pulled off the boots leaving his shoes in them along with the pants, suspenders and underwear all in a tangle. Ida watched with a smile. When his attention was again focused on her, she pulled down her bloomers and removed them leaving her shoes. She never made it to the buttons of her shoes. As she stood straight again, he embraced and for the first time they felt flesh on flesh and their combined eagerness to consummate this relationship.

Ida stepped backward toward the bed, never letting go of John, and pulled him down on top of her. She wrapped her legs around his torso, and they fit together as if they had been doing this for years. It took very little time to find that they were compatible.

Afterward, after the sighs, and sounds of delight had faded away, they lay spent in each other's arms, and Ida's lips brushed John's ear as she whispered, "You know what this means, right?"

John nodded. "I'm in love with you."

Ida chuckled. "Well, yes. I hope that is true, because I love you. But this means that we must get married very soon. It's good to find that we are well suited to each other before we marry, but we also don't want to have a baby too close to the wedding date."

John sat straight up. "You are going to have a baby? Whose baby is it?"

Ida looked at him. "You are so sweet. There is only you, my dearest. I might be going to have a baby because of what we just did, but we won't know for a few months. When do you want vows?   I will talk to Mama and Papa Stoffel and see if they have conflicts, but how about the beginning of November? That will give me enough time to make a dress and to invite people. And that will be enough time to get things in Woodstock set up, right?"

"November? I was thinking more like a year from now."

"Funny boy. No, we must do it soon because IF I am pregnant, you do not want me walking around nine months pregnant next summer with no husband right?"

"Well, no, of course not." The satisfaction he had felt only moments before was now full-fledged panic. "But I'm not ready. We don't have a house, and I don't have a profession and….I'm not ready."

"Well, I'm ready. And it's time, John. Girls don't like such long courtships. It's time. I would call the pastor right now, but we are both too rosy-cheeked at present, and he'd surely catch on." She put her hand on his inner thigh and felt the tension. "Let's just say that we are not going to do this again until we are married. Is that enough incentive?"

John considered waiting another year to lie with her again. How could he have given in so easily? His mind raced. He was not ready financially, but he was truly ready physically. He needed a wife. He needed Ida. But surely, they could wait until they knew for sure and if there was no baby….

"I'm not ready."

"But, my sweet man, when WILL you be ready. We are already into our prime. We want a family, right? If we wait a year or two or three until you are ready, I may not be able to bear because of my age. We must strike while the iron is hot!" Ida smiled broadly and patted the comforter right over his crotch.

Reflexively, he reached to cover it with both his hands, too late. He felt the desire well up. He cleared his throat. A flush spread up his body and sweat broke out on his upper lip.

"Of course, I want children." John's hand covered hers. I've seen many women bear when they are…um…older. There is no hurry. I am also glad to know we are so well…suited, but…" He paused and looked at her. *Gott im Himmel*, this woman was exactly what he needed.

"John, do you want me?" Ida's free hand came up and took him by the chin forcing him to look directly into her eyes. "Do you really want to marry me?"

"Yes, Ida, I do." John smiled, holding her eyes for courage.

"Then, November it is! First week if possible!"

She let go of him and stood, and the click of her high-topped shoes on the hardwood floor as she gathered up their clothes echoed in the room.

"I'll be there." John couldn't take his eyes off her as she stood there confidently in just her shoes. She was a force to be reckoned with.

***

Women Should Sleep More

A physician who is a specialist in the nervous diseases says that women should sleep at least nine hours at night and one in the daytime, says the New England Farmer. A woman will plead that she hasn't the time to lie down for a few minutes in the daytime, and she will infringe upon the hours at night, which should be given to sound, healthy, needed sleep, in order to finish some piece of work which could as well be completed on the marrow. She will rush and hurry all day long, and then when the household is hushed in slumber at night, she will sit to read the daily paper thinking she will not have to pay for the time she is stealing from the health-giving sleep that comes before midnight.

Woodstock Sentinel, November 6, 1902.

From Louisville Courier-Journal

There is an evangelist going about from church to church in northern Illinois announcing his terms as $40 a week and fifty converts guaranteed or money refunded. He seems to be doing business, and yet if he were say a Mormon, the very people with whom he is doing business now would probably do it with tar and feathers.

Racine Journal Times, November 6, 1902.

LOCAL INTEREST

The Oliver Typewriter Co. announces that the month of October was a record breaker for them in the typewriter business, and that November starts out as though to eclipse its predecessor.

PERSONAL MENTION

John Wienke left for LaCrosse, Kansas, Sunday morning. It is rumored that he will do a little courting. We hope it is the right kind.

Woodstock Sentinel, November 6, 1902.

Doering – Wienke Matrimonial

Miss Ida Doering was united in marriage yesterday afternoon at the home of her parents,

Mr. and Mrs. J. H. Stoffel, 926 Huron street, to John W. Wienke of Woodstock, Ill. At three o'clock the guests began to assemble under the strains of a mandolin orchestra, and the bridal couple proceeded to the east parlor where they were met by the Rev. Burger, pastor of the German Lutheran Church, who in a few words united them as man and wife.

The bride was attired in white chiffon, trimmed with point lace and carried a bouquet of white chrysanthemums. She was attended by her sister, Miss Clara Doering, who was attired in white. The groom was attended by his brother, Robert Wienke. The beautiful home of Mr. and Mrs. Stoffel was decorated with white and green flowers and formed a neat appearance. Immediately after the ceremony, a supper was served, and the newly married couple departed on an afternoon train for an extended wedding trip to the northern part of the state. The dining room was decorated with autumn leaves, carnations and roses. The bride is a popular young lady of the north side, having resided in this city all her life, and the groom is a hustling businessman of Woodstock, Ill. Guests from out of town were Frank, Robert, Charles and Fred Wienke of Woodstock, Mrs. C. Wienke, also of Woodstock, Mrs. William Kuff of Portage and Miss Emma Ardelt of Whitewater.

Racine Journal Times, November 6, 1902.

***

John and Ida lay cuddled in each other's arms on their last morning at the grand Hotel Doering located in Marshfield, Wisconsin. While they had selected the hotel for its name, it turned out to be modern and delightful with a dining hall and maid service. It was like heaven, no work, and much play.

Marshfield was a quaint little town with gambling halls and muddy streets. It was surrounded by forests and rolling hills. They had taken several carriages out into the surrounding environs. The weather had been excellent. Cool and crisp, but with no snow. The people were hospitable Scandinavians for the most part, but they had also encountered native Indians. The Indians looked much less frightening than Ida thought they might, dressed as they were in the everyday clothes of the white man, but predictably, they wore straw hats with one or two eagle feathers poked in the band. Overall, it had been a relaxing and exciting honeymoon, but today they would catch the train back.

Ida's fingers played along her husband's chin, feeling the stubble of whiskers. "Have you ever thought about growing a beard?"

John considered a moment. "I will if you want me to. I always thought I'd look mighty strange with a beard. Bare-footed head and a flowing beard don't seem to go together."

"Mm. I don't know. Maybe we can find a fake beard and try it on…see how it looks before you take the plunge."

He laughed. "Sure. It would be nice not to have to shave. Frank grows a beard for winter sometimes."

"Does he? How does he look?"

"Good, but he says it itches once the weather gets warm."

Ida cuddled closer if it was possible, and her voice took on a little pout. "Are you sure we must go back today?"

He squeezed her before answering, "I'm afraid so. Duty calls. They won't hold my job forever."

"I'm glad we shipped all my goods to Woodstock before the wedding, so we can go right to your mother's."

"Yes, you are a smart cookie that's for sure. You think of all the things I don't. We make a good team."

"Yes, we do." Ida hoped it was true. "Take me home to Woodstock, John."

And he did.

***

Wienke – Doering

John Wienke, one of the popular typewriter force, surprised his many friends in the factory and about home the past week by taking unto himself a wife. Mr. Wienke started by way of Chicago for Racine, Wis., the fore part of the past week and informed his associates that he would not be here to cast his vote as he had important legal business to attend to. His friends all unsuspicious believed this to be the case and were considerably surprised several days later on hearing the nature of the business, which was legal all right but of a different character than they were led to believe.

The bride, formerly Miss Ida H. Doering, was a popular young society lady of Racine, Wis., in which city the ceremony was performed, Nov. 5, 1902, at the home of Mr. and Mrs. Stoffel, of No 936 Huron street, the Lutheran pastor officiating. Mr. and Mrs. Wienke will no doubt make this city their home and will be given a hearty welcome by the many friends of the groom, who extend congratulations and wish them much happiness and joy.

The above news item was handed to us for publication last week but through an oversight of ours was omitted, for which we humbly ask pardon.

Woodstock Sentinel, November 13, 1902.

CROWD HEAR EVANGELIST
Sunday and the Devil Both Fighting to a Finish

The Woodstock meetings in the Armory, under the direction of Evangelist Sunday and his singer, Mr. Fisher, are marked for increased attendance and interest. The interest in the coal strike is subsiding, politics is not in it; no one talks of the coming cold wave. Instead of hearing inquiries concerning the weather, fuel, health, etc. they are all about the meetings. Scores are being warmed at the glowing altar of experience, multitudes sweat under an awakened and aroused conscience. Last Sunday standing room was at a premium and many were unable to find even a place to put one foot.

It is simply wonderful what the stranger, the new preacher, is doing. Preaching is certainly his business and he is working it, not as a mere figurehead, not an automation in the pulpit, not a dried up old fossil who puts you to sleep, not a dignified cold blooded crank who will try to save you for so much a dozen – money in advance, not a narrow-minded, one-sided egotistical conglomeration of imbecility and superciliousness, nothing of the sort, but a simple man, true, forcible, with rich religious experience, bold for the right, who shoots cold facts at you and straight from the shoulder, with the penetration of a Dewey shell bound for a Spanish boat. One who makes you feel you are in the arena and an awful conflict is on – Sunday and the devil, fighting to the finish. Come and help, dear people of Woodstock, let your presence at least sanction the withering, blighted, damning denunciations of sin by the evangelist, and the sweet, loving, tender songs of the singers.

Woodstock Sentinel, November 13, 1902.

***

Elect Officers

At the annual meeting of the German Lutheran society, held last Sunday, the following officers were elected for the ensuing year: Chas. Hobe, Sr., Chairman; Frank Beth, Secretary; Fred Schroeder, Treasurer; Herman Hallier, Collector; Louis Churchman, Frank Wienke, and Louis Kniebush, Deacons. A committee of six were elected to arrange for Christmas exercises.

Woodstock Sentinel, December 4, 1902.

***

FINE WOMEN FOR LOUD PRAYING

Racine, Wis., Dec 15 –[Special]—Arrested on the charge of disorderly conduct, found guilty, and sentenced to pay a fine of $3 and costs, Emma Leopold of the Metropolitan Holiness church of Chicago was advised to return to Chicago, the $50 bond being furnished by F. J. Hanche, who recently joined the church.

The woman admitted that the police told her to stop screaming, but said she could not, as the inspiration had entered her soul. The prisoner desired to remain in jail until given a trial or the walls of the jail were torn down to release her.

Chicago Tribune, December 16, 1902.

***

Factories Close

Three factories in the Fox river manufacturing district in northern Illinois have been shut down because their employees, numbering more than

1,500, refuse to promise, in individual agreements, not to strike. These factories furnish rods and sheet metal to a number of manufacturers, and we are likely to see a ripple effect.

PERSONAL MENTION

John Wienke was layed off last Wednesday on account of a lack of stock.

Woodstock Sentinel, December 18, 1902.

***

"But John. How could this happen? What did you do? People don't just get fired over nothing." Ida was beside herself. She and John had been married but a month and already – tragedy.

"I didn't do anything, and I wasn't fired, just laid off. It has to do with getting the materials that they need when they need them. The suppliers are struggling with the unions and have shut their doors, so Oliver isn't getting the raw materials to make typewriters. It's good for a business to be flexible."

"Did other's get laid off? How long will you be laid off?"

"I was the first one to go since I'm inspecting finished machines, but there will be more. And they didn't say how long – a few days or maybe a few weeks. Could be as much as a month or two, depending on the labor negotiations."

"Well, I am sorry, but it doesn't make sense. You are a supervisor. Why would they lay you off and not someone who had been there only a short time? Or give you a different job? Something is fishy. You go back in there and tell them that this isn't right, and if you are being fired *for* something, what is it?"

"Ida." John rubbed his face, trying to think of a way to explain. "I wasn't fired for anything. I was laid off. I am an inspector, and without stock, there is nothing to inspect. I couldn't do other jobs."

"Why not?"

"Because I don't have the training."

"Why can't they train you?"

"Well…it would take too much time."

"You bring me down here to live in your mother's house and now you have no job." Tears sprung into Ida's eyes. "What am I to think? Did you miss too much work for the wedding and honeymoon? Did you do something wrong and that caused the shortfall of stock? You can tell me."

John looked down like a guilty little boy unable to meet her blazing, tear-filled eyes. They were sitting at his mother's kitchen table. Sophia had excused herself to her bedroom early on in the conversation, thank goodness. He didn't know what to say. As far as he knew, he had done nothing wrong at work, but he agreed that the layoff was a bit strange, especially when the factory had claimed they were going to increase production. But he was sure they had good reasons.

"I don't know, but they will most likely call me back soon and until then—"

"Until then we will live on bread and water!" Ida's voice was too loud.

John looked at the ceiling wondering if Sophia was listening. "No, of course not. Ma will feed us, and I'll look for a temporary job."

"No, I'm not going to live off your mother! I will go back and live off my own mother and hope that I can get my job back at the laundry, or I'll sew."

"Couldn't you sew here?"

"I don't know anyone here. How would I get customers?"

"I could—"

"You could what? You don't even have a position! You could end up at the poor farm."

"Come on, think about this. Think about what your parents will think of me if you go running home at the first challenge."

She looked at him, incredulous. "The only thing I can think is that you are hiding something from me, and I won't have it! That you have been lying to me about this steady job that kept you away from me for months. I'm not thinking about your reputation at present." Ida's eyes were cold, and her voice hissed in an attempt to be quiet, but also emphatic. "You must work! You are a married man, and you might have a baby to think of."

John looked up sharply and color rose to his cheeks. "Listen! I told you that I wasn't ready. It was you who wanted to rush into this. So now we feel the results of that rash action. This house was purchased from a pooling of the brother's funds, so we have every right to be here. All I can say is that I warned you that I wasn't ready, but all you could do is push."

Ida stared at him. "Rash action? Push? I don't remember you slowing things down on that afternoon. How dare you blame me! Are you sorry we came together? Are you sorry we might be expecting a baby? Are you sorry you met me?"

"Of course not! How could you say such a thing." John's voice got louder. "I don't need one moment to decide about you or a baby. But it wasn't me who was so gung-ho to get married. You do remember I said that I was expecting another year before we'd marry. You do remember that, right?"

Ida shook her head and looked at the ceiling. Her face was also flushed. "Do I remember what?"

"That I wanted to wait for another year?"

"Oh, come on. You couldn't wait another minute as I remember it." Ida was no longer controlling her volume.

John sighed. It was true. He had wanted to bed her and when the opportunity presented itself, he had not hesitated. He let the silence draw out examining the pattern in the tablecloth on his mother's table, in his mother's house.

"You are right. I was all in favor of the fun without embracing the possible consequences. At that moment, I wasn't thinking very far into the future. But now I am."

John rose and took her in his arms. She struggled briefly but then let him. "You are the love of my life." He said, speaking softly into her hair. He paused. She relaxed, and he held her more tightly. "Yes, I agree. Go to Racine for a few days, and I'll work on arrangements….for our own place and a job. I don't want you to worry about anything. It will be all right, I promise."

"It better be, John. It better be."

***

PERSONAL MENTION

Mrs. John Wienke is visiting her parents, Mr. and Mrs. J. M. Stoffel, at Racine, Wis.

Woodstock Sentinel, December 25, 1902.

***

John sat, eyes staring into the distance, nursing a drink and his ego at the Pleasure Club. It wasn't jumping for the last day of the year. A few men came and went, working with weights or jump rope or punching bag. They greeted him but then retreated without question. He would stay here as long as they would let him.

He had secured a job at the same grocery he had worked at as a kid and gone back to being the stocking, delivery, and clean up person. It would be steady until something else came up. He could also sell some of his lots to make ends meet, but he was *not* going to draw from his savings. Still, he was unwavering in his decision to marry Ida. It was by far the best choice he'd made in the last year no matter this difficult situation. He put his head in his hands and took a deep cleansing breath.

"Hey, brother! What are you doing here?" Bob's voice rang out in the practically vacant hall. "Shouldn't you be home with your wife and mother?"

Ache meine Gott! Bob. This is all he needed to complete the fall from grace.

"Ida is in Wisconsin, and I am here drowning my sorrows." John always believed that honesty was the best policy.

"I came in for calisthenics."

"Go ahead. You won't bother me."

Bob sat down. "What's going on?"

John looked up, "Oh Bob, don't worry yourself. Go get strong." He took a sip of his drink touted as a healing elixir.

"What are you drinking?"

"Sarsaparilla."

"Hm. Wanna go get a real drink?"

John considered. A waste of money, but then hadn't he broken other rules this year? "OK," he said, "Lead on."

Bob led him down the stairs and out into the night. A little beer wouldn't hurt him and might help him through this night – particularly this night – New Year's Eve.

As they headed toward Wienke and Schneider's, John asked, "How are you? Got a real job, yet?"

"I'm still thinking about the factory."

John sniffed, "Well, I can't help you there anymore."

"What? Why not?"

"Got laid off. Got married and got laid off."

"You're kidding. Why?"

"Lack of inventory."

"Anyone else laid off?"

"You and Ida ask the same question! I don't know if anyone else was laid off. I'm the only one who made the paper."

Bob let the silence stretch a bit. "So, what now?"

John hesitated. In for a penny, in for a pound. "Back to being the boy at the grocery shop."

Bob's voice was upbeat. "You better let me buy tonight."

"Gladly," John said. Maybe having a saloon-keeping brother at a time like this was a good thing. No judgment. "Thanks, Bob."

"Not a problem. Thanks for going out with me. I needed some company tonight, too."

Ida Doering and John Wienke
Circa 1903
Around the time they were wed.

Learning to Play Ball
(1903)

PERSONAL MENTION

Joe Connors and Robert Wienke were initiated into the mysteries of the order of Elks at Elgin the past week. It is said that they didn't do much to Joe.

Woodstock Sentinel, January 1, 1903.

Happenings

Mrs. John Wienke of Woodstock, Ill. Is spending several days with her sister, Miss Clara Doering, of Huron street.

Racine Journal Times, January 2, 1903.

Bob hustled up the board walk as he rounded the square toward Austen's grocery shop, his feed carrying him swiftly. He crossed Main Street, leaping across puddles still there from the freak rain on New Year's Day. He jumped up onto the walk and whooped, causing a man in an earflap cap and his lady to pull back in distrust, but he smiled his infectious smile and got one in return.

He burst into the shop. "Oh my God, John. John! Oh, my God!"

John hurried out of the back room where he had been cleaning up onion skins from a new shipment. The onions were beautiful, baseball-sized, firm, and ready to eat. He could just taste a thick slice on a ground beef patty sandwich, his favorite.

"Sh-h-h-h. Language." John grabbed his little brother and ushered him to the back. Mr. Austin looked up from the paper. Luckily, there were no patrons in the store.

"Oh, sorry," Bob whispered, but then burst out. "I heard at the Elks meeting that the leagues are going to a WORLD SERIES! Can you believe it! The National leaguers against some no-name American League team. A real shootout! What a day it will be! Can't you just see the crowd! It's the best news in…well…forever!"

Wow. That's great, Bob." John dropped Bob's arm. "But how can you be so sure it will be the Orphans and not the Cardinals or the Beaneaters?"

"I just know! And don't call them the Orphans or the Remnants or the Microbes or even the Colts. They are Selee's Cubs now, and the best team in the world. You'll see.

John's demeanor sobered. He took up his broom and looked down at the job still to be done. His voice was flat. "Well, best of luck to them. I hope you get to go."

Bob's enthusiasm seemed to drain. "She's not back yet."

"Nope."

"Have you talked to her?"

"Nope."

"Does she know you have a job?"

"Nope."

"Stop being such a stubborn Deutscher! Call her."

"Call her? I can't make my case over one of those damned contraptions."

"John. Language." They looked at each other and began to laugh. The laughter continued a bit too long and was a bit too hysterical, but in the end, they patted each other on the shoulder and started over.

"Maybe it's time for a trip to Racine?"

"I didn't leave…I'm not going up there begging. I suppose I could write to her."

"Great idea."

The front bell tinkled. John looked up and started for the front, but stopped when Bob said, "Mr. Austen's there. He can handle it. Okay, if you write, what would you say?"

John turned back to Bob, looked at the floor, and considered for a full minute. "Well, I'm not sure…. I think I'd say something like…'Ida, I love you, and I want you to come back to Woodstock. I know we hit a rough patch right out of the gate, but I love you and all I want to do is make a good life for you and our family. And you can trust me when I say I will do it, because—"

"I know you will," a female voice interrupted.

John froze looking at Bob's smiling face. Bob nodded over his brother's shoulder and moved around him, attempted to tip his hat to Ida, but realized at the last minute that he was wearing a knit stocking cap and changed it to a salute of sorts and continued out to examine the groceries on the main floor.

John turned and dropped the broom to the floor with a *SMACK!*

Ida!

She rushed across the room and into his arms. "I'm back, and I'll never leave you again." Her tears wet his grocer's apron.

"Oh, Ida!" He closed his eyes and held her close. Thank you, God!

***

Blizzards for January

According to Rev. Irl R. Hicks, January begins in the midst of unsettled weather with rain and snow striking many localities. A short, sharp change to cold, northwesterly winds and rising barometers will follow closely these reactionary storms.

The second storm period will be central on the sixth. As this change moves eastward, falling barometer will attend with growing cloudiness, causing general rains with winter lightning and thunder, ending in sleet and snow. Snow blockades and blizzards over the northern and western sections need not cause surprise.

Four other regular storm periods are scheduled for the month, attended by sharp, cold weather, snow and blizzards. They are central on the 12th, 15th, 23rd and 29th. As a rule, one to three bright pleasant days are enjoyed before the actual storm periods, and readers are cautioned to plan during these days for the stormy ones which are sure to follow.

Put yourself in sympathy with nature and provide fuel and provisions at your command. January is one of the most severe months of the year so heed these timely admonitions.

Woodstock Sentinel, January 8, 1903.

A Pleasant Evening

A number of friends of William Snyder and Charles Bachman gave them a happy surprise last Monday evening at the home of Charles Bier. Before they were hardly aware of the fact, the party had taken possession of the house and held it from that on until a late hour when all departed, declaring it one of the most enjoyable evenings spent for some time. Music and social amusements were the prime attractions of the evening, and a bountiful supply of refreshments were served. They made Mr. Snyder a present of a beautiful opal ring and Mr. Bachman a fine watch chain and locket. Those present were:

Messrs. and Mesdames—

Joe Connors	C. A. Stone

Messrs.—

Robert Wienke	Albert Snyder
Albert Wienke	Clayton Harding
Nat. Ostenberger	Fred Dirrenberger
Walter Schwamb	Edward Maldoon
Miss Lillie Schwamb	

Woodstock Sentinel, January 8, 1903.

***

January 17, 1903
365 Lincoln Avenue
Woodstock, Illinois

Dear Mama,

I hope this finds you healthy and glad for your sound house in this cold and snowy winter. This last storm had everything, rain, thunder, sleet, and piles of snow. We were nearly at a standstill for a full day. It was nice, John even had a chance to go to one of the infamous Woodstock evenings a few nights ago but chose to be at home with me. Such a loving husband.

I think I can tell you now that, yes, I am with child. My red headed aunt failed to appear again this month, and we are so excited. I do hope it is a boy so we can get that whole thing about junior out of the way. But we had best start thinking about girl names also. What do you think of Frances? John's middle name is Francis so it would seem appropriate if the baby isn't a junior.

We are still under Mother Wienke's roof, of course, and will be for some time I suspect, although in his excitement of seeing me, John did begin talking about building "me" a new home with a large kitchen. John is getting called back to the typewriter factory as of February 2, as he says now that he expected to be. I doubt he did. He thinks his brothers made it happen by talking to the powers that be. And Bob has applied for work at the factory, also. That would make four of the brothers building typewriters. They'll soon be taking over the whole company, I suspect. John is none too happy working there. I think he was happier pushing a broom in a grocery shop this past month. He genuinely loves grocery work.

When I was home, Herman and I talked about his desire to open a mercantile. Interesting how my two favorite men both are drawn to the same things. I must write to him about John's plans. Do you think he'd consider moving to Woodstock?

Well, I better run this over to the train. I miss all of you. Please greet Papa Stoffel for me and give my love to Clara and Herman. Tell them I'll write soon.

Love,

Ida

***

"Mama," Clara called out distractedly, as she glanced through the mail. "Lots of mail today. A letter from Emma. Also, one here from Ida."

Louisa came hurrying into the parlor from the kitchen wiping her hands on her apron. "*Gib mir die von Ida.*"

Clara handed over Ida's envelope. "Why are you so wrought up? *Warum bist du so aufgeregt?*"

Louisa tore open the letter and tried to read it. "*Ach, es ist auf Englisch.*"

"Here, give it to me." Clara began to translate Ida's letter into not perfect, but understandable German.

"Ach, you Deutsch ist no gut." Louisa's English was just as strained, but also understandable.

Clara forged on and upon reaching the second paragraph, she squealed with glee. "*Ein Kind!* She's going to have a baby!"

"*Lessen!*" Louisa commanded. Read!

"I *am* reading! She says, "*Ich denke, ich kann jetzt sagen, ya, ich bin mit Kind.*" Clara danced around the room as she read, and a large smile broke out on Louisa's face.

Louisa closed her eyes and muttered under her breath, "*Danke gnadiger Herr.*" Thank you, gracious Lord!

Clara finished off the letter and handed it to her mother, with a smile. "I'm going upstairs and writing to her, right now. She wants to name a girl Frances. How horrible. I'm going to push for Daisy. Isn't that a nice name? Like in the comic strip. A little girl named Daisy Mae that I can dress up and take to the Hotel Racine! Oh Mama, *das ist wunderbar!!*" She took two steps at a time as she raced to her writing desk.

Louisa sat down on the davenport, letters in her hand. She would read Emma's in a moment. It would be in German. She folded her hands and said a short prayer asking God to bless her middle daughter and her husband and their life together. She had been surprised when Ida showed up in Racine barely a month after the wedding and stayed so long without contact with John. Ida had said that she was thinking. Louisa had told her to remember that even the best plans don't always work out the exact way that one sees them from afar. One must be flexible. Ida had also told Louisa that she had missed a period.

"*Viellenicht ist* John *nicht ganz bereit eine Familie zu haben,*" Louisa had said to Ida.

"*He's* not ready to have a family! You are jesting. He is thirty-three years old…how long should we wait, until he is forty, fifty or how about sixty, when we are too old to have children?" Ida countered. "He had better be ready."

"*Ja, aber jetzt könnte es ein Kind geben, an das man denken muss.*"

"I know. There could be a child to think about." Ida's eyes welled up with tears. "I'm not telling him about the possible child until I know for sure. *Das sollte nicht die Lösung sein.* That should not be the solution to our disagreement."

Louisa had hugged her daughter and let her cry, and finally had given her space to think. When she had said on New Year's day that she was ready to go back to Woodstock, Louisa had been glad but worried. And now this first letter verified their reconciliation. *Gott ist gut.*

***

Fat Lady

Don't sleep too much; exercise; don't eat fats and sweets. To reduce flesh rapidly take Rocky Mountain Tea. Acts directly on the fatty tissues.

Woodstock Sentinel, January 20, 1903.

***

"*Wohin gehst du?*" Sophia asked as Ida made her way, as quietly as she could, down the stairs toward the front door.

Ida paused. "I'm going to my friend Len's house for lunch and some catching up."

Sophia came around the corner and looked at her. "*Bist du warm genug angezogen?*"

Ida looked down at herself. "Yes, Mother Wienke, I am dressed quite warmly. I'll be fine. It's a bright sunny day."

"Okay. Haft gut time." Sophia gave in with reluctance. Ida was pregnant and shouldn't be out walking on the ice and snow. What if she fell? But Sophia didn't have any authority to keep her housed up. If one of the boys had been around, she would have insisted Ida be taken by buggy, but no boys today.

"*Achtung*, Vatch stepping," she called as Ida made her way down to the plank sidewalk.

"I will," Ida called back. She walked away briskly and fumed silently at her mother-in-law. She wants me to just sit in that house and do nothing for the next five months. Maybe if I was further along, it might be smart, but I'm fine right now, barely showing. She was quite toasty and confident with the hat, muffler, and boots she had splurged on last winter at the Gimbels in downtown Milwaukee. She had never been better.

It was a bit of a journey from Sophia's house to Lena's but less than a mile, or wouldn't have been, except that Ida got turned around and ended up at the square. From the square the path was very straightforward. Ida walked up Jackson until she recognized the house. There were places where the walks were blocked by snow, and she had to move out into the muddy street, but overall, it was a very satisfying walk.

You *walked?*" Lena gasped when she saw Ida at the door.

"I'm fine. I walked everywhere in Racine. The only time I hopped a streetcar was when I was going up to Milwaukee."

"Racine has streetcars to Milwaukee?"

'Why yes, we do. That's how I got these fashionable boots. Bought them last Spring at Gimbel's." Ida moved her foot, this way and that, to show off the boots.

"I would love to go shopping at Gimbel's. Here, give me your coat. Come and sit. Evie is asleep so we'll have at least a few minutes of adult conversation. How are things at Sophia's?"

"Fine, except she treats me like a basket of eggs," Ida grumbled.

I can't imagine living with her. Maybe she is overly protective because she never had girls, and now she has one."

"Oh, didn't you know?" Ida leaned closer. "Sophia and her husband had two girls before they had the eight boys."

"What? What happened to them? Al has never said anything about girls in the family."

"I think they must have died in Germany. All John can remember is that there were no girls in the house by the cemetery. We'll have to ask William or Ed about them."

Lena waved her hand dismissively. "Good luck getting an answer out of Ed."

Ida laughed. "He is somewhat reticent, isn't he?"

"Reticent is one way of putting it. Unfriendly is another."

"Anyway, I feel like a prisoner in that house, I'm hoping things get better as the weather improves this summer."

I have to agree with her about walking in this weather. It's very…um…obstacle filled. I'm glad you were able to manage it without falling." Lena looked up sharply at Ida. "You didn't, did you? Fall that is."

Ida shook her head. "No, it was very uneventful except getting lost and ending up at the square."

Lena laughed. "We've all done that. I'm glad you didn't slip on the ice. Don't want to jar anything loose too early. Al will be home for lunch around one o'clock. He can take you back, so you don't have to take chances in both directions."

"Okay, but for heaven's sake, you'd think a woman had never had a baby in this town before."

Lena smiled. "I'm not as worried about you as I am about your precious cargo. Would you like lemonade? And I made some little sandwiches like I used to make before Evie joined us."

"Good. I love those." Ida got up and went to the cradle in a corner of the parlor. Evie was sound asleep and dreaming. Every so often, her lips would pucker, and she would suck a few times getting only air.

Ida tiptoed away to the dining room. "She is such a good baby. Look how hard she's sleeping so that Mama and Aunt Ida can talk."

"She is a good baby, but I don't want to talk about children. I want to talk about buying shoes at Gimbel's and your family and John and well…anything…except for children."

They settled onto the dining room chairs and Lena poured tea into cups with a beautiful yellow rose pattern.

"How lovely."

"Wedding present."

Ida helped herself to three petite, crustless sandwiches. One was white cheese and knockwurst. One was cream cheese and apple. One was sauerkraut, a thin slice of corned beef and a dab of creamy dressing.

"These are wonderful, Lena. You should sell some to the local restaurants."

"Oh my. Thank you, but they are too much trouble to make all the time. I just make them for my special friends." Lena reached over and squeezed Ida's arm.

"What gossip do you have for me?" Lena reached for one of the Reuben sandwiches.

"Well, let's see. Herman got married." Ida took a bite of the knackwurst and smiled.

"He DID!" Lena said too loudly. They both held their breaths, but the crying did not start.

"Yes." Ida's tone was hushed. "He married Bessie Leahy; I don't think you know her. They got married in the parsonage of the Congregational Pastor. Looks like we've lost another Lutheran to his wife's religion. She didn't have a gown but wore a traveling dress. They came in together, said 'I do,' accepted a toast from the best man, and hopped the train to Chicago. They will be gone for a month touring down South where it is warm."

"How nice."

"I suppose. Clara was beside herself. No gown, no party, no dinner, no—"

"I bet she was."

"You know what the paper said about the bride? Mama sent the clipping to me. I think it says it all." Ida pulled the clipping out of the pocket in her gray woolen skirt and spread it on the table.

"And I quote, 'The bride is an estimable young lady with an interesting personality.'"

Both women burst out in laughter and hushed each other.

Lena was finally able to ask, "An interesting personality? I wonder what that means."

"Here's some more. 'Herman Doering is well known among the businessmen and is connected to the Zahn Dry Goods company.'"

"That is faint praise, also. Maybe it's just the paper. They make up something when they don't know the bride or groom. Here in Woodstock, the praise is always filled with hyperbole, the best, the greatest, the prettiest, -the most well-known. Everything in Woodstock is the most prosperous and up to date!" Lena's voice had gotten more strident as she listed this litany of the virtues of their chosen hometown.

"You mean it isn't true? My fine and beloved husband has told me wonderful stories about this grand city. Am I not to believe them." Ida's eyes were wide in faux surprise.

"If you must. Don't listen to me. I've been here only a year, and I'm so glad to have a good friend in Woodstock at last. The people are all nice and polite, but best friends are hard to find if you didn't grow up in the area." Lena took a long draw from her teacup.

"Hm. Interesting. Have you and Al been going to church?"

"We have a few times, but he is less than enthusiastic about going. He and Bob like to…um… 'travel' on Sundays." She put quote marks around the word with her fingers..

"What does that mean? Travel?" Ida copied the gesture.

"Go places, see things, enjoy events. Like going up to Lake Geneva for the day."

"Don't you go with him?"

"At first, I did, a few times, but then I got pregnant, and it was unseemly. And then I had a baby, so now I'm stuck here." Lena's eyes filled with tears.

"But he still goes?"

"Not as often, I guess, but yes, he still goes." Lena dabbed her eyes. "Oh, listen to me! Let's not talk about husbands, either. Let's talk about Gimbel's. When were you last there?"

The two lapsed into a comfortable conversation about styles and the city of Milwaukee, but Ida was left with an uneasy feeling. She was sure that John would not be going off with the boys constantly, but who knew for sure. She felt so sorry that Lena was less than happy and vowed to be the best friend she could possibly be in this alien land.

***

IN THE SOCIAL WORLD
Mr. and Mrs. Wittenberg Entertain

A score or more friends of E. C. Wittenberger
were invited by that gentleman to a "stag" party

at his home on Washington street, last week Thursday evening, where they were entertained in a most sumptuous and royal manner. The host and his estimable wife proved themselves to be generous entertainers and their hospitality was much enjoyed by those present. "Let joy be unrestrained" was the motto for the evening and our readers can rest assured that it was lived up to in a true old-fashioned manner.

At an early hour, or late as you may wish to call it, the guests departed. They were as follows:

C. C. Harding	Robert Wienke
Albert Wienke	C. A. Stone
W. T. Conn	J. L. Carroll
E. C. Bodenschatz	Joseph Connors
E. C. Watson	Chas. Bier
James Sullivan	Chas. Bachman
William Kiel	E. C. Boyce
Chas. F. Renich	Lynn Stone
John C. Rowe	Frank Martin
John Wienke	

Woodstock Sentinel, January 25, 1903.

***

PERSONAL MENTION

Born to Mr. and Mrs. Frank Wienke, Wednesday, February 4, 1903, a son, Clayton.

G. W. Webster had a runaway last Tuesday. His team became frightened at the factory whistle and ran three or four blocks before they could be stopped. In endeavoring to stop the team, Mr. Webster was slightly injured but will be able to take up his milk route soon.

Woodstock Sentinel, February 5, 1903.

LOCAL INTELLIGENCE

Mr. Sueji Miyamori has written that he will reserve Saturday evening, Feb. 14, for the people of Woodstock and will, without fail give us his lecture on 'Japan and the Japanese' at the Baptist church.

Report on Woodstock Public Library for the week of February 1, 1903. Number of visitors, 479; number of books loaned, 247.

Mrs. C. M. Curtis, Librarian.
Woodstock Sentinel, February 5, 1903.

***

NEWS FROM THE FACTORY

New typewriters are being invented every week, but there is only one that will do the business. You know.

Wanted, to rent, houses—any number. Enquire at the factory.

Howard Brubaker left the factory yesterday and he and Mrs. Brubaker will leave for Freeport Saturday.

The factory now had a well-organized fire department, with Fire Marshall Wienke in command.

Woodstock Sentinel, February 12, 1903.

***

AN OPEN LETTER
To the Woodstock Friends of
The Chicago Industrial Home

Supporting friends of the homeless and orphans and those who would like to hear what we are doing at the orphan home; we take the pleasure of writing to you.

In the last week we have taken in six little helpless ones, one a babe of four weeks. Three of these were taken from our own county. This makes nineteen children we have taken in and cared for from our own county in the last year and a half. Of this number we have placed six in good Christian homes.

We would be much pleased if more of our friends could make it convenient to call any day (except Sunday) and see our happy family and go through our home. We endeavor to give the children good, well-cooked food, and good, comfortable, clean clothing also to keep the home in sanitary condition.

Whatever He (Jesus)
Saith unto you, do it.

Yours to care for the helpless
MRS. Minnie Bardell.
The Matron.

Woodstock Sentinel, February 25, 1903.

***

PERSONAL MENTION

Walter Schwamb, Will Snyder and Robert Wienke were in Chicago, Sunday.

Woodstock Sentinel, February 28, 1903.

***

PERSONAL MENTION

Connors & Stone are fixing up their saloon on Main Street in an elaborate manner. They are putting in a steel ceiling and papering and painting the side walls and giving their place of business a general overhauling and intend, when completed, to have one of the finest rooms in the county. Albert Wienke is doing the work, which in itself is a guarantee that it will be properly done.

Woodstock Sentinel, March 5, 1903.

***

March 20, 1903
365 Lincoln Avenue
Woodstock, Illinois

Dear Herman and Bessie,

I just wanted to drop you a note and say how nice Mama thought your wedding was. I'm sure you are back from your honeymoon and settling into your house by now. Everything is fine here, and we are healthy if not wealthy – ha. Time marches on. I am anxious for Spring to come so I can get out and walk as I was used to in Racine. Woodstock still has wooden walkways although the issue of improving them is under continual discussion at the city council meetings. John brings back detailed accounts of those for my edification. I'm learning the players slowly, and John certainly has a desire to join them.

Herman, I was thinking about our conversation last December about your desire to open a store, and how you were finding that a very difficult thing to do in Racine where so many are already established. The thought has been flitting around in my head since then that you and John might be able to join forces to start something here in Woodstock that would be more successful than in Racine. This is a very nice little town that prides itself on being up-to-date and cultured. John has had the idea of opening a grocery shop or bakery since I met him, and he is working toward that by making good investments and saving his wages. That is a big reason we are living with his mother, to save the rent money we might otherwise "throw to the wind."

Would you consider talking to John about this possibility? He is a hard worker and very dedicated to making a life for us here in this growing town. You could lean on each other's strengths. It would be a very nice place for you and Bessie to raise a family. Anyway, I hope you will think well of us and our predicament. Talk to him…please.

Bessie, Mama said your traveling ensemble was beautiful.

Your favorite sister,
Ida

***

IN THE SOCIAL WORLD

On last Saturday, March 21, Miss Florence Schroeder gave a party to a few of her friends at the home of her parents, Mr. and Mrs. John F. Schroeder, in honor of her 11th birthday. Refreshments were served and a jolly time was enjoyed by all. A large number of presents were left by those in attendance to show the high esteem in which Miss Florence is held by them. Those present were:

Misses—

Eva Enlow	Minnie Kirchman
Grace Schuett	Maude Schwamb
Alice Wienke	Letah Wienke
Alice Green	Ethel Wienke
Myrtle Myers	Bessie Beatty
Marian Senger	Leona Jacobs
Florence Renich	

Messrs.—

Arthur Metzger	Harold Kemmerling
Edwin Kemmerling	Willie Schwamb
Frank Kirchman	Arthur Sahs
Henry Kindt	Percy Forman
Leon Sprague	Ray Wienke
Frank Klann	

Woodstock Sentinel, March 26, 1903.

(Author's note: Alice and Letah Wienke are Ed Wienke's daughters, Ethel Wienke is Frank Wienke's daughter, and Ray Wienke is William Wienke's son).

***

John, always the grocer, scanned the paper. A headline caught his eye, so he read on.

EAT TONS OF PRUNES

A Frenchman planted a prune tree out in California in 1870. It was the only prune tree in the state. All the prunes used in the United States at that time came from France. But now as a result of that prune tree that M. Pellar planted, California every year ships enormous quantities of prunes not only to France, but to all European countries, says the *Chicago Tribune*.

John was amazed. We export prunes to Europe. That's a feather in the American hat, and these prunes would most likely be cheaper than the imported ones, too.

The growth of the prune industry in California will come from Pellar's single tree. It was found that the prunes, which is a species of purple plum, thrive on the Pacific coast, and that the hot, dry weather of the country brought out its saccharine qualities. The first orchard was planted in the Santa Clara valley, just south of San Francisco, a region which is now the prune center of the state. It was only ten acres in extent and began to yield in 1875. In four years, the trees produced $14,000 worth of fruit.

The size of the prune crop in California is so enormous that the most cynical boarder in any boarding house in Chicago would be surprised. In 1901, the state produced 150,000,000 pounds of prunes, and the total crop of the year just passed exceeded that of the preceding year by several thousand tons. If put into ten-ton freight cars, the California prune—

"John, where are you?" Ida called out. It was Sunday afternoon, a time for family, but John had disappeared.

"I'm down here…in the basement."

Ida poked her head around the corner at the top of the stairs. "What are you doing?"

"Nothing. Just relaxing and catching up on my reading."

"Can't you relax up here in company? William and Lizzie just stopped by." John's oldest brother was the city engineer. He had been in the ranks of civil service since he was in his twenties. William was as steady as they came.

"Okay. I'll be up in a minute." John sighed and went back to his article.

…freight cars, the California crop of 1902 would fill a train reaching from Chicago to Buffalo.

The American prune has found its way into the European Market for the same reason that it is sweeter and pleasanter to the taste than the fruit raised there. The California prune, for instance, is dried wholly out of doors, for the long period of absolutely rainless weather, which prevails in California from July 1 to October 1, permits the drying trays to remain out of doors day and night. The French and other kinds of European prunes are dried in kilns for fear of exposure to rains, and the artificial heat fails to bring out all the rich sugar products of the pulp.

San Jose, the county seat of Santa Clara county, is the chief prune center of California, and in its mountain encircled valley, there are 3,567,140 bearing prune trees. There are, besides, great orchards of apricot, cherry, peach and olive trees, so that in this one county there are about 5,000,000 fruit trees. Fruit raising is carried on there on such a grand scale that for some orchards of prunes, 30 acres are required in the busy season simply as a drying field for the fruit trays.

John folded the newspaper. Imagine that…he pictured drying racks covering most of the area of Woodstock. Well, now he knew how—

"John, *what* are you *doing* down there?" Ida had advanced several steps down the basement stairs, and she sounded irritated.

John got up, "I was reading about the prunes grown in California, the best prunes in the world." He came up the stairs and kissed her on the cheek.

"Prunes? Are you not feeling well? Do you have constipation?"

John chuckled. "No, I'm fine, but now I know that we will have California prunes at the grocery shop."

"Oh. Well. At least that is settled, but

"Yes, I know…William and Lizzie. Are the boys with them?" He took her hand, and they went up the stairs to the kitchen and into the parlor to entertain.

PERSONAL MENTION

Mrs. Theo Lake, a sister of Mrs. Albert
Wienke of this city, died at her home in Beloit,
Wis., Tuesday, March 24, 1903, after an illness

of only one week. She left a baby one week old beside her family to mourn her loss.

Woodstock Sentinel, March 16, 1903.

***

"Lena?" Ida found her friend at the Austin Grocery fondling a bag of coffee beans, lost in thought.

"Ida. I can't quite decide if I should buy this or not. What do you think? Is this the best coffee I can buy or is there better? Do you think Al will like it?" Lena looked like she had been crying.

Ida looked around. "Where is Evie, Lena?"

"Evie? I left her…."

"Left her where?" Ida's heart began pounding in her ears.

"With Ma Wienke. I'm filling the coffers with coffee." Lena continued to stare at the coffee but smiled a little at her own joke.

"Good. We all need to do that now and again. I was so sorry to hear about Lillie's death. Did you go to Beloit for the funeral?"

Lena turned angry eyes on Ida. "No! No, I did not! Albert had important things to accomplish, and he didn't want me traveling alone with the baby."

"Oh no. I'm so sorry. It's so sad."

"Yes. Impossible."

Ida paused wondering where to go in the conversation. "How is the new house coming? Do you need help getting moved?"

Lena threw down the bag of coffee. "No, I don't need your help. I don't need anything." Tears streamed down Lena's face, and she buried it in her hands. Through her fingers, Ida heard her say, "I should be in Beloit. The next woman can have the house. I don't want it."

Without hesitation, Ida put an arm around Lena and guided her toward the storeroom. She caught Mr. Austin's eye and indicated the backroom with a nod in that direction, and he nodded back. Nice understanding man.

"Here, pull up a barrel. I'll take 'Pickles' and you take 'Olives.'" Ida sat Lena down on a barrel and handed her a handkerchief.

As Lena cried into the handkerchief, Ida patted her back. "Tell me what is happening."

Lena laughed without warning. "I feel such a fool. Al is about ready to throw me over for a more sunshiny model, if he hasn't already."

"Oh, I doubt that."

"Do you?" Lena looked at her eyes ablaze, but then she blanched and looked at the floor. "It's just…it's just…all I do is take care of his baby here when there is a baby in Wisconsin that has no mother to care for her." Lena again melted into sobs.

Ida let her cry a bit and then tried again. "Do you know what is happening with Theo and the baby."

"Berty. The baby is Berty."

"Theo and Berty."

"As far as I know, they are still in Helenville, near Jefferson, miles from Beloit. But…" Lena looked Ida straight in the face. "But who is feeding her? She is only a few weeks old. Theo can't nurse her. She will die just like my sister." More tears.

"What does Al say?"

"Oh, he says, I'm crazy. Doctor thinks I'm crazy. Probably Ma Wienke thinks I'm crazy."

"I don't think you're crazy." Ida waited a beat. "But—"

"Everyone always follows 'I don't think you're crazy' with a 'but.'"

Ida let a few moments pass and tried again. In the calmest voice she could muster she said, "I don't think you are crazy. What needs to be done to protect the child?"

Lena paused and blew her nose. "She needs to come live with us. I'm nursing Evie, who doesn't take all she can now that she is getting some solid food. I have more than enough for Berty also."

"Okay. How will Theo feel about this?"

"I don't know."

"How will Al feel about this?"

"He won't care as long as it doesn't stop him from doing what he wants to do."

"Okay. The first step then is to see if we can find out how Theo would feel about allowing the aunts to furnish care for Berty. If he says 'yes,' we are all set, but if he says 'no' then we'll have to bring in the reserves to persuade him."

"Why would he say 'no'?" Lena's tears had dried, and she seemed somewhat brighter as they mapped out a plan.

"I don't know. Let's just check before we act. Let's go see if we can figure out that telephone and call him. Do you have a number?"

"No."

"Then let's call your folks and see if they have it."

Smiling her thanks to Mr. Austin, she led Lena out of the shop, across the square, and up Jackson to her home. Ida dreaded trying to get the phone to go through to Beloit, but if it would help her friend, she was willing to try. At the house, the two women stood looking at the brown box on the wall of the kitchen.

"Do you know how to make a long-distance call." Lena's sounded as nervous as Ida felt.

"I've only done it twice on the receiving end of the line, but I'm sure the hello-girl will help us." Ida picked the receiver from the wall box and stood up straight. She brought the mouthpiece down level with her mouth. "Do you know your parent's number?"

"Yes, 4382 in Beloit."

Ida double clicked the receiver cradle switch as she had seen John do.

"Hello. Number please," said the hello-girl.

Ida swallowed hard. "Hello. This is Mrs. John Wienke. Mrs. Albert Wienke is here with me, and she would like to talk to her mother in Beloit, Wisconsin."

"Fine. What is the number, please."

"It's 4382 in Beloit, Wisconsin."

'One moment, please." Silence. Then a buzzing on the line which seemed endless.

"I don't think it's working." Ida made a motion to hang up but then heard a tiny far-away voice say, "Hello?"

Ida handed the earpiece to Lena mouthing, 'Mama.'

Lena stepped up to the mouthpiece. "Hello? Mama?"

***

New Regulations for Pitchers, Fielders, and Men at Bat

At a conference in Washington, D. C. between President Pulliam and his staff of the National league umpires held at Old Point Comfort, radical measures were taken to enforce rules against kicking and rowdyism. The following important construction was placed on rule 29, relative to the pitcher's position: It is construed as meaning that the pitcher, in taking his position, shall place no part of either foot back of the rubber, nor shall he take more than

one step in delivering the ball to the batsman.
The enforcement of this rule will do away with
all preliminary steps, either to the rear or side of
the pitcher's rubber.

A stricter interpretation of the rules
prohibiting the batsman from balking the
catcher and that of the fielder's interfacing with
base runners when caught between the bases
was agreed on. No batsman hereafter will be
allowed to take first base when hit by a slowly
delivered ball, the umpire to be the judge of such
speed. Emphasis is laid on the rule requiring
runners to keep within the three-foot lines in
going to first, and in general notice is given of
the literal enforcement of playing rules.

Chicago Tribune, April 4, 1903.

***

"Ida, are you asleep?" John whispered as he slid into bed.

Ida sighed. What else would she be doing in bed at midnight? Without opening her eyes, she mumbled, "You jest getting home? Long meetin'?"

"Yes. But guess who you are sleeping with." John cooed into her ear and spooned with her.

"Tebby Roothevelt?" Ida's tongue was thick.

"No."

"King Edward?" It sounded more like 'Ethwood.'"

"No."

"Governor Lahf...La...Follette?"

"No. That's three guesses. All you get!"

"Good. Night."

"You are sleeping with the newest member of the Dorr Township Committee!"

"Wondaful." A long pause. John thought she had gone back to sleep, but then, "I…rather you were Tebby."

"Roosevelt? Why?"

"I'd be sleeping in da White House," and she began to snore lightly.

***

NEWS FROM THE FACTORY

Frank Martin left last Thursday for Florida where he has gone to regain his health. He was accompanied as far as Chicago by Joe Connors and Robert Wienke, who saw him safely started on his long journey.

The Oliver factory has a well-organized fire department, with Fire Marshall Frank Wienke in command.

Woodstock Sentinel, April 9, 1903.

CITY COUNCIL
Woodstock, Ill., April 3, 1903
REGULAR MEETING

E. C. Jewett, mayor, presiding.

Ald. Burger, Cunningham, Schuett, Stupfel, Walters, Whitworth answered to their names at roll-call constituting a full board.

The following bills, approved by the finance committee, were read:

Dacy Lumber Co, lumber and tile...…..$ 26.31
Whiton Bros, plbng etc. for city hall... 262.64
Oliver Typewriter, rebate taxes……....   55.35
Albert Wienke, painting in City Hall…   51.10
State Bank, int on orders……………..   66.82
Farmers Ex. Bank, same……………....   15.51
A C Adams, electrician……………….   75.00
Chas Backhaus, helper……………….....   35.00

> William Wienke, engineer 55.00
> Fred Sahs, trimmer........................... 40.00
> John Bolger, supt. waterworks............ 15.00
> John Bolger, marshal....................... 50.00
> J F Eckert, nightwatch.................... 50.00
> E C Jewett, mayor......................... 10.00
>
> *Woodstock Sentinel,* April 9, 1903.

***

Ida sipped her coffee. Easter had been very strange here in Woodstock. Was it just the German Lutheran Church or had all the churches here approached Easter with the sadness of Good Friday rather than the joy of the resurrection? She had come away from the church service without the satisfaction she normally felt that God was in his heaven, and all was right with the world. She perused the front page of the *Woodstock Sentinel*:

Festival and Carol and Triumph Songs and Joyful Words in all the Churches

More space would be required than can be allotted by even *Sentinel*-like liberality, if one were to faithfully report the many services held in this young city, expressing nobly the glad Easter day just past. One is reluctantly content with partially indicating the joyous spiritual feasts which were prepared by the faithful in the various churches.

The shades of Lent were chased away when the morn of resurrection dawned in the east and the world awoke to a new life.

Ida leaned back in the kitchen chair. Well, this reporter certainly has a way with words. Ida's eyes slid down the column. The Catholic claim to fame was being the earliest worshipers. The Baptist's service was described as "delightful and quite original." The Methodists were lauded for their offering being "in furtherance of the system of 'benevolences' adhered to by the Methodist church at large, for the education of the colored race in the south." The Congregational church service sounded interesting with the choir and organ "re-enforced by violins, flute, and saxophone," – a saxophone in church? The paper claimed that the Presbyterian's "beloved pastor wore a smile broad enough to cover and comfort every sorrow of his great flock." How wonderful! She found the entry for the German Lutheran church:

> The German Lutheran church, Rev. Johannes Bertram, pastor, was a solemn temple of praise. Then 116 communicants advanced to the altar rail and received the symbols of bread and wine and with all the more grateful hearts because a company of boys and girls joined them in taking their first communion. The chorales were: Auf Auf meim Hers mit Freuden, and Freuet euch ihr Christen alle.
>
> *Woodstock Sentinel*, April 16, 1903.

Auf Auf meim Hers mit Freuden? "What in the world is meim Hers? 'Up, On my face with joys?' Or maybe 'Up, On my lord with joys?'" Ida translated the name of the hymn aloud and then laughed. This reporter might have a way with words, but he surely had challenges with German. The 'meim Hers' could be 'mein Hertz.' "Up, On my heart with Joy."

She chuckled again. "I suppose I wouldn't mind having a joyful face." But the article was right about the service. Here it had been Easter, the most joyous day of the Christian year, and the paper described the service as *solemn*. These joyful songs, the second one being 'Rejoice, All

Christians," were sung like dirges. Of course, the German language enhanced their dirge-ness if that was a word. Maybe they *did* need a more progressive Lutheran church in town as John talked about so often.

Easter in Woodstock had been solemn overall compared to her experience in Racine. Ida was used to blowing eggs and hiding them for Emma's children to find from the *Osterhase* – the Easter Bunny. Mama would order chocolate eggs and bunnies from Germany, and everyone, including the adults, had to wait until after church AND after dinner to eat them along with the German chocolate cake in the shape of a lamb with coconut wool. Sometimes the eggs and bunnies had a surprise inside – nuts or jam for the children and a bit of alcohol for the adults.

Ida remembered that when they were all young, Mama would spend the months from New Year's Day to Easter in preparation for a celebration of new life. In Racine, Easter was celebrated for at least four days!

Grundonnerstag, Maundy Thursday's supper had to include something green. The eggs in green frankfurter sauce had always been one of Ida's favorites.

On *Karfreitag* – fish and only fish, since Good Friday was a day of mourning – no singing, no laughing, no church bells ringing, just one meal of fish. Ida wasn't a big fan of fish and without bread and butter to 'wash it down,' she always dreaded this meal. Sometimes she would convince her mother that fasting was even more spiritually cleansing that fish.

Saturday was spent decorating the house and the yard with bright spring colors and flowers. Painted eggs, blown over the previous weeks, were strung together like a garland to decorate the *Osterbaum* – Easter Tree.

Best of all was Easter Sunday! It was joyful. The sermon was often funny and engaging. Emma and Frank brought the children to Racine for church and then to the house for the *Ostereiersuche* – Easter Egg Hunt. The food was plentiful as was the laughter. Ida's eyes had glazed over, and a smile played on her lips as she spent a few minutes helping Emma's little ones find eggs hidden in the grass and bushes.

She shook herself back to the present. What had happened in John's beloved Woodstock to make the Lutherans so serious and solemn? A time to pummel the sinners rather than rallying the saved. Next year, when she had a house and a child to help her blow and paint eggs, she vowed she would change the mood around Easter and keep the German traditions alive – except maybe only fish on Good Friday. That tradition may have to go by the wayside.

***

LOCAL INTELLIGENCE

Gingerbread at Doten's bakery.

B. S. Austin has a new covered wagon.

The best physic: Chamberlain's stomach and liver tablets. Easy to take; pleasant in effect. For sale by all druggists.

The opera "Pinafore" will be given at the opera house by home talent on Friday evening, May 1. Reserved seats on sale, Tuesday, April 28 at 7 o'clock.

John Wienke, who recently bought the Lambert property on Washington street, is fixing it up in first-class style and will have, when completed, a fine residence.

A. B. Pratt & Son have recently purchased through Schuett & Schaaf a new two-wheeled cart for delivery purposes. It is quite a novelty and ought to be very handy for the purpose for which it is intended.

Woodstock Sentinel, April 30, 1903.

Colored Butterine

The Bloomington Pantagraph has told of "uncolored" butterine of quite a yellowish or cream color, which was very much more attractive than the white stuff and yet did not pay the tax of colored butterine. This kind was sold readily on the Bloomington market. At Des Moines, Ia., a jury has disagreed in a test case brought against Armour & Co., for selling butterine described above. It was proven that no coloring matter was used but that the tint was due to cream, natural butter and cotton seed oil, all legitimate ingredients in oleomargarine. But slightly increasing the quantity of certain ingredients and by changing the quality of the vegetable oils used, a variety of yellowish oleomargarine is produced which looks enough like certain shades of butter to pass for that commodity. It has yet to be decided by the federal courts whether such butterine can be taxed as "artificially" colored.

Woodstock Sentinel, April 30, 1903.

***

NEGROES TO FOUND EMPIRE ON THE ISLAND OF HAYTI

NEW HAVEN, Conn. May 4.—William Pickens of Little Rock, Ark., the colored orator of Yale, '04, who captured the Ten Eyck prize in February, has received an invitation to become the head of an Afro-American empire to be established on the island of Hayti. The proposition comes from N. L. Musgrove of Sturgis, Ky., who is agitating a movement tending toward the seizure of the island of Hayti by the American negroes. The plan is for Pickens to enlist interest in the movement in the East, especially at Yale university, and collect money for the equipment of an army, the purchase of a warship, transports, and provisions. Then the negro army hopes to attack Port au Prince, the capital of Hayti, and if successful to place the island under the protection of the United States. The government will be administered as a gigantic corporation, with all the citizens as stockholders.

All land titles and franchises are to be vested in the state. There will be no penitentiaries or jails, but all dangerous and incorrigible criminals will be provisioned and set adrift on the sea to seek other shores. Agriculture, manufacturing, and all other profitable industries are to be encouraged. Public schools are to be established, and liberty is to be universal, but the rights of each are to be bound by the equal right of every other person. The movement has developed greatly in the South, and to a more limited extent in the North.

Chicago Inter Ocean, May 5, 1903.

***

Awful Horrors in Russia

Dispatches from Odessa, Kishineff, and St. Petersburg say that another massacre of the Jews is expected between May 18 and 24, old style, which would be about June 1 of the English calendar. There has been an almost general exodus for the Jews. Wealthy Hebrews are disposing of their property for whatever they can get. Many have abandoned homes and businesses rather than remaining to face the terrible slaughter which is anticipated. Many have already taken their departure. There is a Jewish population of 37,000 in Kieff, and all are affected. The agitation in Kieff is so great that the Jews are in dread of an immediate massacre.

A ministerial circular forbidding the Jews to defend themselves has been issued. It is expected that this step will stimulate Jewish emigration to America.

Chicago Inner Ocean, May 19, 1903.

***

Personal Mention

Albert Wienke was in Chicago last Tuesday looking after business connected to his large painting trade.

Woodstock Sentinel, May 21, 1903.

***

Ida folded the paper and looked for something to do. This would be the time of year when her own mother would be spring cleaning, throwing the devil out with dust. Did she dare start cleaning her mother-in-law's house? Ma Wienke had not said anything about spring cleaning. She wandered around the large room that she and John shared. She could at least clean this room well and then see what happened. She pulled up the throw rugs and placed them in the hall to be taken out and beaten – she would ask John to do that – and went down to the kitchen to retrieve a broom and dustpan.

"Vat's wrong. Vat are you doink?" Sophia's voice came from behind her as she leaned down for the dustpan.

"Nothing, Mother. I was just going to clean our room...you know. Easter is the time for spring cleaning, my mother always says." She tried to sound jovial and turned to smile at Sophia.

"*Ist es dreckig?*"

"No, it's not very dirty," she replied in what she hoped was not an afront. "But I haven't done a real cleaning up since we moved in. It's the right time of year to clean, in the Spring, right after Easter."

"*Du* not work. No gut for Kind."

"Why shouldn't I be working? It isn't going to hurt the baby. I feel fine and just thought I'd do something productive. We have two women in this house. We should split up the work more so I'm earning my keep."

Sophia's brows drew together. "Du tink my *haus ist nicht sauber* – not clean?"

"Oh no. I just want to clean our room, beat the rugs and look for wool mice – *Wollmause* – under the bed, wash the linens and so forth. It is the least I can do for my husband and for you. But if you need help with other things around the house, please tell me. I've been very lazy and would like some chores to do."

"*Du* vant to work? *Das ist gut auf Kind?*"

"A little work will not hurt the baby at all. If I had my own home, I'd have to clean it. I won't lift anything heavy and if I get tired, I'll rest. I bet you didn't stop working when you were carrying the boys, did you?"

"*Nein. Bei Enkelkindern ist das anders.*"

Ida laughed. "Ja. It is different when it's your grandchild, I suppose. I will be careful, I promise."

"*Wie du willst!*" Do as you will! Sophia disappeared back into the parlor.

Ida stood for a moment, her hands shaking a little, not quite knowing what to do. She took a deep breath and decided to soldier on. Picking up the dustpan and broom, she retreated up the stairs to their room and closed the door. This wasn't her house, but this was her room, and she could clean it if she wanted! She smacked down the dustpan and broom and then dropped to the bed sobbing. How long, John, how long?

***

COURT HOUSE NOTES
Real Estate Transfers
M W Lambert to John Wienke, lt 8 and 4 ft lt 7, Wicker's in Woodstock....................$1.00

Woodstock Sentinel, May 7, 1903

***

EXCHANGE GLEANINGS
HAPPENINGS IN McHENRY AND ADJACENT COUNTIES.

Woodstock Republican: Woodstock will have nine saloons the coming year, the city council having already issued licenses for eight as follows: John McGee, Wienke & Schneider, Connors & Stone, Art. Stupfel, Gustav Behrens, Jacob B. Schwamb, James Guest and Nester & Pfeiffer, and Vincent & Lee will open the ninth in the building to be vacated by Wittenberg & Bodenschatz as soon as they can fit it for the purpose.

McHenry Plaindealer, May 14, 1903.

***

Floods and Wind Work Havoc
in Middle West

Many landslides and washouts have resulted from the high water, and railroad traffic, in Wisconsin especially, is practically at a standstill. A huge tidal wave yesterday swept up the lake striking Racine with terrific force. Vessels lying in the harbor were lifted to the level of the docks. St. Joseph, Mich. and many other points in Wisconsin reported similar experiences.

The devastation in the Middle West by wind and flood continues. Within the week past nearly 100 persons have been killed and many hundreds injured and millions of dollars' worth of property has been destroyed. Scarcely a town between Ohio and the Rocky mountains has been free from the fury of the storm, and numerous villages have been completely wiped out by tornadoes.

Chicago Inter Ocean, May 18, 1903.

***

Deaths of Many Babies
Blamed Upon Mothers

Many babies die every year because their mothers, for selfish reasons, refuse to nurse them and are, therefore, guilty of the crime of child murder. This is one of the statements made by Dr. C. A. Lindsley, secretary of the Connecticut board of health and professor emeritus in Yale medical college.

Dr. Lindsley asserts that more than 600 babies died last July, August, and September from cholera infantum, and that most of them were bottle-fed babies or in other ways the victims of improper feeding.

Dr. Lindsley believes that the mother who can nurse her baby, but who, for selfish reasons, refuses to do so is often guilty of crime. The natural nourishment of the human offspring during the first year of its life is found only at its mother's breast. No substitute for this can ever be made without risk of disturbance of its digestion. While this is always true, it is more emphatically so during hot weather. A nursing baby, the mother being healthy, is immune to summer complaint if no other food is given to it than that provided by nature.

Chicago Daily Tribune, June 15, 1903.

***

June 1, 1903
Racine, Wisconsin

Dear Ida and John,

What a week we have had. Did you get hit by "the storm of the century" as they are calling it here? We had a storm seiche — do you know what that is? I was walking home for lunch in the rain, the worst of the storm had gone by, it seemed, so it was just sprinkling a bit, but suddenly people were yelling and screaming and running back up the hill from the lake as if a lake monster had been sighted or worse. I, of course, ran toward the lake hoping to get a story that the paper would like — I think I told you I'm going to be a reporter, but I need a good story to get them to notice me. It was amazing, but not something easily written about. The schooners and tugs and other boats in the harbor just started to lift up. Higher and higher they went until they were floating above the dock, and of course, crashing their hulls into them. I never saw anything like it, and I dare say neither have most of the people in Racine. They were running and yelling, "Tidal Wave!!" Since I didn't know how high this floating would go, I didn't go right down to the edge of the water, but I got close — maybe fifty yards away. A huge wave rushed forward bringing the boats with them. And then as quickly as it had started, the water began to recede. Some boats came down hard on the posts of the docks and got holes poked in them. A few came down on land, as at least one person was swept out into the lake. The larger schooners and tugs just demolished what they came down on. It was somewhat interesting to watch, but how does one write about something like that?

Then a police officer came over and told me I had to move back up the street to where others were standing. That was too bad because as soon as I turned my back, one of the schooners rolled on its side, and I missed it! I told the police officer that it was his fault that I had missed the best part of the event. I was extra mad because up until then there had not been anything to write about, and I missed the only newsworthy part.

Of course, he thought my anger was funny and laughed at me! I turned around without so much as a howdy-do and walked home. I'm sure his name was Officer Common Bob Spoilsport.

We are fine here. I am working hard to save up some money so I can make future plans. I told Mama that as soon as I have $500, I'm moving to Chicago. I have about $86 already so still have a way to go. Mama said she won't hold her breath. No one believes in me.

I know she thinks I'll just get married like all the other girls and fade away. I keep meeting nice men, but no one I'd want for the long term. They are so blah, with blah names, and blah Racine ways. But don't worry, I'll keep looking.

The girls and I have been singing a bit, but for only a pittance…a donation that I am obliged to split three ways or donate to the church. Sad to have a talent and not be able to make money from it.

Have you thought more about the names for the baby? Did you like my suggestions? I especially think Daisy is a winner. I wish my name were Daisy instead of Clara. Maybe if you don't use it for the baby, I'll just start introducing myself as Daisy and see what happens. If I counted correctly from your wedding day, the baby should come in August, aina? I will put in for time off when it happens. This is one time Mama is going to want to go by train to Woodstock.

I hope this finds you well and happy. Let me know if you have leads on any reporter jobs. I'd even move to Woodstock for that.

Love,

Daisy

***

Harting-Stanke

The host of friends of C. C. Harting will be pleased to learn of his marriage to Miss Linda Stanke of Beloit, Wis., Wednesday afternoon, June 10, 1903, at the home of Albert Wienke of this city. Rev. Bertram officiating. The ceremony was performed in the presence of but a few immediate relatives of the contracting parties.

The bridegroom to this happy union has been a resident of Woodstock for seven years. He is the skillful and efficient patternmaker of the Oliver Typewriter factory. Everyone knows Clayt and know him to be large-hearted and generous and an exceedingly popular young man who numbers his friends by the score. He is one of the oldest of the Oliver operatives, always attentive to business and has ever proven himself to be a valuable man to the Oliver management.

The bride is a comparative stranger in the city. She is the sister of Mrs. Albert Wienke, and is a young lady of fine disposition, of pleasant address and is well qualified to make their domestic life pleasant and agreeable.

Immediately after the ceremony the happy couple were driven to Nunda, where they took the 5:30 train to Chicago, thence to Freeport, Rockford, and Beloit, expecting to be gone about one week, after which they will be at home to their many friends at the residence of Mr. and Mrs. Albert Wienke.

Woodstock Sentinel, June 11, 1903.

***

"John! Haven't seen you in a month of Sundays," Frank settled himself at the wooden lunch table next to his older brother.

"Well, what's the world coming to. They're giving *you* a lunch break now too? What's the world coming to?" John punched Frank's shoulder softly.

"Wahdid Ma pack you? Oh wait, I mean, wahdid Ida pack you?" Frank stole a look in the paper sack in front of John.

"Yes, yes. They even argue about who will pack my lunch. Ida is trying to be patient, but Ma is as stubborn as an old Deutsche dame. It's her house and don't you forget it! And the fatter Ida gets, the more she complains. She says she feels fine and doesn't need watching over, but then she carries rugs out to the line and beats them silly, exhausting herself."

Frank laughed. "Looks like you got two stubborn Deutsche dames! Too many women under one roof. So, when are you breaking ground?"

John smiled as he unwrapped his Braunschweiger sandwich. "Already have. Got your builder, Frank Keshard, on that lot over east of McHenry Road. But I also want to…" John paused, looked around conspiratorially and leaned close and lowered his voice. "…get out of this place and into my own business. Two prongs, one fork. Maybe it would be smarter to sell the new house for a profit that I can use to start the business. On the other hand, we might need a place before then, after the baby is born. Can't you just see those two women having to go to King Solomon to decide who is more adequate to care for the child?"

Frank laughed again. "When is the anticipated arrival?

"August, Ida says. And the surprise house is also a distance from the business district. I have those two lots up in Wicker's addition, but they are also farther from the square than I would like. Being close to the square will mean being within walking distance of everything including my own shop if I end up opening one. I've been reading up on goods I should carry and have decided on a grocery shop with all the best."

"Hm." Frank's mouth was full of his own Braunschweiger sandwich. The spicey liver sausage was on special last week at Austen's. He swallowed. "The best wurst in town, eh?"

John laughed. "That's not half bad...not half good either."

"So, can't you borrow some money from your bank? Aren't you vice president or something? I suppose they would be more willing to lend to a business than a house, right?"

John snorted and almost choked. "Vice president? Not hardly. Just a shareholder. And of course, the business will need more money to establish than the house to build. So, I keep working, and Ida gets fatter as the weeks go by, and Ma just holds on tighter and tighter."

"To her very last mama's boy." Frank held up the cap of his thermos as a toast and drank a swig of the black coffee therein.

John punched his shoulder again, harder this time. "Stop! She still has Bob to worry about."

Frank shook his head. "Don't we all?"

"I'm sure he will move back in as soon as Ida and I are gone. And your new place is just across the street practically, so you'll be close. She'll have plenty to do."

"And what do you know about the crowd at Al's house?"

"Ach, it will be short-lived. Clayt and Linda will take over the rental when Al and Lena move into the house on Lincoln Avenue. Ah, there will be many grandchildren for Ma to tend eventually. How about sharing your little chitlins a bit more…take the load off Ida?"

"Ma does want babies to hold. I'll see what I can do." Frank crumbled up his lunch bag and sent it flying into the trash barrel. "Talk to Al. He owns lots all over town. He's working on a deal with Hoy to sell one near the square for three thousand."

John choked on his coffee and had a coughing fit. Frank slapped him on the back.

"Three THOUSAND dollars?" John managed between coughs.

"Ja," Frank confirmed. "I should have been a painter." He smiled and got up. "I gotta run. Fire meeting…putting on a drill later in the week. Be ready."

"So long, it's been good to know ya," John sang him away. Three thousand dollars! For a single lot? John sighed. He'd never have the money for a lot close to the square. But before that, he had a house to finish so that his son didn't come into the world homeless.

***

Ida Wienke struggled up the three stairs to Misses Donnelly's haberdashery. All she wanted was a summer hat and the Donnelly sisters were famous for their flowery spring bonnets. She took the few steps across the porch to the door of the establishment and suddenly simply had to go water. She opened the door and called out to the white-haired woman rocking and knitting near the door. "Miss Donnelly, I must use your outhouse. Where is it?"

The still-beautiful woman, although she couldn't be a day under eighty years, smiled, and pointed toward the back door. Ida pushed her way through the too-narrow doorway, almost too wide to fit, but with a bit of work, she got inside and started toward the back door.

But she was too late. She felt liquid trickle down her legs, wetting her stockings, filling her—

Ida's eyes flew open in horror. Wasn't it bad enough that she was as big as a house: Wasn't it bad enough that she felt like the fat lady in a circus. But now she had wet the bed. She reached for John. Not there. She rolled out of bed and observed the damage to the bed linens.

At least the embarrassing scene at Donnelly's was a dream. How humiliating that would have been. What time was it? Light was streaming in the window so it must be—

The pain. Ida doubled over grabbing a bedpost for support. Oh no. The baby must be coming.

She pulled a housecoat around her shoulders and went to the top of the stairs. "John? Mother Wienke? Are you there? John? The baby is coming."

John rushed to the foyer with the paper he had been reading still in his hand. He looked up at her, concern written all over his face. "But…but…." He glanced at the date on the paper. "…but it's only July second. You can't have the baby today."

Ida had to laugh at his confusion as she gave him a knowing gaze. "Right on time."

The rest was a blur as the doctor was called and after six hours of contractions and a good deal of pushing, it turned out she *could* have the baby today.

John sat at bedside holding his fussy little girl as an exhausted Ida came out of a nap. "Ugh. Mothers don't tell daughters how much bearing will hurt."

John reached over and squeezed her hand. "Maybe there's a reason they don't tell. Daughters might shy away from marriage if they knew."

"I doubt it. Here let me see if she'll suckle. Maybe she's hungry."

John handed the little bundle swaddled in a flannel bunting, and Ida presented the child with supper.

"How much did she weigh?" Ida winced as the baby latched on to a swollen nipple.

"Just over eight pounds. About as much as a good pork roast." John's hand showed how big the pork roast would be.

"Oh, mercy, John! She's a baby not a meatloaf." Ida tried to look stern, but she was smiling. "So have you decided on Helen Frances or Frances Helen?"

"Helen is a good first name, I think." John touched the back of the baby's blond head.

Ida nodded and touched the soft cheek. "Helen Frances Wienke. So be it!"

***

Woodstock's Population

That Woodstock is growing at a rapid rate is shown by comparing the figures of the school census for 1902 and those for 1903. While there is an increase in the number of persons of school age to the number of 52, there is shown an increase in the population of 266 over the year 1902. Total population in1902 was 3146 and in 1903 it is 3413.

Woodstock Sentinel, July 2, 1903.

Local Intelligence

Next horse sale, July 8.

Rev. N. A. Sunderlin's subject for Sunday morning will be *Hurrah*! And for the evening service, *Which Kingdom*!

Report of Woodstock Public library for the week ending June 18, 1903: Number of visitors 301; Number of books loaned, 138.

We are requested to remind all of an ordinance regulating the size of firecrackers that can be shot off in this city, which is not to exceed three inches in length. The use of toy pistols, revolvers, and guns of all kinds is absolutely prohibited.

The attention of the parents of a number of boys living on Washington street is called on to the fact that said boys must stop their play at the new houses being erected for Holz, Connors and Wienke. They are destroying property and unless they are compelled to stop, some of them will get into trouble.

Woodstock Sentinel, July 2, 1903.

***

Dorr Assessment
Township 44, Range 7
Wicker's Addition

August Wienke (ex e 4ft) lt 7...........$180

John Wienke 4ft lts 7 and 8...........$144

Spring City Addition

Wm Wienke, lt 1......................…..…..$208

Wm Wienke, lt 12.....................…...$ 18

J Wienke, lt 8...........................…......$ 14

Woodstock Sentinel, July 2, 1903.

***

July 3, 1903
Racine, Wisconsin

Dear Ida,

Oh goodness, we are so surprised by Helen Frances' arrival nearly a month early. She must be a tiny baby, and we are so glad to hear that both the baby and you are doing fine. Mama practically shrieked when she heard the news. She so wanted to be there with you when Helen made her appearance, but that was not to be.

Thank John for his phone call yesterday to inform us of your happy and healthy little girl.

We will come Saturday on the noon train. I can only stay the weekend, but Mama will, if all goes well, be with you until you kick her out. I jest, but she is backing quite a large trunk for the trip. Better bring the buckboard to meet us.

We assume that her baptism will be this weekend or next and I can't wait to give you the dress that I made with my own hands, working my fingers to the bone for my newest niece. So don't buy one if you thought to.

I want to get this in the mailbox before the postman picks up so you will get it tomorrow or Friday. I can't wait to meet little Helen, and of course to see you and John also.

Love, Clara

***

"Oh Ida, she is just precious. Hello, little Helen Frances." Lena nuzzled the top of the fuzzy head of the baby she was holding.

"You have a precious one here, too." Ida looked down at the tiny three-month-old in her arms. "Just think Bertha, you are going to grow up with a friend named Helen."

Lena smiled, "I'm not sure how long Theo will be able to do without her. He was very thankful that Mama and I stepped in to help, but I know he is heartbroken and misses her so much. It's good that the weather has improved. He says he will come down every week to see her, and I believe him."

"And how are you holding up with Evie pulling at your apron strings, Berty at your breast, and another baby on the way? You haven't promised too much, have you?" Ida adjusted Berty to her shoulder. She was so tiny.

"I'm lucky that Evie has stopped breastfeeding just when Berty needed help. You know Berty had stopped gaining weight on cow's milk and was promising to be a sickly child, if not worse. But she has gained three pounds since coming home with us, so we are hopeful that no permanent damage was done. How has your first month of motherhood gone?"

"Fine. She is a happy baby so far and keeps me on a schedule of two to three hours between feedings. John groans when she cries at night, but I love getting up with her, letting her eat. and then falling asleep in the rocker with her until the next feeding. Is that wrong to do?"

"Ida, whatever you must do to get your sleep in, do it. I spent several nights when Berty first came sitting in the rocker next to her bassinet, just so she wouldn't be alone if she woke up. It seemed to work, and she is much less fussy now. Mothers do what they must."

"Thank you, my dear friend. You have taught me so much about being a mother.

"Oh no, it's I who should be thanking you. Where would I be without Pickles and Olives?"

They laughed and then noticed that both girls were sound asleep in their arms.

***

Olivers are Again Declared Victor

Wow! What? Another? It was indeed a nice game. Four shutouts in the last five games played. The Olivers should get an incubator and hatch out a few of those goose eggs. Hill pitched a superb game. The visitors, who undoubtedly know how to bat, couldn't do a thing with his zigzaggers, pollywaggers, and twisters. When they did hit the ball, it went straight up in pop flies, easily handled by the infield. Saturday the Olivers play the Union-Giants, the crack-colored aggregation. Will it be a goose egg? If so, will the fruit go into Farmer Ryan's market basket?

Woodstock Sentinel, July 23, 1903.

***

Open a New Addition to City

John J. Murphy has opened a new addition in the west end. It is known as the Bellevue addition and comprises eighteen lots. Already eight have been sold, the purchasers being as follows: 1. Will Glazier, 2. George Donnelly, 3. F. W. Doten, 4: Albert Wienke, 5, Benj. Anderson.

Woodstock Sentinel, July 30, 1903.

***

Lazy Liver

For a lazy liver try Chamberlin's Stomach and
Liver Tablets. They invigorate the liver, aid
digestion, regulate the bowels, and prevent
bilious attacks.

Woodstock Sentinel, July 30, 1903.

***

August 5, 1903
365 Lincoln Avenue
Woodstock, Illinois

Dear Mama and Clara,

*Oh, little Helen misses you so much, Mama! And so do I.
Thank you for coming to help with our move and taking care of the
little one. She is pleasant and good-natured and smart. I do believe
that she knows you are no longer here. And Clara, thank you so
much for bringing Mama down and coming to accompany her home. I
hope the two round trips in a month didn't wear you out so much
that you had to miss work. You are a sweet sister.*

*I was never so surprised in my life…first a month early
baby and then a new house. Isn't John thoughtful? When I think of
all the complaining I've done over the last few months about sharing a
house with Mother Wienke, well…my face turns red just thinking
about it.*

*I got the curtains hung last night, with my fine husband's
help, and they make all the difference. One hardly notices the
unpainted walls. Al has promised to make time to paint in the next
month or so, but he is so busy right now, it might be later. I suppose
I should have put off moving until he could do the painting, but I
couldn't wait a moment longer. My own new house!*

*Clara, the baptismal dress was just beautiful. Helen looked
like a little angel in it. You have become quite the seamstress. I pride
myself to think that I had a small hand in that. And the bonnet*

from you, Mama, made quite an ensemble. I also loved that she cried when the water hit her forehead. Do you think she will actually be a singer?

Mother Wienke has been very attentive this week since you've been gone. Each day, she has brought food over for dinner and sat and rocked Helen to sleep for her afternoon nap, so I could rest. I feel I may not have had Christian thoughts about her or maybe it's true that distance makes the heart grow fonder, even if the distance is blocks instead of miles.

Helen says hello to her Oma and Auntie and that it is now time to eat, so I must close. John will take this to the station this evening so that you will get it before the weekend. Again, thank you for all your help. I hope Papa Stoffel was well cared for by Clara during your absence, Mama. It's good practice for her. Ha!

Ida

***

Selee's Cubs Play Woodstock's Olivers
Friday

Tomorrow lovers of the great national sport in Woodstock will have the first opportunity of seeing a major league team in action on the home grounds when the Chicago national leaguers, variously nicknamed, the cubs, the microbes, the colts, and the Selleeities, do battle royal with the Olivers.

It is confidentially expected by the local management that fully 2,000 spectators or more will see the game, as advices from the neighboring towns and cities indicate large delegations. Reports from some of the country districts show that every farm wagon and team in the county will be in use and special provisions are to be made to take care of those that patronize the game.

Having the leaguers here seems to indicate that the Olivers find the average amateur and small league team about the county as too easy picking and want to tackle something that will prove more interesting. While there are few of even the warmest supporters who are willing to back their opinions with collateral by saying that the Olivers will come out victorious, still there are many that are willing to wager a considerable amount that the locals will not be shutout.

Selee's team stands second in the per centage column and is a warm contestant for first place Pittsburg.

Woodstock Sentinel, August 6, 1903.

COURT HOUSE NOTES
Real Estate Transfers

A Wienke and w to J M Hoy, lt 1, blk 11, Woodstock..............................\$ 3000.00

Woodstock Sentinel, August 6, 1903.

***

PERSONAL MENTION

Mr. and Mrs. Charles Wienke of Beloit arrived on Sunday for a visit with Woodstock relatives.

Woodstock Sentinel, August 6, 1903.

***

"John, Frank, Charles!" Bob sang out their names loud enough that several people turned to see what was happening. Bob had caught them walking toward Sophia's on Washington.

"Bob!" The three brothers returned the greeting in unison.

"I'm taking some action on the game tomorrow. Win-Loss odds are stacking up against the Olivers, but how about a point split or the number of strikeouts or Moriarty's putouts or runs? Anyone want some action?"

Charles shook his head. "Not me. I'm an out-of-towner. I only bet on the Beloiters."

Frank tried to control a guffaw and failed. "Do you actually think Moriarty is going to score runs? Plural?"

"Of course, I do…or don't…it depends on which way you are leaning." Bob's smile never faded.

"What odds do you have of a shut out by the Cubs?" asked John.

"Five to one." Bob opened his book ready for a bet.

"I'll take that." John reached into his vest pocket, found a quarter, and held it out.

"Two bits? Two bits? Can you afford it? How about a dollar?" Bob's voice had once again risen to a level that gained the attention of others on the walk. Several men John knew stopped nearby as if waiting for the bookie.

John put his hand on Bob's arm. "Bob, please, a bit of decorum. I don't want to get to be known in this town as a gambler."

Bob snorted. "Oh, you don't have to worry about that with a two-bits bet."

"That is all I want to chance. A quarter dollar will do. I'm a father now and must be conservative."

"Frank?" Bob was nothing if not persistent.

"Hm." Frank scratched his chin. "I'll bet a dollar that the point split will be ten or more. What kind of odds can you give me on that?"

"How about three to one? Are you sure you only want to put a dollar on it? If you give me five dollars, you'll get fifteen dollars back if you win."

"Okay. Five dollars! Why not?" Frank found his money clip and pulled off five bills. Al held one up to the light as if checking for a counterfeit. The one-dollar Silver Certificate had the U. S. capitol behind a bald eagle perched on an American flag with small portraits of Abraham Lincoln to the left and Ulysses S. Grant to the right.

"Looks legit," Bob teased as he pocketed the money. "Ha-ha! Gotcha both! No way Moriarty is going to let the National Leaguers shut out the Olivers…and ten points or more? I just don't believe it can be done. Say good-bye to your money!" Bob rubbed his hands together.

Frank shook his head at Bob's histrionics. "We'll see. We'll be there…and don't you dare tell *anyone* that we bet against the Olivers."

"Don't worry I won't. See you there, Frank and Mr. Cheapskate! See you later, Charles." Bob's eyes had already found his new patsies as he spoke. "Hey Clayt, Phil, want some action on the game tomorrow?" And off he went to make his millions.

Charles shook his head. "I wish he'd get a real job."

Frank looked after his brother who was laughing with the other gamblers. "He will. He's gotta settle down sometime. If the Cubs don't win the championship, it will be a sign."

John chuckled. "A sign of what. That he has lost everything?"

Frank shrugged. "That would be a start toward the reality of life, wouldn't it? You can't always win. He's having so much fun with it. He'll never stop if he's always winning."

***

SELEE'S CUBS SHUT OUT
THE CRACK OLIVERS

Selee and his microbes have come and gone, and they so thoroughly infected the Olivers with the germ of defeat, no matter how Dr. Ashmore, and his bunch labored, he could not find the anti-toxin that would stop the progress of the disease, although he did hold it in check for six straight innings.

The germs of defeat permeated the systems of the local lads to the tune of 12 to 0 which geometrically speaking along the base lines means that a shutout was scored.

Woodstock Sentinel, August 13, 1903.

***

Moriarty Plays with Chicago

Last Sunday George Moriarty, the crack third baseman of the Oliver Typewriter baseball team of this city, played that position with Selee's Cubs of the National league at Chicago. That he made good is evident by the nice things said of him by the Chicago papers. The Chicago Daily News of Saturday evening had the following to offer:

A well-known local baseball manager said today.

"Watch that Moriarty that Selee has signed for a utility man. I watched him in the Spaldings, and I watched his work in the Three I league where he was with Springfield and again at Woodstock, where Selee picked him up. He is young, about 19 or so, and big and plays the third bag as if he were made for it."

Woodstock Sentinel, August 27, 1903

***

Carl...Sophia's hand stopped stirring the eggs she was scrambling. Her eyes stared out the window, over the railroad tracks, and into the past. How long since Carl was gone? Almost twenty years now. She would soon be joining him. Already she was sixty-seven last birthday. So far so good. She was not really alone; she had her boys nearby.

She went back to mixing the eggs and milk, added the goose grease to the frying pan, and poured the mixture in. The eggs sizzled in the cast iron skillet that had cooked many meals for her children and husband over the years. Not fancy, but it did the job and would continue to do so for some years to come.

As she watched the eggs cook, her mind traveled back to Germany and to meeting Carl for the first time. It made her smile. He was so young, they both were, and so shy. Why are men always so shy? It had taken Carl almost a year to marry her, but she had known from the first moment she saw him. He didn't want to drag her into his problems, Those years in Germany had been nothing *but* problems. The expectation of a baby was what had changed his mind.

She stirred the eggs in the pan, flipping them over so they would brown slightly on both sides.

Frederick Wienke had been drafted into the Prussian navy in 1850 during the Revolution, when he was nineteen years old. After five years, he couldn't take the fighting anymore, and he walked away from his ship when it docked at Bremen. Instead of going home, he went to Seedorf in Lower Saxony, and started calling himself Carl. It was there that Sophia met him and where they had fallen in love.

The grease in the pan popped, and Sophia realized that she was about to cook the eggs too long. She quickly turned them out onto a plate and brought them and a refreshed cup of black coffee to the table. She added salt to the eggs and put butter on a piece of bread and took a bite of each. Not bad. A little dry, but not bad.

As she chewed, her thoughts floated back to those early days when they lived every day in fear of discovery. They quickly had two girls, Caroline and Doris. Carl worked in the tanning barns, and Sophia took in laundry, and each week they made ends meet – just barely. They talked of going to the new world, to America, where they wouldn't have to worry about being found out. They moved to Parchim into a bigger house where they could take a border or two, and they were able to put a few *vereinsthalers* (coins of the realm) into their purse, and that became their traveling money.

Sophia finished the last bite of egg and bread and pushed her plate away from her. She pulled her coffee cup in front of her and looked into its dark depths. A gray-haired old lady looked back, but soon vanished in unfocused memories.

Every time it looked like they were nearing their escape to America, disaster fell. Sophia would lose a laundry client, or she'd find herself pregnant again. So it was, with William and then August. They had given up on the trip to America when the fifth pregnancy occurred. How could they pay for a passage for two adults and five children?

With each child there was more need for clothing, blankets, beds, and especially more food. The girls were nine and seven when the school was hit with cholera. Within a few days of the announcement, both girls were sick. Carl took the boys, then four and two, out into the country to a place where he had hidden when he had first walked away from navy servitude; a place where they would not commingle with their sisters or other children.

Tears blurred the patterned oilcloth covering the tabletop as she remembered 'her girls.' What a loss they were to the family. Sophia had held each girl's hand as she took her last breath. How was it that the mama did not get sick when her children did? Why did she live while they died? Sophia picked up the cloth napkin and wiped her eyes. Remembering their passing still brought a stab of pain to her chest. She took a deep breath and blew it out.

After the girls died, she hit a low place from which she didn't want to return. But then Carl came home and took up the reins. He washed the floors and walls and bed clothes and street clothes to banish the sickness. Then he told Sophia to start packing. William and August were healthy, and the baby was due soon. It might take their last coin, but they were leaving for America as soon as they had the baby in their arms.

Sophia took a long draw on her lukewarm coffee and then warmed it from the pot on the stove. She smiled remembering the birth of Charles in a dark damp room near the docks in Bremen without a doctor or midwife. *Gott sei dank*, he had slipped out into Carl's waiting hands with a short labor and no trouble. She was able to rest for only a day before the ship was leaving.

They went onboard right under the eyes of the authorities in the dark of night and were bound for America before dawn.

Sophia smiled. Charles was such a good baby and didn't make a sound during the whole escape. They took very little with them. Three carpet bags and a duffle with food and other valuables.

They bet on the idea that the *Regierungsbeamten*, the government officials, would have more important things on their minds than watching a small merchant ship filled mostly with French wine heading to America. After a few stressful minutes of quietly climbing the wooden gangplank without dropping the children into the sea, the five of them were safely onboard. It took five weeks to cross the ocean and food was scant at best. Carl insisted that Sophia and the *Kinder* eat more because she was feeding two and they were…well…*nur Kleine Kinder* (just little kids).

Thinking about that *Aufregende Erfahung* (exhilarating experience) still left her breathless. Sophia's hand went to her chest. She could feel her heart beating quickly and took a deep breath to calm it.

How had Carl arranged their escape? She had never asked. She had a *Neugeborene* (newborn) to care for and two little *Jungen* (boys) to keep quiet until they were underway.

That was 1866. They were young and ready for hard work. And the babies just kept coming…one boy after another. Oh, how she missed the girls and hoped that there would be another, but it wasn't to be. In the end, eight boys sat around this table and ate scrambled eggs from that cast iron skillet.

Then one evening Carl had come home with a cough, and a week later he was gone. Pneumonia took him. There was nothing that could be done.

Sophia had looked around the table at all those boys. She had no option but to find a way to care for them. They had become her life.

Fixing meals for only one felt *ziemlich engenartig* (quite peculiar) and eating meals with no conversation was lonely. Most of her daughters-in-law were good cooks, so she was rarely called on for help nowadays. And Sunday dinners were even rare with all the babies being born. Not that she was complaining about the babies, but it did keep the children in their own homes more often than not. The house groaned as if it was feeling the loneliness, too. She got up and filled her coffee cup again. The cup was the last of the morning coffee, dark and rich.

Sophia returned to her chair at the kitchen table. And then reached up and boxed her ear with one hand.

"Hör auf! Wir haben nichts zu beanstanden!" she said to the house. Stop it! She had nothing to complain about. She was glad to have this house – so warm compared to the old house and so close to downtown. She could walk to the square in good weather. She had healthy children and grandchildren who visited quite often.

Life was finally being good to her, and she should just sit back and enjoy it, at least for a while. She could use the time to get caught up on her sewing and she would reestablish the Sunday dinners for whomever could come. It was a time to be a grandmother. Who knew how long she'd last, but she was going to make these last years happy ones.

"What else can I do?" Sophia took the last swallow of coffee and put the dishes in the wash pan. She was not ready to stop using that frying pan!

***

CITY COUNCIL
REGULAR MEETING
WOODSTOCK, ILL, Oct. 2, 1903.

F. A Walters, Mayor, presiding.

Alds. Burger, Cunningham, Green, Murphy, and Schuett answered to their names at roll-call, constituting a quorum.

The following bills, approved by the finance committee, were read:

Chas E. Gierty & son, build'g catch basin..$ 42.50
Same, labor on power house....................... 437.00
Hartford Steam Boiler Imp & Ins. Co.
Insurance on Boilers.............................187.00

Huntzinger Bros, meals for prisoners...... .80
Geo Grote, cutting thistles................. 15.00
F B Swale, electrician...................... 82.50
Wm Wienke, trimmer....................... 45.00
Fm Fritz, helper........................... 45.00
John Bolger, marshal....................... 50.00
J F Eckert, nightwatch..................... 50.00
John Bolger, supt w w..................... 15.00

Woodstock Sentinel, October 8, 1903.

***

O. T. Factory News

Frank Wienke moved into his new house in Dacy's addition on Saturday. Chas. Bier will move into the Glennon house which Wienke vacated and Cha. Schmidt and wife (nee. Hobs) will begin housekeeping in the Stuffel house Bier vacated.

Woodstock Sentinel, October 15, 1903.

COURT HOUSE NOTES
Real Estate Transfers

J. Wienke and w to A. Wienke, pt lt 8 blk 7 Wicher's addition Woodstock............ $1.00.

A. Wienke and w to J. Wienke pt lt 7 block 7 Wicher's ad Woodstock.................... $1.00.

J. J. Murphy and w to A. Wienke, lt 6 and 7, blk 1, Murphy's ad Woodstock......... $1000.00

Woodstock Sentinel, October 15, 1903.

BIG YACHT IS LAUNCHED
By Clara Doering

The day that the whole city of Racine had been waiting for has finally arrived. The launch of John W. Gates, a $50,000 yacht built by the Racine Boat Works. This day *was especially heart-rending because this yacht will be the last launch of any boat by the Racine company as they are moving their boat works to Muskegon, Michigan, taking with it a number of upstanding Racine citizens who will be sorely missed.*

By the two o'clock published launch time, a large crowd had gathered for the auspicious occasion only to be disappointed as the afternoon passed with a large force of men working steadily to get the ship ready to roll majestically down into the Root River. There seemed to be quite a discussion going on regarding the safety of sending such a tall boat down the rollers, the culmination of which was the removal of the pilothouse that was placed aground to be added later.

As the afternoon reached the three o'clock quitting time and beyond, workmen on their way home swelled the crowd on both sides of the river waiting for the spectacle to commence. As 4:30 p. m. approached, the crew began knocking the blocking away cautiously trying to knock the same block on either side of the yacht at the same time. While the crowd had hoped to see Mr. Gates watch his "baby" fall into the sea, he did not make an appearance, although a few of his company officers were sightseers in the crowd. No society belle broke champagne over the bow, although this reporter did offer her services for same.

At around five o'clock, the last piece of wood holding the boat was liberated and the boat began to move toward the river. "She's off!" cried the crowd as the yacht slid into the water, the stern diving deep.

A tremendous splash wet down parts of the crowd and then the bow came up and the boat rested erectly on the water.

Applause washed through the people watching signifying the success of the venture which they had patiently waited for, some for over three hours. The crowd dispersed more quickly than it had gathered, and the crew was left with the work of reassembling the pieces that had been removed.

The yacht will be taken in a few days, after it is deemed shipshape, to LaSalle to be presented to the great man himself, and thereafter, it will be sailed down the Illinois to the Mississippi to Arthur, Texas for the millionaire's pleasure and pastime over the winter.

Fare thee well, Racine Boat Works. Ye shall be missed.
Racine Journal News, October 15, 1903.

***

October 20, 1903
Racine, Wisconsin

Dear Ida, John, and Helen,

Just a quick note to go with this article from last week. I'm sending a copy of what I sent to them rather than the edited down piece. It was edited and published in the paper, and they even paid me for it!!! I am so excited. Maybe I can be a reporter after all. Being a performer is getting pretty old already. Write soon and tell me what you think. The editor especially liked the line where I volunteered to break the bottle over the bow. I actually did that...volunteer that is. I had a front row seat on the bank to watch the whole spectacle. What fun! The crew was very nice and beautifully strong...oh, I shouldn't be saying such things when John might be reading this.

Now that I have "real credentials," I hope to do more reporting on more than buggy crashes. Wish me luck!

Love,
Clara Doering,
Newspaper Reporter

***

BATHS! BATHS! BATHS!

Woodstock City Bathrooms.
South side of the public square.
READY FOR BUSINESS.
Tubular.
Needle and Shampoo Combination
Showers
The most exhilarating Sanitary and
Thoroughly Cleansing Bath Given in
the city.
Open Sunday Mornings from 7 to 12
o'clock.

Woodstock Sentinel, October 29, 1903.

Personal Mention

Harry Cross, F. G. Arnold, Joe Connors and Robt. Wienke drove over to Elgin Monday evening in automobiles and attended a meeting of the Elks Lodge.

Woodstock Sentinel, October 29, 1903.

***

John rushed up the steps of his new house. He paused just a moment to relish the beautiful oak door newly stained. The house was small with only two bedrooms but large enough for his small family, and he was drawing up plans for a more prominent situation to begin in the spring, he hoped. Still, the door looked stunning. He pushed it open and called out, "Ida?"

"In here, John." John turned toward the parlor and took in the scene of motherly bliss. The baby and mama were happily playing with rag dolls on the floor. Helen looked up at him and smiled. He swept her up into his arms, and she giggled as he kissed her and twirled her around.

"John, a bit less enthusiasm. She just ate." Ida's raised eyebrows gave warning.

John set her gently back aground. Helen lay on her tummy with hands and feet punching the air. "Da, da, da, pmmm."

John smiled with pride. "See she knows her Dada."

Ida rolled her eyes. "Here we were quietly having a conversation before nap and now she's all worked up again. Doesn't she look like a grounded turtle trying to get purchase to crawl away?"

"And well you should be excited, my little turtle. Guess what I just heard."

Ida looked at the baby who didn't seem to be inclined to answer. "I assume that question was addressed to me? Hm. I don't know…the Cubs took the pennant after all?"

"No…sad to say, no. You should have seen the look on Bob's face when it became clear that the Pirates were going to take the league and the Cubs would be third. A lot of pints were lifted that night, for sure. Guess again."

"Let's see. Mother Wienke has decided to stop feeding us so much because we are getting fat on her cooking?"

John laughed, "Good try. No. Successful Germans are supposed to be fat."

"Well, then I don't know. I guess the only thing left is politics. Who won this time?"

"You guessed it…well not exactly, but close. Judge Donnelly is looking at a run for Governor!"

"Wow. I'll get lunch while you tell me about it. Okay? Little Helen, you just play Here for a while. Mama will be right back." Ida accepted a pull from John as she got up from the floor.

"Dap," said Helen.

"The thing is that no one likes the other candidates, and there are a lot of them…but no one looks like the cream that will rise to the top. So, we are going to keep a close watch on them and if after a few rounds, there still isn't a front runner, Judge Donnelly will be encouraged to throw his hat into the race. You know what that means, right?" John's face was rosy with excitement.

Ida looked blank-faced at John. "What?"

"There will be jobs, lots of them, on the campaign and then after he's in Springfield. How would you like to live in the capitol?" John's eagerness was palpable in the room.

Ida pulled out the left-over pork roast and put it on the table. "Springfield?" Color had risen to her cheeks also. "Might as well be Washington, D. C."

"Maybe later, but this is still a wonderful opportunity for those of us close to Donnelly. Of course, who knows who he'll hire as aides, but the campaign will be great! Traveling with the Judge, and convincing people all over Illinois that he is the man for the job." John stared out the window contemplating the fun of the campaign.

"That's wonderful." Ida added bread, butter, mustard, applesauce and cold potato pancakes, and two glasses of milk to the table. "What about us while you are traveling?"

John paused in his reverie and looked at Ida. "You can come with us." He sat down and looked across the fare. "You like to travel, right? Trains, streetcars, automobiles. It will be fun."

"And the baby?"

"Ma can watch over her. We aren't talking about right this minute. We'll start planning now but the campaigning will be next summer and fall. She'll be big enough to be without us for a while, won't she?"

Ida turned toward the window, ostensibly to gather plates and utensils, so he wouldn't see the tears that had sprung into her eyes more from anger than hurt. Leave her baby? Was he crazy? She knew John was watching her. No sense in fighting about it now. There would be plenty of time to make her position known. She turned back to the table and busied herself making sandwiches from left-over pork roast, shared by Mother Wienke midweek, a treat.

"Ida?" John's voice had calmed. "Are you mad?"

Ida looked up at him. Her anger dissipated just looking into those blue eyes. "No, John, but talk of leaving the baby is upsetting. Let's see what the future brings before we make plans for such an occurrence."

"Okay. I was just excited by the possibilities. We don't have to leave Helen anywhere you don't want to. We will work it out." John accepted the plate with his sandwich. She had cut it in half on the diagonal. He took a big bite and nodded.

"You remember that tomorrow we are going to your mother's for dinner after church, right? I'm making German Potato Salad to take."

"Good. I love that." He took another bite and washed it down with a swallow of milk.

"It's my mother's recipe passed down in her family."

"How appropriate." John smiled. "I'm sure it will be delicious. Everything that your Mama makes is delicious."

Ida's hands went to her face.

"Ida? What is it?" He placed a large hand on her arm.

"I don't want to leave Helen."

John stood up and pulled her to her feet and into his embrace. "It's okay. I'm sorry I upset you. What can I do to make it up to you?"

"I want to see my family."

"Of course, we can go to Racine."

"For Thanksgiving?"

"Of course, we can. Helen would love the train ride, wouldn't she?"

Ida wiped her tears with a dish towel. "Yes, I think she would."

***

CITY COUNCIL
Regular Meeting
Woodstock, Ill, Nov. 6, 1903.

The following bills, approved by the finance committee, were read:

National Carbon Co., carbons………........$ 15.74
Lawrence Jesson, cow killed in ditch… 40.00
E E Richards, subscriptions for library 35.95
Mrs. C. M. Curtis, librarian…………... 20.00
F B Swale, electrician………………… 82.50
Wm. Wienke, engineer……………… 65.00
Fred Sahs, trimmer………………….. 45.00
Wm Fritz, helper…………………….. 45.00

Woodstock Sentinel, November 12, 1903.

***

There was a pounding at the door. Just back from their visit to Racine, John, Ida and Helen were upstairs readying themselves for bed. Helen was tired, fussy, and demanding time with Ida while John took on the task of unpacking the suitcase. They looked at each other. Who would be at the door on a Sunday night at ten o'clock? John headed for the stairs. For some reason Ida called out, "Be careful, John."

He left the lights off and approached the door. *Bam, bam, bam.* Someone was kicking the door. The pounding startled John, and he jumped to the side, not knowing what to expect. From the side he peeked out around the curtain. What he saw was horrifying. He threw open the door. "Bob! What happened?"

"Oh good. I sought m'be you wernt home, and I'd havta hide on da porch." Bob fell forward into John's arms.

John took a furtive look around and then pulled his brother through the door and closed it tightly. Bob had been beaten and was bloodied around the face. His hands were skinned and swollen. He seemed to be guarding his right side as John let him slump gently to the floor.

Ida padded down the stairs and turned on the parlor light. "She is already asleep. Who was at the— Oh my!" Ida looked down at Bob bleeding on her braided entrance rug. "What has happened?"

"I'm not sure. Let's see if we can get him up and calculate the damage."

Ida came to one side and John took the other and they were able to get him to the davenport.

"I'll go boil some water for cleaning and coffee." Ida bustled to the kitchen, turning lights on as she went.

John got down on his knees beside his brother whose beautiful face was misshapen and bleeding. "Bob? Hey Bob? Can you hear me?"

"Yesh," Bob didn't open his eyes. John suspected that opening them was going to be a challenge for a few days.

"Can you tell me what happened? Who did this to you?"

"No money, beat sup, all bets off." Bob slurred his words, but the meaning was there.

"Are you saying that someone wasn't paid off fast enough from a bet?"

"Yesh, shtupid, shtupid, shtupid." Bob's left hand hit the floor with each 'shtupid.'

"Okay, let's see if you can sit up and we'll clean out some of the wounds and assess damage. What hurts? Does anything seem broken?"

"Teeth, nose, hand, face…." Bob's list went on.

When Ida returned, John was just removing Bob's muddy shoes. "How is he?"

"Well, he's drunk, so that's one thing. I assume someone beat him or he jumped or was thrown off the train, which would explain him coming here. I'm glad he didn't go to Ma's. He seems to be breathing all right except for what is probably a broken nose, but he could have a broken rib or two. He might just need some cleaning up and bandaging and a good night's sleep."

"Should we call the doctor?"

"I think he will keep until morning." John was trying to remove Bob's coat. Ida leaned in to help. "I'll try to get him down to his skivvies so we can see where the bruising is."

"And I'll get the soap and water and tear up an old sheet…I think I know right were one is."

John reached over and took her hand. "Sorry about this."

Ida leaned over and pecked him a kiss. "Not your fault."

After Bob's shirt, undershirt, and pants were removed. John lightly covered him with an Afghan.

A bruise was forming on his left side which worried John. Other than that, he had splits in his lips, crooked nose, and a gash in his scalp at the back of his head which continued to ooze blood, so they bandaged his head. He looked a bit like a Revolutionary war hero and swaddled his hands in strips to keep the knuckle cuts clean and to protect the davenport cover.

Bob bore it well with a few moans, but it seemed that the alcohol was doing a good job of numbing his senses. They tried to get him to drink a little coffee, but he rejected it, and finally dropped into a fitful sleep.

John put his arm around his faithful wife. "Go on to bed, Mama. Your little bear will be up at dawn. I'll stay down here and sleep in the chair just in case he wakes up and doesn't remember what's going on. Or seems to be having trouble."

"That's good. I think we should be watchful. Wake him up every so often and assess. But if it would make you feel better, we could call the doctor now before it gets any later."

"I think if he were bleeding inside, it would be coming out of his nose or mouth or ears, don't you? I don't see that, but I'll keep a close eye on him overnight. Tomorrow, we'll get him over to Ma's. She'll be glad to nurse him."

"Okay, Papa. I hope he and Helen both sleep through the night." She pecked him again on the cheek. "You are a good brother."

"Oh, there's enough time to be angry tomorrow. It wouldn't have had any impact tonight. Sleep well, my girl."

Ida made her way upstairs turning light switches as she went, and John settled down in a chair with the afghan. Bob moaned as he tried to move a bit.

John shook his head. "Stupid, stupid, stupid."

***

ITEMS OF INTEREST

Next horse sale, Dec. 9.

This is the season of the deadly corn husker.

Albert Wienke has moved into his new house on what will be called Lincoln Avenue.

Be sure to read the news on the second page.

Crystal Lake has been frozen over since Nov. 20.

Candidates are beginning to show up all over the county.

Judge Donnelly is now holding court at home after a bad bout of influenza and will complete his term.

Barkeep Bob Wienke was injured in an accident the other night in the train yard and is recuperating at his mother's on Washington street. We wish him a speedy recovery.

Woodstock Sentinel, November 26, 1903.

***

WOODSTOCK'S WONDERFUL GROWTH AND PROSPERITY
OVER $180,000 EXPENDED IN NEW BUILDINGS

Woodstock is enjoying an era of prosperity that seldom falls to a town of its size, and the prosperity and growth is not of the mushroom variety that springs up in a night and dies away with the first frost of business adversity.

Within the past building season, which is not drawing to a close, starting in with March 1, there have been erected in Woodstock over one hundred residence houses, the total cost of which foots up $185,000.

[I]n addition to this evidence, there is the increase in the banking business of the city, one of the surest signs of a healthy financial condition, and a decided improvement in all commercial lines.

The population of the city has kept pace, too, with its building growth, and today it is estimated that fully 4,000 live and labor in Woodstock, some of whom, perhaps, being forced to temporarily reside either in the country or in neighboring towns and villages for want of homes.

[T]here are scores of families "camping out," living in barns temporarily fitted for living purposes, crowded in rented rooms, in the hotels, or wherever they may find an abode, and winter is coming on with its cessation of building operations. The prospects are not very flattering, to say the least, for the homeseeker.

One of the chief causes for all this prosperity, and it might almost be said, the only cause, is the Oliver Typewriter factory.

At a considerable expenditure of energy, The Sentinel interviewed each contractor in the city and secured the number of houses erected since March 1, 1903, to the present date. Together with the name of the owner, the size of the house and the cost.

By Henry Keishard

John Wienke, 8 room residence.........$ 1800
Frank Wienke, 8 room residence........ $ 1800

By J. O. Cunningham

Albert Wienke, 11 room residence.......$ 3000

Woodstock Sentinel, November 26, 1903.

***

Keeping Christmas
By Henry Van Dyke in Youth's Companion

It is a good thing to observe Christmas Day. The more marking of times and seasons when men agree to stop work and make merry together is a wise and wholesome custom. It helps one to feel the supremacy of the common life over the individual life. It reminds a man to set his own little watch, now until then, by the great clock of humanity.

But there is a better thing than observance of Christmas day, and that is *keeping Christmas.*

Are you willing to forget what you have done for other people and to remember what other people have done for you; to ignore what the world owes you and to think what you owe the world; to put your rights in the background and your duties in the middle distance and your chances to do a little more than your duty in the foreground; to see that your fellow men are just as real as you are, and try to look behind their faces to their hearts, hungry for joy; to own that probably the only good reason for your existence is not what you are going to get out of life, but what you are going to give to life; to close your book of complaints against the management of the universe and look around you for a place where you can sow a few seeds of happiness? Are you willing to do these things even for a day?

Then you can keep Christmas.

Are you willing to stoop down and consider the needs and desires of little children; to remember the weakness and loneliness of people who are growing old; to stop asking how much your friends love you and ask yourself whether you love them enough; to bear in mind the things that other people have to bear in their hearts; to try to understand what those who live in the same house with you really want, without waiting for them to tell you; to trim your lamp so that it will give more light and less smoke, and to carry it in front so that your shadow will fall behind you; to make a grave for your ugly thoughts and a garden for your kindly feelings, with the gate open? Are you willing to do these things even for a day?

Then you can keep Christmas.

Are you willing to believe that love is the strongest thing in the world, stronger than hate, stronger than evil, stronger than death, and that the blessed life which began in Bethlehem nineteen hundred years ago is the image and brightness of the Eternal love?

Then you can keep Christmas.

And if you can keep it for a day, why not always?

***

Ida sat by a west window in a meager beam of sunlight reading the newspaper on Christmas Eve afternoon. Helen was taking a nap, and the house was quiet. The paper was full of interesting articles today.

Banker Hoy had broken a hip in a fall and at eighty-three it was doubtful that he would recover. How old was Ma Wienke, Ida wondered? What would the family do without her help? Seemed like the first words out of their mouths was to call on Sophia for help.

There had been a bad train wreck in Harvard. The tracks in Woodstock were so close to the buildings on the square. If there was a wreck here, it might wipe out the whole downtown area. And they practically ran right behind Ma Wienke's house on Washington. Ida shuddered just thinking about it.

A man in Cleveland killed himself and his whole family "due to despondency over the impoverished condition of the family purse and then near approach of Christmas." How sad. Are their people in Woodstock feeling that way? Who was reaching out to them? Anyone? Ida decided she'd ask next Sunday at church. They must not make Woodstock famous as Cleveland was now.

A cartoon on page six showed Santa tucked neatly into a small roadster next to his bag of toys with the headline, "Santa Claus Up-To-Date." Ida chuckled and tried to imagine how Santa could move more efficiently in an automobile than in a flying sleigh.

Mead and Charles advertised, "Turkish layer figs and hollower dates." Maybe Figgy Pudding would be good for Sunday dinner. She'd have to ask Ma Wienke to see if she was to bring dessert this week.

Ida's favorite page of the newspaper by far was page eight where inspirational readings, poems, and stories were found. Ida felt tears rise as she read Henry Van Dyke's "Keeping Christmas." She thought of all be bad thoughts and deeds she had had and done during the past year. How would she ever make up for them? Maybe by trying to keep Christmas all year long.

***

John opened his eyes. All was black. Something had awakened him. A noise? Helen? He waited for it to be repeated. Could have just been the house creaking. It was bitter cold outside. Who knew what might be popping and snapping. But then he heard three distinct evenly spaced raps. It was the door. Oh no, not Bob again. Come calling in the early hours of Christmas morning in a drunken stupor to ask for forgiveness? If it were Bob, he'd be sent packing.

John slid out from under the covers, his feet hitting the cold floor. He felt for his robe and slippers, trying not to wake Ida or Helen. He had taken to bolting the doors at night, so whoever was knocking could not get in. He moved stealthily down the stairs; only a few steps squeaked. Without turning on any lights, he looked out the window to the front porch. A man, bundled against the cold, stood on the front porch. He raised his hand again and rapped, 'A shave and a haircut, two bits.' A friend then. A thief wouldn't have continued rapping for so long.

John slid back the bolt and cracked it just enough to speak through, his slippered toes given some security pressed against the bottom of the door.

"Yes?" John's voice carried out into the still night.

"Oh good, John. It's Frank."

John threw open the door. "Frank? Come in. What's wrong? Is it Ma? Anna? The children?"

"No. Ma's fine. My family is fine, but there is a search going on for someone else's children. Some kids ran away from the Home."

John closed the door against the icy wind, and they made their way to the kitchen in the dark where the stove still gave off a little heat. John turned on the light and stoked the firebox with several sticks to warm the room.

"Three of them ran away two days ago when they were supposed to be walking to school." Frank warmed his hands over the stove. "Yesterday, Mr. Austen saw them in his shop trying to filch food. He gave them a loaf of bread and some peanut butter and sent them on their way."

"Just like him."

"But he also called the sheriff and was told they were missing from the Children's Home. The boys told Austen that they were going to Rockford to be home for Christmas.

"How old we talking?"

"Youngest is eight; oldest is ten."

"Mm." John pulled his robe a bit tighter around him and redid the tie.

"The home administrator has gone up to Rockford to look, thinking they might have jumped a train, but the sheriff thinks they are still local, trying to hunker down in the cold. So, he called for searchers from the various groups that have donated to the Home. I got the call because I'm a church elder."

"Okay, what do you need? Food, hot coffee, feet on the ground?"

"A group is going northwest toward Rockford and looking in ditches a few miles out of town. They asked me and this other sled to head toward McHenry. I have our sled out in front and wondered if you could join me in the search for a few hours. Four eyes are better than two."

"What time is it?"

"About three. Tomorrow is Christmas, you remember, so you don't have to work. Just church. I promise to get you back for that."

"Okay. Let me go get some warm clothes on and tell Ida so she doesn't worry about where I've disappeared to. Make yourself at home. I'll be as quick as I can."

Frank unbuttoned his coat and removed his ear-flapper cap. He didn't want to get overheated and then have to go back outside in the cold.

John took the stairs two at a time not worrying about squeaks. He turned on the hall light and then opened the bedroom door wide so he could see to dress.

When he was dressed in several layers of cotton and wool, he leaned close to the bed. He could just leave a note but decided to wake Ida and give her the story before he left.

"Ida?" he whispered. Her eyes flew open, and she sat straight up in the bed and began to bring her feet out over the side.

"Helen!" she said.

"No, no. It's okay. Helen is fine. Just stay in bed. Here lay back down." John lifted her feet back up and coaxed her to lay down under the covers.

"What's happened, John?" Her voice was shaky. A note might have been better.

"Some children from the Home are lost. Frank is here and we are going to go help look for them."

"Alone?" Ida was trying to sit up again.

"No. Many are out looking." John gently pushed her back down and brought the covers up.

"On Christmas Eve?"

"Really Christmas morning. I will be back in time for church. Okay?"

"I suppose it will have to be. Be careful."

John kissed her. "I will."

***

The moon was a slim crescent against the black, star-filled sky, adding virtually no light to the ground below. There had been new snow yesterday evening, which gave off a glow but also blended the ditches into the road. While they would have to be careful not to drive the horse into the ditch, anything dark lying in the ditch would stand out. The lantern was ineffectual against the dark, and they eventually doused it, allowing their eyes to do their best in the dimness.

Frank's horse Nick walked along until up ahead they could see a shape. Nick nickered a greeting that was returned, and they pulled up beside the other sled.

"Any luck?" John's question was met with silence. "Oh sorry, stupid question. You wouldn't be out here if you'd had luck."

"Right so." The man was a stranger to John. "Glad you're here. You take the right ditch and well take the left. It will go faster than trying to see both at the same time."

"Sounds good." Frank slapped the reins and the sleds moved off in tandem.

They made their way along slowly, side by side, searching the ditches, their eyes looking for something dark against the snowbanks or any kind of movement. After a long while, the unknown man again. "How far out should we go, you think?"

John deferred to Frank as the elder who was called. "Well, let's think. They were seen in town in the late afternoon. Got some food, and if they hightailed it out right then, they could have walked three or four miles in an hour or until they got hungry or tired. Let's say five hours maximum so a max of fifteen miles."

"We be almost to McHenry. That's twelve miles. I'm sure they are searching there just like we are in Woodstock."

"We'll go a bit more and then turn around and go back. Maybe we should stop at some of the farms and check hay mows or outbuildings. Farmers should be getting up just about now. Or they might have heard us on the way out and come out of hiding and we'll see them on the road or catch them as the sky lightens."

"Good plan!"

Several hours later, they were almost back to Woodstock, nearing the Children's Home on the edge of town. John now had the reins, and Frank scanned the ditch. One of the men in the other sled said, "Hey! Look up thar!"

As they looked up the road, they saw a figure on the road silhouetted against the white of the snow ahead. The person was running toward them and screaming. John clapped Nick on the back, and he broke into a trot. The other horse followed suit.

Soon they could discern that it was a woman in a lightweight, dark coat with no hat or boots screaming what sounded like "It's a child. It's a child!" As they got abreast of the spot where she stood, she said again, pointing beyond the ditch. "It's a child crawling out of the cornfield."

Frank was out and toward her before the others. She turned before he quite reached her and ran back up the road a bit and into the ditch bordering the cornfield. He followed. John brought Nick to a stop next to the ditch. Frank quickly scooped up the boy, not even half-grown, and carried him to the sled. He pulled out a few blankets to cover him and John took off his warm wool scarf and tied it gently around the boy's head covering his ears and lower face, so only his closed eyes were showing.

"Go, John, as quick as you can to Dr. Windmueller's. I'll stay here and help with the search for the other two."

"G'dy-up!" John slapped the reins rudely against Nick's back urging the horse into a fast trot which he maintained back into Woodstock. John looked back at the boy and was not sure if he was breathing. He alit from the sled and banged on the doctor's door. It opened immediately, and the good doctor emerged. Both men ran to the sled, but it was John who gathered the boy up along with the blankets and brought him into the warmth of the office laying him on the examination bed. So light; so thin. The boy looked frozen with frost on his forehead and cheeks.

"How long was he out there?" The doctor was sweeping away the scarf and blankets to expose a tiny figure in a light coat with no hat, gloves, or boots.

"I don't know. Overnight. But he was conscious within the hour, crawled out of a cornfield toward the road about a mile from the Children's Home. Can you believe it? Frank and the others are searching the fields for the other boys."

"Alright. I'll do what I can. Go tell the sheriff if you can find him. I think he's running the town search."

"I'll do that." John hurried back to the sled and began his search for the sheriff by going to the jailhouse, which was where he found him and several deputies. On hearing the news, they jumped on their horses and took off toward McHenry Road.

John looked around the quiet town. There was a dull light in the eastern sky although it was not quite time for the sun to rise. He decided he wouldn't go back out along the road, but rather gave Nick his head, and the horse went straight to the stable at Frank's. He brought the tired horse into the barn still attached to the sled and closed the big doors against the cold and lit a lamp. Nick went without comment to a bucket standing in the aisle and got a long drink while John took off the harness hanging it from the empty wooden pegs along the back wall. As soon as he was free, Nick went to his stall and lay down, rolling in the deep bed of straw which John was glad to see Frank had furnished earlier in the day.

"Good boy, Nick." The horse got up and got another drink and began munching on a leaf of hay. John closed and latched the stall door and made his way back out into the yard. The windows of Frank's house were dark, but as he began his three-block walk back to 365 Lincoln Avenue he noticed that many houses already had lights in the kitchens. As he walked, he said a prayer for the two boys still out on the cold McHenry Road.

***

Ida held John's hand tightly when the minister announced at the beginning of the Christmas service that two of the boys had been found dead. A great sigh of sadness filled the room dampening the joy of the day. Ida pulled her handkerchief out of her sleeve and dabbed her eyes and then gave it to Helen to play with. A prayer was offered for the boys' families and for the Chicago Industrial Children's Home's keepers.

Later as they walked toward Ma Wienke's on Washington Street with Helen in John's arms and Ida hanging on tightly to his elbow and carrying the basket with the figgy pudding, John told her the whole story of the harrowing night.

"Goodness, it was a miracle that you found even one alive. What were they doing in the cornfield?" Ida slipped a little on some ice and tightened her grip even more.

"I really don't know. Maybe the boy we found will explain the logic. I heard the others were found in an old house foundation on the other side of a small wood. Maybe they thought it would protect them, but without a fire, it was a lost cause after they went to sleep."

"I don't blame the matron of the Home, do you?"

"My first thought is not to, but they did wait a bit to call in the searchers. I'm sure it is hard to know when to raise the alarm when a child goes missing of an afternoon. Lots of distractions walking home from school. Maybe the village should be given some guidelines when they see boys or girls just hanging around the square or walking aimlessly on the streets. If I saw that, I'm not sure what I'd do."

"That's a good point, John. Maybe bring it up at your next political meeting."

John smiled. "The Children's Home is an excellent moral way of handling orphans, but when it comes to delinquents who are brought out from Chicago or other cities, they become our problem. Probably the sheriff's office should be introduced to the…um…bad boys and maybe even take an interest in reforming them."

"The sheriff? You're kidding right? That would be the last person those boys would listen to." Ida shifted the pudding basket to her other hand and moved around John to take his other arm.

"But who better? Church people? They'd probably be too kind and would be easily taken advantage of. I guess it could go the other way also, and they'd be too strict which wouldn't help either." John's breath made puffs as he spoke.

"True. What about getting them jobs after school so they could earn a little money to spend or maybe the money should be given to the Home for their keep. I could see someone like Mr. Austin and his boys, working with a boy to bring him up as a good community member."

John smiled. "Or Mr. Stafford at the furniture store. He could teach them to drive the horses for funerals."

"I can't quite see that. But...."

"But there are others who might be willing. Just having three meals and schooling might now be the best way to approach boys that come from the streets of Chicago. Here we are. Are you and your figgy pudding ready?"

Ida smiled. "As ready as I'll ever be. Watch out Wienkes, here we come."

***

"It's just so sad. I can't shake the feeling of dread." It was a week later, and Ida's fingers were flying as she knit a scarf to replace the one that John had lost on that trying night. "I suppose this scarf is going to remind you of those boys every time you put it on, isn't it?"

"It's fine. I was part of saving one rather than finding the others. I will wear it like a badge of honor."

They were sitting in the parlor enjoying some adult time. Helen was in bed, hopefully to sleep until morning, unless they made too much noise over the New Year comin' in.

"How's Frank? He seemed a bit perturbed with you last Sunday."

John snickered. "He's okay. He was just upset that I didn't go back out to get him Christmas morning. I explained that the horse was tired, and they seemed to have an excess of searchers at that point."

"How'd he get back?"

"He walked. It was that or ride in the sled with the corpses of two little boys."

"Oh, now I'll have that image in my head forever. How far was it?"

"A mile at most. He was fine. Kept him warm in the cold."

"You could have said that you let him walk back because he needed the fresh air after the discovery. Or because it was faster than waiting for you and the sled."

"I suppose either of those might have worked better than a tired horse and brother. At any rate, he had to walk back. He admitted that he was glad to see that I took care of Nick before heading home. But I doubt he'll not let me live it down for a while."

Ida looked up from her knitting and caught his eye, signaling a change of subject. Her hands continued their work. "I guess on this auspicious night, we have a lot to be thankful for."

John rose from his chair and came to sit next to her on the davenport. He stopped her hands with his own and looked into her eyes. "Last New Year's Eve we weren't even together."

"You're right. That was when I was so scared and acting crazy. I'm sorry." Tears sprung into Ida's eyes at the memory.

"No need to apologize again. It was also my fault for being such a competent communicator." A self-depreciating shake of John's head made Ida snort. He looked up smiling. "We are very lucky that we are here together in our own house and that our little one has both parents to furnish her a good upbringing. In truth, thinking about all those orphans got to me. Maybe we should consider going out there to have a look at them once Helen is a little older."

Ida looked down at her hands, clutched in his, and back up at his now very serious eyes. She didn't know what to say. It wasn't often that he left her speechless.

"They do sometimes get babies who wouldn't have been damaged by running wild with hooligans or having barely survived drunken fathers."

Ida cleared her throat and pulled her hands away to extract the knitting and return it to her sewing bag. Then she took his hands again and looked at him but still said nothing.

"Ida?"

"John…I…I don't know what to say…I…I'm not against the idea. I don't want Helen to be our only child, and certainly, a child from the Home needs a good family, but…."

"But what?"

Ida thought about how she had, just a week earlier, promised to *Keep Christmas* all year long. She needed, right now, to put her own feelings aside and open her heart and home to…no she couldn't do it. Not yet.

"But what?" John's face was anxious brows drawn together.

"But not right now. Let's see what God provides first."

John loosened his grip and let his eyes stray from hers. "I only thought—"

"I know, and it was a good thought. Let's think about it more, and we'll see what the future brings."

John's eyes came back to hers. "So that sounds like a definite maybe."

Ida smiled. "A definite maybe."

John held her gaze, and they both felt the melting of barriers and the stirring of the desire that had brought them to this place. John pulled her in for a kiss.

And then, Helen began crying.

Ida pulled back from the kiss. "Oh my, what is she doing awake at this time of night?"

John stood. "Have we been too loud?"

Ida stood. "I don't think so. I'll go get her. She might be a bit hungry. She didn't eat much supper. You stay here."

Before she went to the baby, she reached out and hugged her loving husband. "I love you, John. I will think about it. I promise." Then she was away.

John sunk into his chair. It had been a somewhat spur of the moment idea about the adoption. He didn't want to see that boy's frozen face in his dreams. He didn't want any of the children to face that awful death. But Ida was right. They needed to think about it more. He shook his head. There was a good chance that every home in Woodstock with two loving parents was having this same conversation. He'd wait and see what the new year brought.

Ida walked in with Helen, wide-awake and still sniffling a little. John rose to greet them. "Hi there, little Helen. Did you get up to ring in the new year?"

Helen put two fingers to her mouth and uttered a shaky sigh.

"She says, yes, she's hungry. Do you mind if I feed her right here?"

"Not at all. My girls know what they want. I'm just along for the ride."

Ida winked at him. "And what a ride it's been so far. We are so glad you brought us home to Woodstock, aren't we Helen." She stood on tiptoe and placed a proper kiss on John's lips, and Helen giggled.

Ida sat and opened her multi-button bodice, and Helen eagerly began to suckle.

"My Madonna and child." John's wistful look as he watched Helen suck made Ida giggle.

"Oh, for heaven's sake, John! Sit down and read the paper." Ida sounded brusque but a smile curled up the corners of her mouth, and she blushed slightly. "Don't worry. She'll be asleep in no time."

And she was.

Helen Frances Wienke
(Circa Winter 1903)

From Maryon's Recipe Book
(February 1948)

In case you didn't know it, I just got married but I know almost nothing about cooking for a family, so my mother, Mame, gave me a recipe book with some of my great-grandmothers' favorite recipes as a shower gift. Between this and Gramma Rasmussen's guidance, Earlie and I won't starve to death.

Mom said that her sister, Helen, sat and watched their grandmother Louisa and grandmother Sophia cook, putting to paper the recipes that the old women made relying only on their memories. Aunt Helen was a home economics major, so I'm not surprised. Mom said she hoped I could translate them to today's oven. I never met either of these grandmothers, but I've heard stories, especially about Gramma Sophia. I remember Grampa John once saying that she was "a force to be reckoned with." Kinda like Gramma Rasmussen, I suppose. Those old ladies have an inner power which I will never have.

Nenna – that's my Aunt Edna – said that she was glad that these recipes were being passed down "to the next generation of great cooks." I almost spit out my root beer when she said that. Me? A great cook? Come on! I'd rather be working outside on a farm or reading a book or drawing or pretty much anything else rather than being holed up in a kitchen doing womanly things. I just hope I can get the hang of it before I poison my new husband.

Maryon Rasmussen Range

Oma Sophia's Recipes

German New Year's Cake

Baking a New Year's Cake makes you think about your hopes and dreams for the new year coming.

Cake Dough (the night before)
  A little more than three cups of sifted flour
  About a cup of soft butter
  A quarter less than a cup of powdered sugar
  Two fresh candled eggs
  Two or three dollops of sour cream

In a big bowl begin by cutting the butter into the flour and adding the powdered sugar. Add the eggs and the sour cream. Knead the whole until smooth. Cover the bowl with a damp kitchen towel and put it in the icebox or on an enclosed back porch overnight or at least an hour or two. Do not let it freeze. Should be cold when cut later.

Poppyseed Filling
  Enough ground poppyseed to cover the top of a twelve-inch cake – more or less depending on your liking of poppyseed.
  Three or four dollops of butter
  Two handfuls of sugar
  Two handfuls of raisins
  A cup of milk
  Big spoon of honey – two if more sweetness is desired.
  A few drops of vanilla
  Put all the ingredients in a small pot and put it on the warming spot of the stove. Stir it so that it does not stick or

burn, maybe two minutes or so, until well combined. Set on the sideboard.

Nut Filling

Two large handfuls of ground almonds (hazelnuts will also work)
Big spoon of sugar
Half a cup of milk
A dash or two of cinnamon
Combine all the ingredients. Set on the sideboard.

Apple Filling

Four or five apples – peeled, cored, and sliced
Two big spoons of butter
Two big spoons of sugar

Melt the butter and sugar in a saucepan over medium to high heat. Add the apples and cook them quickly stirring almost constantly. Stop just before the apples get mushy. Set to cool on the sideboard.

Putting The Cake Together

Cut off half of the ball of dough and roll out very thin, to cover the bottom and sides of a springform pan. Let the dough hang over the edge at the top of the pan. On top of the dough at the bottom of the pan add the poppyseed filling for GOOD LUCK in the New Year.

Cut the other half of the dough into three smaller balls. Roll out into circles that fit neatly into the pan. Place the first dough layer gently so it floats on the poppyseed filling. Add the nut filling for GOOD HEALTH in the New Year.

Gently cover the nut filling with a dough layer making sure the nuts stay evenly spread under the dough. Add the apple filling on top of the dough for SWEETNESS in the cake and in the New Year. Top with the third piece of dough thinly rolled and fold the extra dough edges from the first dough layer over the top to seal the cake.

Baking the Cake

Heat the oven to a good baking temperature, one that has worked well for other cakes (Mame's note: 350 degrees F). Add a pan of water to the oven near the firebox to absorb extra heat from the firebox so that the oven keeps an even heat.

Topping

One beaten egg
Powdered sugar

Beat an egg with a tiny bit of water and brush it over the top dough layer. Put the cake in the center of the oven carefully turning it after half the bake-time. Bake for about an hour and a half. Check at each fifteen-minutes after one hour for doneness. Remove from the oven and after cooling a bit, maybe ten or twenty minutes, unload it from the spring pan gently onto a plate. Store the cake in a cool place at least overnight for best taste. Dust with a thick layer of powdered sugar before serving.

Vell, dat's how I do it. Now go make your own.
~ Sophia

Erbspüree
(Split Pea Soup)

For the New Year, there is nothing like hot and creamy *Erbspüree*. Peas and lentils are GOOD LUCK food on New Year's Eve. But if you are to do it the old country way you must start well before Christmas to prepare.

Instructions

Get a large bag of dried split peas from the grocer. The split peas will be gone from the shelves by Christmas, so think about ordering them early. Since they are dried they can be kept in the pantry for a while. When you bring them home, pour them into one of your own bags just in case the bag they came in is damp from the storehouse.

The day before Silvester (New Year's Eve), bring out the peas, pour them into the middle of a cheesecloth and rinse them under a stream of water. Cover the dried peas with fresh water. This should sit on the counter overnight covered with cheesecloth. Dump the soaked peas into the cheesecloth, discarding the water. Rinse the peas again under a weak stream and then put them into the pot in the proportion of two and a half cups of peas for each two quarts of water.

Add to the pot:
> A large ham bone
> Two small onions sliced thinly
> A pinch of salt
> A pinch of black pepper
> A pinch of marjoram

Bring to a boil on the hot spot and then move to a cooler spot and simmer for at least an hour and a half, stirring occasionally.

Remove the ham bone, cut off the meat, shred into small pieces and return the meat to the pot. Give the bone to the dog who has probably been sitting in the kitchen all morning waiting for it. (Authors note: Best 21st Century wisdom is that dogs should not have ham bones).

Add to the pot:
> Three chopped up stalks of celery
> Three chopped up carrots
> One large diced potato

Place the pot back on the stove and boil gently, uncovered, 30 or 40 minutes until the vegetables are tender.

Check to see if the soup is too thick. If so, add water, stir well, and bring the soup to a near boiling before serving. If

the soup is too thin, add thick cream to the pot, stir in well
and bring the soup to a near boiling before serving.

Dis soup best with fresh loaf of white bread for tearing up
when eater hoped for stew instead of soup.
~ Sophia

Glühwein
(Glow Wine)

Glühwein is German mulled wine perfect for New Year's
Eve, a ski party, or a romantic evening. Glow Wine will
make you glow from the inside.

Ingredients:
A bottle of red wine from Bobby's saloon (or alternative
liquor establishments)
A cup of water
Three-inch cinnamon stick
A medium orange
Ten whole cloves

Instructions:

Put the water, cinnamon stick and sugar into a saucepan
and bring to a boil. Move to cooler spot on the stove to
simmer.

Cut one of the oranges in half and squeeze its juice into the
pot. Stick the cloves into the orange peels and put those
into the pot also. Continue to simmer until thick and syrupy
— at least 30 minutes.

Add the wine, stirring the mixture for a few minutes.
Remove the oranges, cloves and cinnamon stick. Cut the

second orange into thin layers and float on top of wine. Serve while hot.

Da cold weather need hot wine. Especially gut wid da fireworks. ~ Sophia

Deutsche Gemüsesuppe

A Saturday night supper to use up all the leftovers. Or when the weather is cold and blustery, and no one wants to face the day.

Ingredients

Five cups of homemade chicken stock (boil the chicken and keep both the meat and the water).
Two stalks of sliced celery
Two sliced up carrots
One diced up onion
One large diced up potato
One cup of chopped up cauliflower
One and a half cups of egg noodles (homemade are best)
One or two cups of diced cooked chicken meat (from making stock)
Pinch or two of salt
Pinch of ground black pepper

Instructions

Put everything except the noodles and the chicken meat in a stockpot and bring to a boil on the hot spot of the stove. When boiling move to a cooler spot but keep simmering for about 15 minutes or so until the potatoes and other vegetables are starting to soften.

Add the noodles and a cup or two of water or more stock, if necessary, and continue simmering for another 10 minutes. Noodles and vegetables should all be tender.

Add the cooked chicken meat to the pot and mix so flavors blend. Serve immediately.

Soup easy. Just water and whatever you got around to put in. Vhy you need recipe? ~ Sophia

Marmorkuchen
(German Marble Loaf Cake)

Marmorkuchen is easy to make. Excellent for expected company. Good for unexpected company too, but how would you know to make it?

Ingredients
Two cups of flour
One and a half small spoon of baking powder
A couple pinches of salt
A cup of unsalted butter, softened
A bit more than five big spoons of butter, melted
A cup of white sugar
Two large, candled eggs, not chilled
Five small spoons of baking powder
Two-thirds cup of milk plus two large spoonsful
Two or Three dollops of sour cream
One large spoon of vanilla
Three large spoons of unsweetened cocoa powder.

Directions
Make a medium hot stove and grease a large loaf pan well.

In a separate bowl, combine the flour, baking powder and salt by sifting them together.

Using a hand beater, beat the softened butter until smooth and then slowly add the sugar and melted butter.

Add the eggs, beating between each egg until smooth. Add the sour cream and vanilla. Do not hurry this process. The resulting batter may be lumpy but well combined.

Slowly add the two thirds cup of milk until it is well combined. Scrape the sides and bottom on the bowl often to make sure all the dry ingredients are included. Do not over mix. The batter will be slightly thick, but pourable.

Transfer a bit more than half to a separate bowl and set aside.

In the remaining batter, stir in the two big spoons of milk and the cocoa powder.

Layer in the vanilla batter followed by less of the chocolate batter using a large spoon until the batters are used up. Shake the pan slightly to level out. Pull a knife through the batters to move the colors but not to mix them.

Bake in a medium hot oven. Place the loaf pan in the middle and a pan of water near the firebox to even out the heat in the oven. When a toothpick inserted in the middle comes out clean – about 60-75 minutes – the cake can be removed from the oven. The cake should have pulled slightly away from the pan around the edges. Start checking cake every 5-10 minutes after 50 minutes.

Cool cake in pan on a cooling rack for about 30 minutes then run a knife around the edges of the loaf pan and turn the cake out onto a cooling rack or a serving plate, top up.

Sprinkle the top with powdered sugar before serving.

Everyone like dis cake especially when next to German boiled coffee.
~ Sophia

Oma Louisa's Recipes

Bratwurst and Schmorkohl
(Braised Cabbage)

Bratwurst

Cook bratwurst as bratwurst. Can be boiled, roasted, fried, heated in the *Schmorkohl* or however it wants to be cooked. [If you don't know how, ask your mother.] If you want to actually stuff the bratwurst, that's another wurst and another recipe. Easy to buy down by the grocery.

Beef Broth

For beef broth roast soup bones in a very hot oven with three carrots, three celery ribs, two medium onions all cut up. After thirty minutes transfer everything to a Dutch oven and cover with water. Add three cloves of garlic, three bay leaves, some peppercorns, and large pinches of thyme, marjoram, and oregano.

Bring to boil then move off of the hot spot so the covered pot continues to simmer for four to five hours. Don't let the water get low. Best to add hot water from the kettle every hour if needed and mix. Skim off the foam when it happens.

After the time is spent, strain the broth through cheesecloth. [Throw everything but the broth out for the dogs; they can even eat the garlic - it is good for them]. If using the broth immediately, skim off the fat. If not, let it cool and the fat will float to the top and solidify and be easy to remove.

Schmorkohl

Schmorkohl is just cabbage cooked in beef broth with sugar and onion.

Start with bacon fat, not a lot of it but enough to grease the bottom of the pan and make the cabbage not burn. If using oil, about three big spoons.

To this, add a large spoon of sugar and a large onion sliced very thinly so it will fall apart on the cooking. When the onion is slightly browned add a head of green cabbage, shredded, just under two pounds. Get that all browned up.

Before it gets too brown add a cup of beef broth or if you don't have beef broth, just add a cup of water. Add a small spoon of caraway seeds to ease the acid of the cabbage as it cooks.

Bring to a boil and then move it off the hot spot and cover it. Let it simmer for about an hour. Check on it once in a while and add more water to keep the level at about an inch in the bottom of the pot.

After an hour, here's where you might want to stir in salt and ground pepper and a large spoonful of white vinegar to bring out the flavor.

Cook da bratwurst and serve up with dark German *bier.* *Beifall* (applause) ~ Louisa

Bienenstich
(Bee Sting Cake)

Bee Sting Cake is especially important when served during courting. The bee symbol is "potential for marriage."

Ingredients for Filling
Two cups whole milk

Two large, candled eggs plus two large egg yolks
Two pinches of salt
Three handfuls of granulated sugar
Four small spoons of vanilla
A handful of cornstarch
Three large spoonsful of cold unsalted butter cut up.

Instructions

Put the milk in a medium-sized heavy pan and set the pan over medium heat. Warm milk until very hot, but not boiling.

While milk is heating, combine the eggs, egg yolks, and salt in a medium mixing bowl. Beat until thickened then slowly add the sugar (2 to 3 tablespoons at a time), beat 50-70 strokes after each addition. Continue beating until the mixture is very thick and pale, about 3 minutes (four hundred strokes) more.

Carefully add the vanilla and cornstarch, mixing until very smooth. Gradually add the hot milk—about one teaspoon at a time at first then slowly begin adding more, beating well (one hundred strokes) after each addition.

Once all the milk has been added, pour the mixture back – scraping the bowl well – into the saucepan you used for the milk. Add the cold butter and set the pan over medium heat. Heat the mixture, stirring constantly with spatula. When the mixture begins to thicken (it will look lumpy) move to low heat and switch to a whisk. Side to side motion works best. Continue stirring the mixture gently for another seven or eight minutes, until very thick. At this point, reduce heat to very low and cook one minute more, stirring with your spatula again.

Remove from the stove and scrape mixture into a medium mixing bowl. Cover with a clean kitchen towel pressing the towel down onto the surface of the pastry cream. [Not to worry. It will come out with hot water in the laundry]. Cool to room temperature and store in the icebox overnight.

Ingredients for Dough
    One cup plus two large spoonsful of sifted flour
    Two large spoonsful of unsalted butter at room temperature
    One large spoonful of granulated sugar
    One small spoonful of yeast
    Two pinches of salt
    One large, candled egg
    Two large spoonsful of well water at room temperature.

Instructions

Combine all ingredients. Using your washed hands slowly knead the ingredients together until well combined, smooth and supple - 10 or 15 minutes.

Put the dough into a lightly greased mixing bowl and cover with another dish towel. Let it rise for an hour or so until puffy.

Grease and flour an 8-inch round cake pan and set aside.

Transfer the dough to a lightly greased counter and deflate gently. Pat into an 8-inch circle. Place the dough circle in the prepared pan. Cover with the dish towel again and let it rise for 30 minutes. After 30 minutes, gently stretch the dough so it reaches the edge of the pan.

Ten minutes before the dough finishes rising, make the topping. Make the oven to medium hot.

Ingredients for Topping
    Four big spoonsful of unsalted butter
    Two hearty handfuls of granulated sugar
    Two big spoonsful of honey
    One big spoonful of heavy cream
    Three or four handfuls of sliced almonds

Instructions for Topping
    Melt the butter in a small saucepan.. Stir in the sugar, honey, and heavy cream. Bring the mixture to a boil, stirring often,

and boil for two to three minutes, until lightly golden. Remove from the heat and stir in the almonds. Spread the topping into an even layer on top of the dough.

Put pan in middle of the oven and bake for 20 to 25 minutes, until the top is golden. Cool cake in pan on a wire rack for 30 minutes, then run a knife around the edge of the pan to loosen the cake. Gently remove cake from the pan, then cool completely on a wire rack, almond-side up.

Once the cake is cool, with a large knife, split it in half horizontally. Top the bottom layer with the chilled pastry cream. Slice the top layer into eight wedges, then place on top of the pastry cream so the cream shows between the almond covered wedges. (Do this to stop the filling from oozing out when you slice it.)

For best, always serve dis cake when love ist sparking.
~ Louisa

Gebratene Ente
mit Apfel-Wurst-Füllung
(Roast Duck with Apple and Sausage Stuffing)

The hardest part about this recipe is getting a duck. Choices would be to raise a duck and then kill, pluck, and clean it; find a farmer who will part with a duck and then kill, pluck, and clean it; or go to the butcher and order a dressed duck. He will kill, pluck, and clean it, and you have much less mess, but also much less weight in your pocketbook.

Ingredients for the Ducks
One domestic duck (about ten pounds) or two smaller ducks could be used to cut the baking time in half.
Salt

Ingredients for the Stuffing
  One pork sausage
  Half a cup of chopped onion
  Half a cup of chopped celery
  A cup of peeled and chopped apple
  A cup of raisins
  Half a cup of water
  One and a half small spoons of salt
  One small spoon of sage
  A pinch or two of black pepper
  Two big spoons of chopped parsley from the garden
  Eight cups of yesterday's bread, crustless, cubed
  Three large, candled eggs, beaten
  Half a cup of chicken broth or water

Directions
  With your hand, rub the salt inside the cleaned duck. Prick the outside of the duck with a metal fork. That's all for the duck.

  In a large skillet, cook the sausage, onion and celery until sausage is well cooked (no pink) and the vegetables are tender. Add the apple and simmer for three minutes, stirring occasionally. Drain off any grease, cover, and set aside.

  In a saucepan, simmer the raisins in the water for about eight minutes.

  In a large mixing bowl, combine the sausage mix, the raisins with water, salt, sage, pepper and parsley and mix well.

  Add the bread cubes, eggs and broth and mix lightly. Spoon mixture into the duck. If need be, lace the back opening of the duck to keep the stuffing in. That's why they call it stuffing.

Place the duck in a large baking pan, breast side up in the middle of a medium hot oven. Bake uncovered for twenty-five minutes per pound and an extra 20 minutes until golden brown and the drumstick moves easily. At each thirty-minute increment, check the level of fat in the pan and drain it off.

Remove all the stuffing into a separate dish and cut up the duck into its specific parts: drumsticks, thighs, wings, breasts, backs, neck, and giblets. Serve hot.

Have du tried baking duck instead of chicken? Da duck is like all the dark meat on a chicken and better.
Try it! ~Louisa

Deutsche Kartoffelknödel
(German Potato Dumplings and Brown Butter Sauce)

German potato dumplings are always a favorite, and they go with almost any meal. Easy with few ingredients, they are also useful in using up left over mashed potatoes or other potato dishes.

Ingredients for Dumplings
Three pounds (10) of medium potatoes peeled and quartered
One cup of sifted flour
Three large, candled eggs, lightly beaten
Just under a cup of dry breadcrumbs
A small spoon of salt
Two pinches of nutmeg
Twelve cups of water.

Ingredients for Brown Butter Sauce
> Half a cup of butter
> One big spoon of chopped onion
> Two handfuls of dry breadcrumbs

Directions
> Boil potatoes for fifteen to twenty minutes uncovered until tender. Drain and transfer to bowl.

> Mash the potatoes. Stir in flour, eggs, breadcrumbs, salt and nutmeg and mix well. Will result in a lumpy, sticky dough. With clean, greased hands, form dough into two-inch balls.

> Bring the twelve cups of water to a boil in a Dutch oven and reduce to a simmer. Carefully with a spoon put the balls of dough into the water. Simmer for seven to nine minutes, uncovered, until a toothpick inserted into the center of the ball comes out clean.

> In a separate small saucepan, melt the butter and add the onion. Cook the onion over a medium heat for five to seven minutes, stirring constantly, until the butter is golden brown. Remove from heat and serve with the dumplings.

Dumplings are first thing girls learn to boil in old country kitchen. ~Louisa

RotKohl
(Red Cabbage)

Red Cabbage is so good and good for you. Keeps you regular and gives you energy.

Ingredients

Two big spoons of bacon grease
One small onion
Half a head of red cabbage, shredded
Little less than half a cup of vinegar
Two big, rounded spoons of sugar
One small spoon of mustard seed
Two or three pinches of salt
A pinch of black pepper

Directions

Using a cast-iron skillet over medium heat sauté the onion in the oil for two minutes.

Add the cabbage and turn it in the pan until it wilts and then add vinegar and turn the cabbage in it. Sprinkle with sugar and turn again. Season with the mustard seed, salt and pepper and move to a cooler spot on the stove top.

Let the cabbage cook and stay warm until ready to serve, stirring occasionally.

A good Oma use cabbage for a quick lunch with Braunschweiger sandwiches. ~Louisa

Obstkuchen
(Fruitcake)

The perfect dessert for a heavy meal especially at the holidays. This recipe will be enough for three loaf cakes so you will be able to give these tasty cakes as Christmas or New Year's gifts unless they disappear before they can be sent. Be aware that you may need to order the fruit from the old country so you should start thinking about these cakes by June. And it is unlikely that you'll find fresh pineapple or allspice in December so you might need to send your grocer looking for canned pineapple and allspice early. Save back some applesauce from the summer canning.

Ingredients

Two pounds of candied mixed fruit
Half a pound of red candied cherries
Half a pound of green candied cherries
A pound of crushed pineapple
A large ball jar of unsweetened apple sauce
Three small spoons of baking soda
One cup of seedless raisins
Half a pound of walnut meats
Two small spoons of allspice
Two small spoons of nutmeg
Three small spoons cinnamon or a bit more but not too much
Several pinches of salt
Four fresh candled eggs
Three cups of sugar
A cup of butter, not chilled
Four cups of flour

Instructions

Oven should be medium cool.

With a hand beater, add the sugar and cream well. Add spices and salt and mix well. Add eggs and beat well.

With a wooden spoon, add the fruits, alternating with flour. The batter will become VERY thick. Stirring in the applesauce will help – a bit.

Grease three loaf pans (if you only have one it is okay to do the cakes one at a time). Put about a third of the dough into each pan to about half full.

Bake the loaves for about three hours in a medium cool oven. Start checking about the two-and-a-half-hour mark with a toothpick every 10-15 minutes. When the toothpick comes out clean, take the cake out of the oven.

Let the cake cool completely in the pan before removing it.

Da children love dis bread. Each get a loaf as Christmas gift, and mine hear, dey often use it when da in-laws come calling. ~Louisa

Clara Doering
16 years old
Circa 1900

Herman Doering
28 years old
Circa 1900

J. Nicholas and Louisa Doering Stoffel
Circa 1903

Next in the Woodstock Tales Series!

If you've enjoyed this book and meeting the Wienke and Doering families, continue the adventure with

A Fine Grocer of Woodstock
(1904-1907)

John is made an offer he can't resist by Ida's brother, Herman Doering. But Ida is again with child, and since the Lincoln Avenue house will break ground at any time, John is hesitant to put any more on his plate. Ida encourages him to fulfill his dream of being a fine grocer.

But events become more challenging when Ida develops dangerous complications with her pregnancy, and John sells their home to finance his other dealings. Now eight months pregnant and homeless, will John and Ida be forced to return to Ma Wienke's boarding house?

A Fine Grocer of Woodstock continues the story of the Wienke and Doering families. John and Ida must meet the challenge of providing for their growing family and nourishing their relationship even in the face of mounting responsibility and fear of loss.

Available at   Read Between the Lynes
Woodstock's Hometown Bookstore
111 E. Van Buren (on the square)
Woodstock, Illinois 60098
(815) 206-5967
readbetweenthelynes.com

Books in the Woodstock Tales Series

Take Me Home to Woodstock - 1900-1903 (2023)

A Fine Grocer of Woodstock - 1904-1907 (2020)

I Will Fly to Woodstock - 1908-1911 (2021)

Ain't Life Grand in Woodstock - 1912-1915 (2023)

Due Out in 2024

At War in Woodstock (working title) - *1916-1919*

Also by Sally Cissna

Fishing for Happiness (with Maryon Range)(2021)

"Come Home Peter" in *Family Stories from the Attic*
edited by Christi Craig and Lisa Rivero (2017)

SANTA CLAUS UP-TO-DATE.

To WOODSTOCK
OR BUST